The Quad Squad

DON FREEBORN

ISBN: 978-1-7330865-0-9 (Paperback)
ISBN: 978-1-7330865-1-6 (Ebook)

AUTHOR'S NOTE

Any references to historical events, real people, or real places are used fictitiously.
Names, characters, and places are products of the author's imagination.

Front cover image by Christina Myrvold
Book design by Michele N Tupper
Editing by Alexandra Ott

PRINTED IN THE UNITED STATES OF AMERICA
First paperback edition 2019
www.facebook.com/TheQuadSquad2019

Use of this publication is exclusively limited to authorized individuals. Contact D.H.
Freeborn at donaldfreeborn@yahoo.com for further information and for authorization
to reproduce, sell, or distribute this novel.

For all those young men who shared their stories with me.

I've never forgotten.

I never will.

CONTENTS

CONTENTS

The
Quad Squad

1. Zack

"**DREW**, hurry up!" Zack Walden yelled in the direction of the stairs. "You're gonna make us late again!"

Zack waited for a reply from upstairs in the bathroom he and his two younger brothers shared. He hoped, prayed even, that his brother Drew was nearly finished brushing his teeth so they could leave. All he got was a muffled yell, which he hoped meant Drew had tried to speak with a mouth full of toothpaste. Satisfied for the moment, he went back to work on finishing their lunches. Three sandwich bags sat underneath three slices of bread, which Zack hurriedly slathered peanut butter on. He followed suit with a smattering of different additions: banana for him, honey for Carter, and strawberry jam for Drew. He slapped a second piece of bread on top of each, stuffed them in their bags and filled each of their lunch boxes with a bottle of water, a bag of chips, and an apple. His brothers probably wouldn't eat the apples, but that was on the list Zack's mother had left him, so he followed it to the letter. He'd come this far. He wasn't about to mess up now!

Zack's parents were teachers at Trace Middle School in Westerhill, a suburb on the outskirts of Columbus, Ohio, and today they'd needed to go in early for some spring conferences. Rather than have their grandparents watch them, as was usual, Zack had argued that since he was eleven, he was old enough to get his brothers ready and walk them the few blocks to school. He'd even volunteered to take care of making their lunches, which he normally didn't like, since his brothers always insisted on different things. At first Zack had felt proud, like his parents had really let him do something special, but now it just felt like work. In fact, Zack considered it a miracle he'd gotten himself and his brothers this far. He'd forgotten to set his alarm for seven o'clock--a half hour earlier than he normally woke up--and from the moment he'd catapulted himself out of bed, the day had been a struggle. Even though he was already worn tired from getting his brothers out of bed, dressed, and eating breakfast, he wanted to make his parents proud and to prove to them, especially his father, that he could handle taking on more responsibility. Still, as he glanced wildly around the kitchen, trying to remember what to do next and worrying he wouldn't have time to meet with his friends Michael and Evelyn as they got off the bus like he usually did, his confidence was quickly fraying.

"Zack?"

"Okay, lunches are done," Zack mumbled to himself as he stared aimlessly at the ceiling.

"Zack!"

"The dishwasher!" Zack exclaimed aloud. His dad had asked him to put away the breakfast dishes and start the dishwasher before they left.

"Zachary!"

Zack jumped in surprise, nearly dropping the bowls he'd picked up as he was snapped from his thoughts. He turned to see the face of his youngest brother, Carter. His eyes were wide, his mouth hung open, and his arms were thrown wide to the sides.

"Hello, Earth to Zack!" Carter scolded.

"What is it, Carter?" Zack shot back.

"I can't find my other shoe!" Carter explained, motioning to the floor, where only one foot was covered by a blue sneaker, the same as Zack's but smaller. Just one of many things Carter copied from him. It was so annoying. It was bad enough he, Drew and Carter looked alike: same sandy blond hair as their mom and the same blue eyes as their dad. Why did Carter have to dress like him too?

Zack grabbed his brother's arm and pulled him along behind him down the tiled hallway toward the front door. Zack slid down on his knees in front of their coat closet to find a chaotic pile of shoes, boots, gloves, and hats. He rummaged through it for a few seconds before his eyes traced a path to Carter's cubby, where his shoes were supposed to be, and saw his other sneaker wedged far to the back. He reached in, grabbed it, and presented it to Carter with the best narrow-eyed, fake angry face he could manage.

"It was where it was supposed to be, Carter!"

"Oh," Carter replied, letting the 'O' sound carry for a few seconds before flashing his brother an innocent grin, absent several teeth, as if to tell Zack he was sorry.

Zack groaned and tossed the shoe at Carter's chest playfully, gave him a friendly shove, and turned to look up the stairs to the walkway.

"Drew!" Zack yelled, as loudly as he could manage. "Hurry up, Derp-O-Potamus!"

Zack knew that Drew hated that nickname. He'd coined the phrase when they'd gone to see the Christmas lights at the Columbus zoo the year before. Zack had seen a hippopotamus in its tank that he thought looked a little dumb--"derpy," as Zack would say--and when Drew began making faces at the hippo through the glass, the word just popped out of Zack's mouth. His brother responded the same way then as Zack hoped he'd do now. Sure enough, he was right.

"I am not a Derp-O-Potamus!" Drew screamed back as he stormed into view from his bedroom and slammed his hands on the banister.

Zack knew Drew had meant that to be threatening, but it ended up just looking funny instead. As he laughed uncontrollably, Drew flew down the stairs to do the second thing he'd always do every time Zack called him the name.

"Punch, punch, punch!" Drew slugged Zack three times in the arm.

"Ow!" Zack yelped through his laughter, putting up a weak defense against his little brother. "Okay, Drew, I'm sorry. I'm sorry! Are you finally ready?"

Drew stared up at him with the most fake frown Zack had ever seen and stuck his tongue out. Though they had very different personalities and were two years apart in age, they shared a similar sense of humor and Zack hoped Drew knew he was only playing around. Zack calmed himself long enough to look at the clock in the living room. It read 8:15. They were running late.

"Oh crap!" Zack yelled. He sprinted into the kitchen, ripped the three lunchboxes from the counter, and sprinted back to the door. He practically threw them at Carter and Drew as they tried to get their jackets on while doing his best to stuff his feet into his sneakers, crushing the heels in the process. Deciding he didn't have time to fix them, he threw on his favorite hoodie and hat and shoved his brothers out the front door.

"Zack, I need my hat too!" Carter begged as his face hit the chill air of the early April morning.

"Hurry up, we gotta go!" Zack demanded. The few blocks through their neighborhood of Kaufman Farms with cold ears was worth not having to hunt for his brother's hat, so he ripped off his beanie and stuffed it onto Carter's head, not giving him a chance to argue.

"Okay, Zack, jeez!" Drew fired back as he leapt from the front porch. He and Carter sprinted across the lawn and down the sidewalk. Zack followed suit, nearly tripping on his not-quite-on shoes as he flung his backpack over his shoulder. He was glad they were finally on their way, but as he ran to catch up to his brothers, Zack couldn't shake the feeling that he'd forgotten something.

As the brothers hurried away, a piercing squeak emanated from the front door of the Walden home as a chill wind blew it open slowly, inch by inch. Zack, panting from exertion, bounded back up the porch steps and slammed it shut. He hurriedly locked it and took off down the sidewalk a second time.

"Being...responsible...sucks!" Zack lamented aloud as he tried to catch his breath; the verdant grass and white houses of his neighborhood were nothing but a blur as he sprinted to catch up to his brothers half a block down the road, the minutes until the final bell ticking away in Zack's head with every step he took.

2. Chase

THE small man sprinted through an empty corn field, leapt a hundred feet onto the top of a house, and hopped down to run along the top of a high fence. Onward he went, smashing through several trees, narrowly dodging a truck and finally kicking a cow before rocketing off yet again. At least that was what Chase Talbert imagined as he ran along the landscape with his hand, his index and middle fingers moving at a feverish pace as they crossed through farmers' fields and the sprawling neighborhoods that had grown around them. As another car flew by, he caught a glimpse of his reflection in the side mirror—a face that was both excited and tired all at once. After all, he'd stayed up far past his normal bedtime waiting for a very important phone call from the west coast, three hours behind them.

Chase's phone had finally rung at almost eleven o'clock after he'd already waited anxiously since the early evening. He still didn't know where he'd found the strength to stay so patient for so long. Now he dreamt of the vacation he thought he'd be having not quite a month from now, over spring break, in a place he'd never been. Chase wasn't sure if she'd let him go, so he'd been working her over since the early hours of the morning using every tactic he knew, but so far nothing had convinced her.

"I can't wait to go, Mom!" Chase cried enthusiastically for the fifteenth time or so that morning as he woke from his daydream. He beamed at his mother from the passenger's seat, his eyes shooting open with uncontained excitement.

"It's going to be so fun!" he continued. "Dad says he'll let me take surfing lessons; we'll go to the beach and maybe even go see the navy base with all the ships! I've never even been close to the ocean before!"

"It sounds like your dad's got everything planned out, sweetie," his mother, Kendra Martin, replied with a half-smile and sad eyes. Chase knew she didn't like talking about his father much if she could help it. The divorce two years earlier was sudden, ugly, and messy, leaving Chase with his father's last name while his mother changed hers back. It was weird having a different last name than his mom. It felt lonely.

"Has he taken the time off work already?" she inquired.

"He didn't say anything about that yet. But he said he'd pay for the plane ticket!"

"It's a long flight to San Diego, Chase. Are you sure you'll be alright all by yourself?"

"Mom, I'm eleven. I'm not afraid of being by myself

anymore," Chase proclaimed, knowing that his mom was trying to convince him to stay so she wouldn't have to say no. "Kids younger than me fly all the time!" he continued. "The airline people make sure they're safe and get on the right plane."

"Wow, you've sure done your homework."

"Yep!" Chase smiled widely, certain his mother was impressed by his research. He leaned back into his seat and stared out the windshield. Out of habit, he reached up and took off his hat. It was a custom-made blue and white baseball cap with the number eight on either side and an "R" on the front in blue print. It was the last real gift his father had given him. He rarely took it off, even at school. His teachers had long since given up trying to enforce that rule with him, and he always grinned when he thought about it. His friend Brady McCormick had told him to keep doing it until they gave up. That such good advice had come from someone who got in trouble as much as Brady did was still unbelievable to Chase.

"I really miss Dad," Chase said with a sigh as he stared down at the "From Dad" written inside his hat with permanent marker. Even with his dad living across the country, somehow keeping the gift with him all the time made Chase feel like he was still close, even though he knew he really wasn't. Even now, not a day went by that Chase didn't wish his father was still there.

"I know you do, Chase," his mother replied.

"Can I please go?" Chase begged, leaning in closer to his mother. "I'll be okay. I swear."

"I'm not sure..." she nearly whispered, her attention turning to the winding snake of parent drop-offs. Chase plastered a giant, hopeful smile on his face, trying hard to keep his mother thinking about it for the next few minutes until they reached the rear entrance.

"Well, we're here. Have a good day today!" his mother said encouragingly, but Chase's expression fell.

"Okay, bye, Mom," Chase mumbled. He grabbed his backpack and opened the car door to slide out onto the cement walkway heading to Frasier Elementary's rear entrance.

"Chase, wait," Ms. Martin called just as Chase was beginning to shut the door.

"Yeah?" Chase replied, pulling the door open again.

"We'll talk about it tonight, okay?" she promised with a smile.

"Really?" Chase exclaimed, his smile returning.

"Yes, really. But you better listen in Mrs. Meister's class, or the promise goes away."

"Thanks, Mom!" Chase cheered, diving back into the car and planting a kiss his mother's cheek. He waved goodbye and took off toward the doors.

"She said we'll talk about it!" Chase said under his breath, already thinking of everything he'd get to do over spring break. His mother saying "We'll talk about it" was almost as good as a yes. He couldn't wait to tell his friends, especially Brady. He'd definitely be jealous!

3 Michael

BUS number seven finally worked its way up to the curb in front of Frasier Elementary, bypassing the long rows of parents waiting to drop off their children in the car lane. "The Big Cheese," as Michael Dzierwa called it, slowed to a stop, its brakes hissing loudly. He looked out the windows at one of his favorite places in the world and smiled. Unlike most of his friends, Michael loved school and enjoyed nearly every day he spent there. To him it was a happy place, a safe place, a place where he could just be himself. After a final, piercing squeak from the wheels, the door popped open and the usual pushing and shoving began.

Michael had made sure to sit alone this morning for exactly that reason; he didn't want anyone plopping down next to him or smashing into him as he tried to get off the bus with his latest injury. More than that, even though he was halfway through fifth grade and had turned eleven three months before in January, he wasn't especially big for his age and always seemed to get sandwiched between larger kids. That wasn't something he could risk today.

He went to grab the shoulder strap of his backpack, stopping just in time when he realized he was about to pick it up with his right hand. That wasn't normally a problem, but his wrist was covered by a blue cast only two days old.

"Not gonna happen," Michael thought to himself as he switched to his left hand. Grasping the strap tightly, he slung his pack over his shoulder before waiting for the right moment to slide out into the oncoming procession of kid traffic. He thought he'd chosen a good time, but a split-second after leaving the safety of his seat, he realized he was wrong.

"Hey!" came a cry of surprise just as Michael's legs entered the thin confines of the center aisle. The yelling and arguing soon began as some of the fourth graders toward the back purposely pushed their friends. The press of bodies was unavoidable, and Michael looked frantically for a way to escape. But with no room to maneuver, he was quickly shoved up against the heavy backpack of the girl in front of him. In his hurry, he'd again forgotten about his injured arm and put it out in front to try to cushion the impact. It may as well have been a hot knife stabbing his wrist. Michael couldn't help but cry out in pain. He squeezed his eyes shut and bit down on his lower lip to stifle the scream as he pulled his arm protectively toward his chest.

"Mikey! Oh my gosh, are you okay?" came the worried words of Evelyn Sanders, whom he'd collided with. She turned toward him, her hands immediately reaching out to cradle his arm gently.

"It's okay, Evelyn; it's not your fault." Michael tried to ignore the stabbing pain and smile through it as he pulled his arm from her grasp.

"Let's get off of here and I'll look at it," Evelyn replied with complete confidence, as if she knew exactly what to do, and it wouldn't have surprised Michael if she did. After all, her mom was a doctor at the children's hospital, and Evelyn had definitely inherited her mother's intellect. When Michael hurt himself, which happened frequently enough, she always seemed to know how to bandage all the cuts, scrapes, and bruises he had a tendency to get with the first aid kit she kept in her backpack. "Just in case," she'd say. But Michael knew better; it was really for him.

The two shuffled down the center aisle together, Evelyn hopping off the bottom step onto the cement walkway while Michael followed. Making their way onto the grass and out of the way of the hordes of kids exiting their buses, Evelyn began their conversation again after they'd drawn closer to the front entrance of the school.

"Okay, let's see it!" she demanded. Michael didn't even think; he just raised his cast for her to examine.

"Cool cast," she remarked, narrowing her eyes and closely examining every detail before firing off the usual volley of questions Michael always dreaded answering.

"Okay, so what did you do this time?" she began. "Did you fall off the trampoline? Brother push you off your bike again? Get hit with a baseball bat at practice? Or was it something your dumb friends talked you into?"

"It was my fault this time," Michael answered sheepishly. "I was climbing the tree in my backyard so I could jump onto the trampoline, but it was still kinda wet from the rain and I slipped and fell off."

"What day?"

"Saturday," Michael responded without missing a beat. "It still hurts a lot."

"I bet." Evelyn studied his cast. "Is it a break or a sprain?"

"The doctor said it's a bad sprain," Michael answered. "It might take three or four weeks for it to heal. The guys are gonna kill me if it's not fixed before practice starts!"

Michael's friends wouldn't actually kill him, of course, but they definitely wouldn't be happy. He'd played with Zack, Brady, and Chase on the same baseball team, the Rangers, since they were seven. It was a club team, and Michael was waiting anxiously for practice to start in a week, though he'd kept up his skills at the batting cages all winter long, and his father had even hired a private pitching coach for him. After all, he was their best pitcher, a fact he rarely let any of them forget, but he was so worried he wouldn't be able to do it this year he'd barely slept the last two nights.

"Eight to ten weeks, actually. And that's only if you don't end up needing surgery," Evelyn replied flatly as she crossed her arms.

"Surgery! No way!" he yelled as his face twisted in shock and a feeling of absolute dread washed over him.

"You're so gullible, Mikey!" Evelyn chuckled.

"Don't do that, Evelyn. You know I hate it!" Michael hissed.

"You're so cute when you're mad," Evelyn teased, poking the smattering of freckles on Michael's face like she always did when they used to play together when they were younger. Chase had some too, so why didn't she ever do that to him? It was so annoying!

"But don't worry, your doctor was right; about three or four weeks. Maybe less, though. How are you going to write in class in the meantime?"

"Well," Michael grinned, "I was thinking maybe you could do that for me."

"Yeah, that is not ever happening," Evelyn said with what Michael called her *annoyed teacher face*.

"Fine. Doctor's handwriting is terrible anyway!" Michael joked, eliciting a friendly slug on his good arm from Evelyn. He always seemed to forget she never had a problem paying his jabs right back.

"Hey, where's Zack? Isn't he always here by now?" Evelyn squinted and scanned the sidewalks that led from the neighborhood to their school.

"Yeah, he's getting his brothers ready by himself this morning!" Michael snickered. "He'll probably be super late because Carter lost a shoe or something."

"Well, give me your hand in the meantime," Evelyn demanded as she rummaged through the front pocket of her backpack.

"Why? What are you going to do?" Michael asked skeptically, narrowing his eyes.

"I want to sign your cast, dingus. You have a problem with that? I promise I won't write something dumb like Brady would." She rolled her eyes.

"Oh, okay," Michael responded with a sigh of relief. He

let Evelyn take his hand gently before taking the cap off her permanent marker and writing her message. It took her a lot longer than Michael thought it would, but after about a minute, she finished. She replaced the cap on her marker, slid it in her pocket, raised his arm her mouth, and kissed his cast.

"There, all better!" she said with a devilish grin before walking away. "See you later, Mikey!"

Evelyn was retreating from him at a nearly a run. Suspicious, he looked at his cast. It read:

"Kissed and made better by Dr. Evelyn Sanders." The purposely horrible signature was followed by a heart. No, not just a heart, a *giant* heart!

"You said you wouldn't write anything dumb!" he yelled angrily after her.

"I didn't!" Evelyn called back in a sing-song voice. "I only wrote the truth!"

Mortified, Michael stretched the cuff of his sweatshirt over his cast as much as he could, but it barely covered half the message. He groaned in frustration and began his trek toward the glass doors of the school. He was in absolutely no hurry now and had to think of excuses why everyone else couldn't sign his cast if he couldn't find a marker to cross it all out in time. Luckily, Michael was very good at making up stories.

4. Brady

THUMP. *Thump. Thump.*

The sound of the basketball being rapidly dribbled on the lacquered floor was just one of a dozen sources of racket reverberating off the walls of the gym. At least thirty students in the before-school program were engaged with anything from board games at the tables back in the attached cafeteria to playing some sort of game in the gym. Some jumped rope, others played tag, but Brady had stopped paying attention to them. Today, only four of the older boys were allowed to use the basketball hoop, and he was making the absolute most of his time.

"McCormick jinks one!" Brady yelled in the most convincing sportscaster voice he could manage. "Oh, jinked again! Get wrecked!" he shouted mockingly as he dodged yet another attempt to steal his ball.

"Brady, shoot it already!" came a shout from his teammate. Indeed, Brady had possessed the ball for quite some time now and was much more interested in dodging and dribbling than actually scoring. It was probably the one time being small for his age was actually useful.

But Brady got the hint. He always did, eventually. After a few more flashy dribbles, he planted his feet firmly on the floor and took his shot. But the ball did not go far as Logan, the boy guarding him, put his arms up and blocked the shot with a downward slap. Brady flinched as the ball careened toward the ground before bouncing hard on the gym floor and straight up into his groin.

"Eep, my boy parts…" Brady squeaked before he fell to the floor and curled up into a ball.

Logan winced as he knelt beside his injured friend. "Brady, are you okay?"

"Logan, Logan, come closer," Brady whispered as he rolled over to face his opponent.

Logan's eyes narrowed suspiciously as he leaned in closer to Brady's face, the other two players moving closer to investigate.

"It hurts so much, Logan," Brady recited. He continued, letting each phrase drag on much longer than it needed to. "If I don't make it… tell my sister... I said you could date her."

"Oh my God, Brady, eww!" Logan spat out as he recoiled from Brady, who was now convulsing with shrieking laughter. The two other boys, Ander and Jack, soon joined in. Embarrassed, Logan turned and sulked off toward the cafeteria but only got a few steps before he was hailed by Brady.

"Logan, wait!" he yelled, reaching out with his arm.

Logan turned and waited expectantly for an apology.

"She likes pink roses and peanut butter cups the most," Brady informed him with the most serious face and tone that he could muster. "And have her home by ten o'clock."

"You suck so much, Brady," Logan replied bluntly, shaking his head even as a small grin came to his face. It was a few moments before Brady got to his feet again and walked to his position to keep playing, but his eye caught the clock on the wall just as it hit 8:15.

Ring!

Brady's ears perked up at the sound of the first bell echoing off the gym walls, immediately reminding him of something he'd nearly forgotten. Not giving any further thought to their game, he immediately ran to scoop up his backpack.

"Brady, where are you going?" Ander asked impatiently.

"Sorry guys, I gotta go!" Brady hurriedly apologized as he turned and sprinted full speed toward the hallway. "I'll see you at recess!"

"Where are you going?" Logan called after him, but Brady didn't answer. There was something much more important to do.

Brady envisioned himself as a ninja as he maneuvered through the hallways, slipping in and out of the herds of kids streaming in through the doors from the buses and parent drop-offs. He threw a few hurried and half-hearted apologies behind him when he bumped into someone as he passed and kept it up the entire winding way to his classroom. But as he tore around the corner to the upper-grade hallway at warp speed, he felt the invisible death ray that was his teacher's stare centered firmly on him and immediately threw on the brakes.

"Good morning, Mr. Dunlap!" Brady greeted his homeroom

teacher enthusiastically as he slowed to a brisk walk. Brady plastered a huge, toothy smile on his face that he hoped would make him seem as innocent and nonchalant as possible in hopes his teacher wouldn't give him a consequence.

"Good morning, Brady," he said, clearly amused but trying hard not to show it. "Go get started on your morning work, please."

"Okay, I will!" Brady promised, yelling over the racket as he picked up his pace into a power-walk.

"It worked!" Brady thought as he giggled to himself like a cartoon villain, hopping up and down twice for good measure. Now free of his teacher's gaze, Brady frantically scouted the crowd, looking for his first victim. He knew what his friends were afraid of and was waiting for one in particular to show himself. Brady hadn't ever been known for his patience, unlike his older sister, but what little he had was soon rewarded when his closest friend Chase walked purposefully up to his locker.

"Yes!" Brady whispered to himself as he stalked closer. Now was his chance, what he'd waited all weekend for. He reached into his pocket and produced the most realistic-looking rubber spider he'd been able to find and held it gingerly in the palm of his hand, trying his best not to giggle at the thought of what he was about to do. Quiet as a mouse, Brady snuck up behind his friend with careful, measured steps and shook his toy's legs so they'd tickle the back of Chase's neck.

Chase turned to see what was touching him, and his eyes went wide. The scream that escaped his mouth crescendoed as he fell back into his locker and onto the floor while Brady laughed hysterically and the other fifth-graders in the hallway, appearing more surprised than anything, looked over to see what had happened and murmured to each other.

"You scream like a girl!" Brady roared.

"Why?" Chase yelled, his eyes still wild and his breathing short and shallow.

"Because it's funny, duh!" Brady laughed.

"Dude, you know I hate spiders!" Chase whined as he pushed himself back up, refusing the helping hand Brady offered. He looked at the toy spider, still jiggling in his friend's hand, and shuddered.

"Is there a problem, boys?" an authoritative voice asked impatiently. Brady and Chase turned to see Mr. Dunlap standing a few feet away, arms crossed, clearly expecting a good answer.

Brady cast a glance toward Chase as he tried to think of a good excuse to give his teacher.

"Mr. Dunlap, he scared me!" Chase blurted before Brady could come up with something creative, pointing his finger accusingly at his friend.

"Snitch!" Brady hissed.

"Brady, if you don't want to get in trouble, don't scare your friends," Mr. Dunlap said bluntly.

"Now, I'll be taking that toy." Mr. Dunlap held out his hand expectantly. Brady gave it to him without complaint.

"Sorry, Chase." Brady said glumly, knowing he'd repeated the same mistake he seemed to make several times a day.

"You have to learn to think before you do things, Brady," his teacher said calmly. Brady had come a long way since he'd stopped taking his medicine, but some days it was a struggle. Probably for both of them.

"Am I going to need to shoot your dad an email about this?" Mr. Dunlap asked.

"No, it's fine, Mr. Dunlap," Chase interjected before his friend could reply. "It was pretty funny. I mean, I do kinda scream like a girl."

"All right, if that's how you feel about it, Chase, then we're done here," Mr. Dunlap said with finality. "Brady, you put this in your backpack, and I'd better not see it again. Clear?"

"Yep," Brady answered, relieved. His teacher turned and entered his classroom, leaving the boys alone.

"Thanks for not getting me in trouble, Chase. You didn't need to tell on me, though."

"And you didn't need to scare me with a spider!" Chase retorted. "I *hate* spiders!"

"It was a *fake* spider," Brady reminded him.

"Doesn't matter. Still mean," Chase scolded.

"Okay, fine, I'm sorry," Brady grumbled. "Anyway we're going to the indoor water park in Sandusky over spring break. My dad said I could bring one friend. Wanna come?"

"Can't." Chase's face lit up. "I'm going to San Diego to visit my dad!"

"Wow, really?" Brady asked, surprised and a bit jealous.

"Yep! I'm going to go to the beach, surf, all kinds of stuff. I even get to fly on the plane by myself!"

"Seriously?" Brady asked with a hint of awe in his voice. "Lucky."

The final bell rang above them, and as it echoed through the halls, the remaining stragglers scurried into their classroom.

"Hey, ball at recess?" Brady called after Chase as he backed up toward his classroom door.

"We're gonna crush them!" Chase said evilly before turning and jogging down the hall. When he reached his room, he called back to Brady sarcastically, "And don't stink it up this time, okay?"

"Shut it, Chase!" he shot back playfully, but not before Chase disappeared into Mrs. Meister's room.

"Mr. McCormick, would you care to join us?" Mr. Dunlap called impatiently from inside his room. "You owe me morning work."

"Sorry!" Brady shouted. He didn't want to get into trouble twice before the day had even started, so he bolted inside.

As far as size and shape went, Mr. Dunlap's classroom was a carbon copy of the other two fifth-grade teachers, Mrs. Meister (Mean Ol' Meister to Brady and his friends) and Ms. Jensen, but that was where the similarities ended. Ohio State flags and posters plastered the walls along with large bulletin boards displaying the student's work. Bins full of math supplies and games sat next to a titanic classroom library kept neatly organized, while the counters toward the windows held a multitude of plants, knick-knacks from all over the country, and their fish tank. The student's desks were organized into six groups Mr. Dunlap called 'pods.' Brady's pod was located in the corner close to the SMARTboard, where he sat with Zack and Evelyn, who he was pretty sure were placed with him because Mr. Dunlap thought they could help keep him on track. He'd sat near the fish at the beginning of the year, but even Brady had realized sitting there was too distracting, and he hadn't stayed long.

Grabbing his supplies from his bin, Brady walked to his chair and plopped down. Next, he kicked off his shoes and sat with his feet on the chair and his legs hugged close to his chest. He always worked this way because it helped him concentrate, but what he loved more was that it drove Evelyn crazy.

"Morning Evil-lyn!" Brady greeted his pod-mate happily. He liked to get in a little fun with her before she left to join Michael in LEAP, their school's gifted program.

"Please put your shoes back on," Evelyn begged without bothering to look up from her work.

"But I got new socks! *See?*" Brady placed his feet on top of his desk and slowly slid them toward Evelyn. He realized about halfway through he was just asking to get in trouble, but luckily Mr. Dunlap didn't notice.

"Get your feet away from me or I swear I'll stab them." Evelyn glared at Brady, holding her pencil like a knife.

"You're no fun, Evelyn." Brady sighed, retracting his feet and replacing them on his chair.

"And you're annoying!"

"I know!" Brady retorted cheerfully, taking out a pencil and flipping to the next open page in his journal. "Hey, where's Zack?"

"Not here yet, obviously," Evelyn replied. "He usually walks in with Mikey and me, but he didn't meet us today. Oh, and speaking of Mikey, you guys aren't gonna be happy at recess."

"Why?"

"Oh, you'll see," Evelyn said dryly.

Brady had planned to continue with his questions, but his train of thought was interrupted by Zack slipping into the room, red-faced and panting. He nervously greeted Mr. Dunlap, who seemed to know he was going to be late, then walked over to his desk and slumped into his chair.

He looks tired, Brady thought to himself as he watched his friend get his materials out.

Brady remembered then that Zack had volunteered to get his brothers ready for school that morning. As soon as Zack looked toward him, Brady regarded him quizzically before crossing his eyes and sticking his tongue out, drawing a snicker from Zack. Brady didn't care if he looked ridiculous; he was always happy to make a friend laugh when they'd had a rough day.

Besides, if they were laughing, they weren't fighting, and that helped keep his friends together. That was the most important thing, keeping everyone together!

"Have fun this morning?" Brady leaned in and whispered. Zack responded by groaning, raising his arms to his neck, making a choking sound, and letting his tongue roll out as if he were dying.

"Drew?" Brady asked knowingly.

"Both," Zack replied flatly. "But yeah, mostly Drew."

"So glad I don't have little brothers," Brady thought out loud before finally getting on with his work.

5 The Quad Squad

MICHAEL'S gaze bore into his teacher like a hawk as he slowly but surely pushed his chair out and held the edges of his desk. He hated how she'd often lose track of time and forget the days they were supposed to have extra recess. Even now, the deafening noise outside--balls bouncing on blacktop, the clanking of the chains on the swings, and the screaming, yelling, and arguing of kids playing games--had become all Michael could hear. What was more, he could see that his friends had gathered under their "Victory Tree," a towering, white-barked sycamore so massive it took at least four kids arm-in-arm to wrap all the way around its trunk. They were too far out to see clearly, but Michael could feel their impatience as he watched them pace back and forth, constantly glancing in the direction of the doors that led outside.

Michael and his friends were in a running basketball league with many other fifth grade boys. So far he and his friends were only up one game, and Michael had no intention of losing despite his handicap. He, Zack, Chase, and Brady had all been friends since they could walk, fought like brothers, and played on the same teams together since they'd first started tee ball. For as much as they argued and got on each other's nerves, *The Quad Squad*, as they'd named themselves in second grade, could handle anything when they were together.

Michael pursed his lips and cleared his throat as loudly as he could, causing his now-flustered teacher to finally dismiss them. He took off like an Olympic sprinter, ignoring the already distant call from his teacher to slow down as he tore through the halls. The only thing he feared at that moment was his friends benching him because of his cast. They'd promised each other after losing their regional championship the summer before that they'd win this year, but when Michael hurled the playground doors outward and ran to join his friends underneath their tree, victory was already starting to seem anything but certain.

"Hey guys!" Michael greeted his friends enthusiastically as he slowed to a stop. "Ready to stomp them?"

"Uhh, Mikey, what's *that*?" Zack asked, seeing the blue wrapping around Michael's hand and wrist.

"Oh, my cast," Michael replied like it was nothing at all.

"Ugh, Mikey, you've got to be kidding me!" Chase groaned loudly as he placed his hands on his forehead as if he had a headache.

"Seriously, *again*? You are so accident prone, dude!" Brady jabbed.

"Mikey, how? What did you do this time?" Zack demanded.

"I fell out of a tree," Michael said with a shrug as if it were no big deal at all.

"You fell out of a freaking tree?" Chase questioned sharply.

"Yeah, the one in my backyard." Michael ignored Chase's usual skeptical comment.

"Dude, we have to forfeit now!" Zack exclaimed. "You can't play with one hand!"

"Sure I can!" Michael fired back confidently while flexing his arms. "I'm just that good, bro!"

Though they were all close friends, Zack was his *best* friend, and everyone knew it. Michael always felt they were more like family, and he didn't like the uncertain, dumbstruck look Zack was giving him one bit. He knew where he'd seen it before; from the countless times he'd stayed with Zack and his family over the years.

"I am not being like Drew!" Michael yelled, shoving Zack's shoulder and drawing a laugh from everyone.

"You and Drew are both way overconfident, though!" Zack retorted.

"Come on, Zack, you're supposed to have my back!" Michael complained, silently hating that his best friend seemed to be doubting him, especially since Zack usually took the lead and Chase and Brady went along with whatever he decided.

"I dunno, Mikey. I mean, can you even dribble?"

"Yes! I'll just use my left hand. I promise we'll still win!" Michael insisted.

"Well, we're screwed," Brady declared, only half joking.

"Are you guys ready yet?" came a restless yell from across the basketball courts. It was Logan, who was captaining the other team.

"Logan, be patient, or I'm telling my sister you can't take her out!" Brady threatened.

"Oh my God, Brady, stop!" Logan demanded, his face growing red as his teammates cracked up.

"Sorry, Logan, we're coming!" Zack called. "Mikey's just being a derp and hurt himself *again*!"

"Shut up, Zack!" Michael shot back, though not too seriously. He was already feeling the relief of not being forced to sit the game out.

"Wait, how long are you gonna have the cast on for?" Zack asked. "Practice starts this week and the season starts next month!"

"Oh crap, are you even going to be able to pitch?" Chase questioned, hesitating a moment before adding, "We need you, dude!"

"Yeah, we were gonna go all the way this year, remember?" Zack reminded him firmly. "We were so close last year before we lost to the stupid Mavericks again!"

"I know, guys, I know! I swear I'll be ready by the time the season starts," Michael promised.

"How can you even promise that?" Chase pressed. "I mean, what if it doesn't heal in time?"

"It just will, okay!" Michael snapped. "I promise I won't mess up this year!"

"Jeez, guys, leave him alone and let's play already!" Brady, always impatient, piped up. He hopped up from their huddle and stuck out his arm into the middle of their circle, his thumb and index finger in the shape of an L.

"We just won't lose until he's better so we won't need to worry about it. Easy!" Brady said confidently. That was Brady, always the peacekeeper. He always knew right to jump in to help, which was weird, since he never seemed to know when to stop talking in class or doing other stuff that got him in trouble.

"Okay, I guess let's do this," Zack conceded with a shrug.

With that, the rest of the quartet stood, each making an L with their fingers and connecting them together until they had formed a square. Their classmates thought it looked weird, but to them it was as important as a secret handshake. As soon as they finished, they broke their fingers apart with a chorus of explosion sound effects and made their way to the court. As they did so, Michael looked at Brady sidelong and mouthed "thanks." Brady gave a warm half-smile in return before making a goofy face at him. So weird...

As they all turned to walk toward the basketball court, a curious look spread across Chase's face as he looked at Michael's cast. Michael froze, his heart quickening, knowing what Chase had seen. Michael had been careful to hide the writing on his cast when he was in class and had tried scribbling it out with a marker, but it wasn't a permanent one and had rubbed off over the course of the morning. He'd gotten lost in the moment when they'd made their square, forgetting all about it, and Michael would have given anything for anyone other than Chase to have seen it.

"Hey, who kissed your hand and made it better?" Chase asked with a wry smile.

"It's a secret," he said quickly, trying to make it seem like he was bragging.

"Why?" Chase asked curiously.

"Because she likes me but made me promise not to tell anyone," Michael replied.

"Really? That's the story you're goin' with?" Chase replied. "You're lying."

"Am not!" Michael looked as smug as he could to sell the lie.

Chase slowed and looked at Michael with narrowed eyes.

"Who is it *really*?" he asked, grinning knowingly.

"Not telling, I promised," Michael said firmly before quickening his pace.

"It's *Evelyn,* isn't it?"

"No, it's not!"

"Hey guys!" Chase yelled toward the basketball court and the six other boys who were present. "Evelyn kissed Mikey!"

"I'm gonna kill you, Chase!" Michael yelled as he ran after his friend, who had already bolted. Chase was the quickest of them by far, but he was laughing so hard he wasn't giving Michael much of a challenge in catching him. It didn't take long before Michael caught up, ramming into Chase and knocking him prone.

"Take it back!" Michael yelled as he sat on top of Chase with his good arm pressing down on his chest, but he just kept laughing. Michael hated being laughed at; it reminded him too much of home.

"So are we gonna play today or not?" asked Ander, who had wandered up to Zack and Brady to watch the spectacle.

"Guys, come on! You always do this!" Zack yelled, but Michael ignored him. By the time Brady finally convinced Chase to apologize, recess was over. Zack had been right all along, and they had to forfeit after all. Even if it was just a pickup game on the playground it, wasn't a great start to their winning season.

6 · Zack-Attack

THE rest of Monday went by quickly, and Zack was thankful for it. It hadn't been a good start to the week, with his morning having been so stressful, and he was still annoyed about having to forfeit their game because Michael and Chase couldn't get along. Even with all that, he still had one more hurdle to jump over: his parents had more conferences after school! Zack dreaded having to watch his brothers until then but hoped he'd think of something. But as usual, his thinking was interrupted by another snag in his plans.

"Carter, loosen up, you're choking me!" Zack gasped for air as he carried his brother piggy-back down the sidewalk as they made their way down Orchard Avenue, the main road that ran through their neighborhood toward their house.

Less than a block into their walk home, Carter had tripped on his constantly-untied shoelaces and scraped his knee and hands on the cement. He'd been inconsolable until Zack had offered to carry him, and Zack was beginning to suspect his youngest brother made a bigger deal out of it on purpose. Sure, Carter was only seven and on the lean side like Zack and Drew were, but lugging forty-five pounds of little brother several blocks was something Zack wasn't built or prepared for. But despite the struggle, he kept reminding himself of a story his dad had told him about when he used to carry a backpack heavier than Carter for miles and miles when he was in the army years before Zack was born. That was enough for Zack to grit his teeth and grunt through the exhaustion.

"Sorry," Carter apologized, loosening his grip around Zack's neck.

"Thanks, that's a lot better," Zack said with relief. "This is hard enough without you choking me!"

"He's gotta weight less than your *backpack*!" Drew complained.

"Suck it up, buttercup!" Zack commanded, just like his father would when he or his brothers made a big deal about something small.

"I'm telling Dad you said that!" Drew threatened.

"Then I'll tell him what happened and that you complained the whole way home and wouldn't help me!" If there was one lesson the Walden brothers had learned from their father, it was to always help people when they needed it. Drew kept quiet the rest of the way home, which told Zack that he remembered that lesson too.

When the brothers finally made it to their house, an exhausted Zack gently lowered Carter to the ground and helped him up the steps and inside the house. Zack quickly got them all a snack to hold them over until dinner, then used what he'd learned from his first aid classes in scouts to clean Carter's scrapes while they finished eating at the kitchen table. That had gone well until Carter screamed and kicked him in the stomach on reflex when Zack applied the antibiotic ointment, knocking the wind right out of him.

"What'd you do that for!" Zack coughed, trying to catch his breath. How could someone so little kick so hard?

"I hate that stuff, Zack! It stings!" A knot of anger twisted around in Zack's gut. He forced himself up and plopped into his seat with a scowl plastered on his face.

"Fix it yourself, then!" Zack grumbled, taking a bite of his granola bar and glaring at his youngest brother, whose expression quickly fell. He was such a pain! All Zack was trying to do was help.

"I'm sorry," Carter apologized. He was probably just saying it because he didn't want to get in trouble, not because he felt bad. At least that's what Zack thought until Carter slid off his chair and hugged him.

"I'm sorry, I didn't mean to," he said. Okay, he was starting to cry, so he meant it.

"It's okay," Zack sighed, returning the gesture. "Lemme put a Band-Aid on it, okay? I promise no more stingy stuff."

"Zack, what can we do until Mom and Dad get home?" Drew asked. He'd already finished his snack and was shifting impatiently in his chair.

"Sorry, Dad said no games unless they're home." Zack wished he could have said yes so he wouldn't need to worry about keeping Drew entertained. But he had a better idea anyway; one he knew his brothers would love. It was their favorite game, after all.

· · · · ·

"**LOCK** and load, boys!" Captain Walden told them in the deepest, most authoritative voice he could manage. He drew the action back to prime his rifle and drew his hood over his hair. The family room had been turned into an impenetrable fortress, the couch and chairs rearranged with great effort into something resembling a castle. Captain Walden noted that they were missing at least two of their guns and some ammo, but that wasn't too surprising, since they were always losing things.

Now the targets were home. His heart thumped as he took careful aim down his rifles sights, exhaling slowly before holding his breath, just as his father had taught him, and waited with the patience of a hunter for his quarry to appear. The lock clicked and the door slowly opened...

"Fire!" Zack ordered, and the racket of springs and compressed air filled the room. Bright blue foam darts shot through the air right into...

Oh shoot...

"Guys, are you actually kidding me right now?" their mother demanded after all three shots found their mark.

"Uh oh..." Carter muttered.

"Sorry, Mom!" Zack hurriedly apologized. "We thought you and Dad were coming home together."

"You're not planning to ambush your father again are you?" she asked, even though Zack was sure she already knew the answer.

"Umm, maybe?" Drew answered innocently.

"Boys…" his mother said, taking a deep breath as if thinking of something to say.

"But we're playing Zack-Attack, Mom!" Zack smiled innocently.

"Yeah, it's our favorite game!" Drew piped up, and Carter nodded vigorously in agreement.

"I'm pretty sure it's your father's *least* favorite game after spending all day at work, guys."

"We'll clean up after, Mom. Promise!" Zack swore. *Please say yes! Please say yes!*

"Well, in that case, I suppose carry on, Commander Zack," she replied with a mock salute.

"*Captain* Zack!" he yelled after her as she disappeared into the kitchen.

"Whatever, just get it done or you all lose your Nerf stuff for a month!" she threatened.

She wandered into the kitchen, and Zack went back to his position. He couldn't put his finger on it, but something felt off. It was never that easy to convince Mom to let them make a mess. What was going on?

POOFT!

The sound of a Nerf gun firing behind them filled Zack's ears, followed by a dull *thump*. Carter yelped in surprise, and Zack looked over just in time to see him flop on the chair he was hiding behind, tongue rolled out with a giant red dart lying next to him. The rules of Zack-Attack were very clear: one hit and you were dead. No exceptions.

Zack looked frantically for the culprit and saw his brother's assassin: his mother, with one of their missing weapons in hand, reloading as fast as she could. But that wasn't the worst of it! Drew turned, vengeance in his eyes, and fired right at him! Zack took cover just in time, and the dart impacted where his head had been just a moment before, losing his cardboard helmet in the process.

"Drew, you traitor!" Zack yelled from his cushion-foxhole. "What are you doing!"

"That's for calling me a derp-o-potamus!" Drew called back. Zack could hear him reloading and had to take the chance. He shot up, let his left eye focus down his sights, and squeezed off his shot. The dart sped through the air right into Drew's helmet.

"Helmet hits don't count!" Drew shouted excitedly as he ducked back down.

"They do so!" Zack yelled back.

"Surrender while you still can!" his mom called in her best villain's voice.

"Never!" Zack screamed defiantly just before he heard it: the telltale cocking of their second missing gun just before he felt the sting of the dart's impact on the back of his neck.

"I win," Mr. Walden said with a wry smile.

"Ahh! Dad-day!" Zack yelled. How had he snuck up on him so easily? He leapt up and charged his father, ramming into him and throwing a flurry of play punches.

Mr. Walton howled with laughter as he defended himself against Zack's mock fit. But after taking a few hits, he took hold of Zack's arm. Zack looked up, wide-eyed, at his father. He wasn't angry, was he? No, his eyebrows were raised and a smile was spreading. Uh oh...

"Zack of Potatoes," Mr. Walden said as he shrugged innocently.

"No!" Zack screamed, but it was too late. His dad snatched him up and flung him over his shoulder. Zack's arms and legs dangled over either side of his father's shoulder. He tried hard to pretend he was too old for this kind of thing, even the tickling, but he liked that his father still took the time to play with him. Michael and Chase's never did.

"Drew! Carter! Help!" Zack shrieked in laughter.

Drew and Carter immediately began their counterattack to save him without a hint of hesitation. With war-cries they both leapt onto their father, Drew putting him in a chokehold while Carter wrapped his whole body around one of his legs.

Zack wasted no time in taking advantage of his father's distraction. He rolled off his shoulder and plowed into his father's midsection, knocking him to the ground. Their wrestling match continued until they were too tired to continue. After his day, Zack didn't have much energy left. His brothers, meanwhile, used their exhaustion as an excuse.

"You're just lucky I'm tired *old man!*" Drew boasted as he tried fruitlessly to break the grip of the arm his father had wrapped around him.

"Boys, stop losing to your father and come set the table

please!" their mother called impatiently from the kitchen.

"Drew, Carter, go help Mom," their father ordered, and though they complained the entire way to the kitchen, Zack's brothers complied. Zack couldn't help but smile tauntingly at them as they left. Once they were gone he let out an exaggerated sigh and allowed himself to fall limply onto his father's arm.

"Long day, huh?" his father asked knowingly. Zack groaned in reply.

"Welcome to every day for your mom and me, buddy!" Mr. Walden said, ruffling Zack's hair roughly. "But I'm really proud of you. You did a great job watching your brothers and keeping them safe today."

"Really?" Zack asked hopefully as his face lit up. He never got tired of hearing those words.

"Yes, I really am," his father clarified. "Hey, do you remember that mitt you wanted?"

"Did you get it for me?" Zack snapped to attention. He wanted it so bad!

"Well, no. But you showed your Mom and me you're responsible enough to watch your brothers while we're away," he began. "So I'll tell you what, if you watch them this Saturday night for a few hours and help me out in the yard over spring break, I'll pay you, and then you can buy it yourself. Deal?"

Zack and considered what his dad said for only a moment before a pleased grin plastered itself on his face.

"Deal!" Zack agreed, offering his hand to his father. The two shook on it, sealing the deal. His dad always kept his promises, and yard work wasn't too hard. Of course, there was the babysitting too, but that was easy enough, right? It didn't take Zack more than a moment to realize that no, it probably wouldn't be easy at all.

7. A Pile of Peas

"**CHASE** Ethan Talbert, what have you done to your clothes?" Chase's mother boomed out the car window as he jogged up to her car. Chase looked a little worse for wear after his tussle with Michael on the playground at lunch followed by a rough game of football during the after-school program. The knees of his pants and the elbows of his hoodie were deep green with grass stains, and both had traces of the same brown mud that caked his shoes. That along with the grime that covered his hands and face made him look more like someone who'd just emerged from a long nature hike than a boy who'd just finished a day at school.

Chase smiled sheepishly, knowing he was in trouble and trying to deflect his mother's anger so she wouldn't rethink her promise to consider letting him go to visit his father.

"Sorry, Mom," he began. "I fell a lot playing football." Finished with his apology, he opened the door and made ready to sit down in the passenger's seat.

"Don't even think about it!" Ms. Martin yelled, hurling her

hands to cover the seat so Chase couldn't sit down. "You're not getting in until I cover the seat and *those* are off." She pointed to Chase's shoes.

His mom went to the trunk and retrieved a towel and a plastic grocery bag.

"Put this on the seat," she commanded, handing Chase the towel, and placing the plastic bag on the floor. Chase compiled but made sure to take his time and sigh loudly and frequently to express how annoying he found it.

"Hey, don't give me that attitude, buster," she scolded. "Clothes and shoes are way too expensive for you to destroy them as often as you do. We don't have as much money as we used to when, when your father was here. If he'd just help more like he's supposed to…" she whispered to herself before trailing off.

"What do you mean? Are we broke?" Chase asked quickly. He'd never tell his mother, since he knew she worked hard so he could still play baseball with his friends, but he often worried that they wouldn't have enough money and they'd have to move again.

"Nothing, sweetie. It's okay, we're not broke. We're doing just fine, you and me. I promise," she said softly. Chase replied with an unsure but nevertheless trusting smile before she put the car in drive and they began the trip home.

The sun was beginning to set when they pulled into the driveway of their modest home: a gray and white single-story with a huge, old oak tree in the front yard. He liked his home but constantly thought about when his parents were still together and they'd lived in the same neighborhood as the Waldens. Back then, he used to walk to school with Zack every day, and it was always easy to find somebody to play with. But that all ended two years ago when his mother sold it and they moved to their current neighborhood a short distance away because it had been too expensive to live in their old house. It was still in the Frasier Elementary attendance area, which was great, but things had never been quite the same.

They pulled into the garage, and he helped unload the groceries she'd bought before picking him up from school. When he finished, left his muddy sneakers outside to dry and went to shower. At first, Chase took his time, since he'd never really warmed up from his football game, but when the smells of dinner drifted into the bathroom, his mouth began to water and his stomach growled. He quickly got out, threw on a t-shirt and a pair of sweats, and scurried to the kitchen, his hair still damp.

"Smells really good, Mom!" Chase proclaimed. He always took care to ensure he made his mom feel appreciated, even when she made things he really didn't like much. Part of the reason was just to be nice; the other was it buttered her up for when he got in trouble.

"Well, thank you, Chase," she replied graciously. "Remember you said that when you see the peas."

"Eww..." Chase moaned in complete disappointment. "But Mommy, you know I don't like peas."

"Don't try that 'mommy' stuff now, it won't work!" She laughed. "You said it smelled great, so now you're stuck with it!"

Chase smirked and sat down at the table. The two sat in

relative silence the first few minutes, Chase waiting patiently for the right moment to bring up his trip. When his mom didn't say anything about it, he stared down at the mountain of peas, his most hated vegetable, and got the hint.

"It's gonna be worth it. Probably. Maybe," Chase thought, trying to psych himself up for the task ahead of him. He took a deep breath and dove in, but no matter how hard he tried, each bite came with a grimace, and he suffered through the whole pile. A disgusted frown adorned his face when he finally finished.

"Well, now that you're finally done, we can talk." She laughed.

"Can I please go, Mom? Please? Please!" Chase pleaded, bouncing up and down in his chair. He couldn't remember the last time he'd been this excited, and his heart felt like it would leap out of his chest. In a way, it almost reminded him of Christmas mornings and being forced to take pictures while the presents sat a few feet away just begging to be opened.

"I have to be honest, Chase, I don't like the idea of you flying alone," his mother began, and Chase felt his smile sink into a frown.

"I think you're too young for it," she stated.

"But Mom!" Chase began before being cut off.

"I'm not finished," she continued. "I think you're too young, but I know how much this means to you. So, if you keep your grades up and work the details out with you father, then you can go."

"Really?" Chase exclaimed, overjoyed at an answer he honestly hadn't expected.

"Yes, really."

"Yes! Thank you, Mom!" Chase cheered, so excited he

slammed his hands on the table and nearly knocked over his glass. Smiling sheepishly, he lowered himself back into his chair and prepared to ask what he knew would be the more difficult question.

"Hey, Mom, do you think Dad could stay with us?" Chase asked nervously. His mother's only response was nearly choking as she took a drink.

"What?" was all she could manage to say through her coughing.

"We're going to make it to finals this year, Mom, and we're gonna win," Chase began. "Dad said if we made it all the way he'd fly in to see it. So could he stay with us?"

"Isn't it a little early for that, Chase?"

"No. We're going to win, Mom. We all swore on it," Chase insisted, thinking if he could just get his dad home then maybe, just maybe...

"Well, if you boys get that far, then your dad would be a dummy for not coming," his mother declared. Chase leaned toward her and raised both eyebrows, silently begging for an answer.

"That means yes, Chase," she said with a sigh and a roll of her eyes. Chase beamed and immediately got to work hurriedly scarfing down the rest of his dinner. Less than minute later, he shot up from the table.

"Where are you off to so fast?" his mother asked.

"Dad said he'd call tonight after dinner, and I don't want to miss it!"

"Did he now?" Ms. Martin asked suspiciously.

"Yeah, he said he wanted to tell me more about the trip."
Chase rinsed off his plate at the sink. "May I be excused?"

"I guess so. Yes," his mother stammered.

"Thanks, Mom! I'll be in my room, okay?" Chase shouted as
he bounded down the hall to his bedroom.

"Do your reading homework while you wait!" she called after
him.

"Okay, I will!" he yelled from his door, which he shut loudly
behind him a moment after.

· · · · ·

KNOCK *Knock Knock.*

"Chase, wake up, it's time for school!" Chase heard from a
place far removed from the dream he was having. A second call
pulled him away, snapping him into reality.

He moaned and lazily raised his head from his pillow, already
feeling the bad case of bed-head he had. But that was fine; his
hat would cover it anyway. Probably even make it look better.
But that train of thought was soon broken.

"Oh no!" Chase said aloud when he saw his phone, still
clutched in his hand. He remembered falling asleep well after
midnight after swearing to himself he'd wait and didn't even
remember closing his eyes. He frantically punched in his
password but saw no calls, no texts, nothing. Undaunted, Chase
sent the same text he did every morning, even though he rarely
received a reply.

"Good morning, Dad!"

8 Broken Glass and Big Brothers

"**THANKS** for the ride, Mr. Scott! Bye, Zack!" Michael shouted as he slid out the door of Mr. Scott's minivan. He shut the door and ran, half turned around, toward his garage, waving back at his friend.

"Bye, Mikey-Man!" Zack called out to him from the window as he and his father drove off down Stoneleigh Boulevard, Michael's street, and out toward the main road.

It had been a short practice that evening. After all, only being early April, the days were fairly short and still a bit chilly. His wrist had a few weeks left before it would be fully healed, so Michael had been commanded to take it easy by his coach-- "light duty," he'd called it. Michael was annoyed that he couldn't practice hitting or pitching, but he could still catch with his left hand and make lighter throws with his right. He wasn't able to do what he loved, at least not fully, but any time away from his home with his friends made him happy.

Michael was the youngest of four children, his brother and sisters all much older than he. His mother called him her "favorite accident," but he never liked the way that sounded or the way his father would scoff when she brought it up. He hated being home. Even though he had every electronic and toy he'd ever wanted, he still hated it. Even with a batting cage in his basement, he hated it. But what he hated most of all was constantly being compared to his siblings.

They always made everything look easy, but it wasn't. He always seemed to be playing catch-up. His brother Jason played club ball, lacrosse, and soccer, so Michael did too. His father would always talk about what a great pitcher Jason was, and no matter how hard Michael worked, he never seemed to be as good as Jason was, at least in his father's eyes. Meanwhile, his sisters had always been on the honor roll, and his dad had no tolerance for Michael bringing home anything besides straight A's. His dad expected perfection from them all, but he always seemed the most disappointed by Michael, who never understood why. Nothing he did was ever good enough, no matter how hard he tried. But this year would be different. This year he'd prove his dad wrong! He'd beat Jason's record, he'd win, and his dad would have to be proud of him. He'd have to be...

Michael punched in the security code for the three-car garage and waited impatiently for it to open. His older sisters, Olivia and Jessica, were away at college, and his mother and father's cars were both gone. No surprise there. Only one vehicle was still there, and it was the one he least wanted to see.

"Oh, crap." Michael sucked in a shaky breath and his pulse quickened when he saw the small SUV that belonged to his seventeen-year old brother, Jason. Swallowing heavily, he entered through the laundry room and closed it as softly as he could manage behind him.

Their home was huge by any account. Michael couldn't have said how many square feet it was, but he knew it was nearly twice the size of any of his friends' houses. He wasn't completely sure what his father's job really was, but he knew that he worked for a large company, traveled often for business and made a *lot* of money. He considered himself lucky that his mom didn't need to work and had been able to stay home when he was younger, but she was involved in so much now that Michael thought that if she had a job it might actually make her less busy. Even with the six of them living there, the house still had two bedrooms to spare and more than enough space to avoid each other if they wanted to, which was exactly what Michael intended to do, but he needed to satisfy his growling stomach first.

Tip-toeing into the kitchen, Michael hurriedly made a sandwich and put it on a plate with as many chips and cookies as he could pile on. After pouring himself a glass of milk, he took off toward the hall to get to his room as quickly as he could and followed the mental map in his head that would help him avoid his brother.

"Mikey!" roared a deep, booming voice, pouncing on Michael as when rounded the corner.

Michael yelped and jumped in fright; his falling plate sent chips raining to the ground and caused his weaker right hand to lose its grip on his glass. It careened toward the ground, exploding on the wooden floor and sending glass shrapnel and liquid everywhere.

"What the hell, Jason!" Michael screamed.

"Ooh, language, Mikey. Language," Jason scolded as he flicked Michael's ear painfully.

"Ow! Screw you, you jerk!" Michael yelled back and pushed his brother.

Jason just let Michael's hands impact on him, letting him see that it did nothing before grabbing both of his arms tightly. His eyes bored into Michael's as he slowly began to squeeze and twist his brother's wrists.

"Stop, Jason!" Michael pleaded, but his brother didn't let up and continued the torsion. Michael hated crying in front of his brother, but with the pain increasing with each second, Michael couldn't keep his eyes from watering.

"Ow! Jason, stop! Stop, you're gonna make it worse!" he wailed when he could take no more.

"Don't cry!" Jason yelled in his brother's face. "You always cry! Man up and fight back!"

"Ow, ow, ow!" Michael screamed frantically. "Please let go!"

Jason sneered at Michael, never taking his scornful gaze from him. Finally, with a disappointed sigh, he released him.

"Fine," he stated with finality before slapping the back of Michael's head. "You gotta learn to fight back, Mikey. If you don't, people will walk all over you. Just. Like. Me."

Michael shrank back, holding his arm tightly to his chest. He trembled, refusing to look his brother in the eye as he tried to stop any tears from falling down his face.

"God, you're such a pansy. You going to cry when you make your team lose again like last year?" Jason spat contemptuously.

"I'm not gonna lose!" Michael shot back with what little bravado he could manage.

"Sure, whatever." Jason rolled his eyes and motioned to the pool of spilled milk and shattered glass on the floor.

"Clean that up before Dad gets home or he'll be pissed." Jason walked down the hall and disappeared through the basement door.

"Jerk…" Michael said between sniffles. He slumped to the floor to retrieve his plate and returned his meal to it before going into the kitchen to get a trash can and a roll of paper towels.

He unrolled a huge volume of sheets and lay them across the puddle, repeating this step until all of the milk had been soaked up.

Then, not thinking, he tried to carefully pick up the shards of glass with his fingers and received a nasty cut for his mistake. He shook his finger in shock before rolling a bit of paper towel around it until he could find a bandage.

"I *hate* him," Michael thought to himself as he fumed, angrily picking up the rest of the glass with a wad of paper towel and thinking of the ways he could get back at this brother. But as he cautiously picked up the last bit of his broken cup, he knew he'd be too scared to do any of it.

Michael was careful to cover up the pieces of glass in the wastebasket with the paper towels before sliding it back underneath the sink, praying his parents wouldn't find it, especially his father. He grabbed his plate and went upstairs to his room, hurled the door shut, and slumped down into his gaming chair, where he angrily ate his dinner in silence. When he finished, he put on his headphones, grabbed his controller and lost himself in a game until Jason pounded on his door and ordered him to go to sleep.

Michael crawled into bed, not even bothering to change out of his clothes, and looked at his phone, finding it was nearly midnight and that he'd forgotten the world for nearly five hours.

He lay in the quiet for a few minutes before rolling onto his side and trying unsuccessfully to go to sleep; the sting of the loss at the end of their last season, which he still blamed himself for, kept his mind awake. He could forget the world for a few hours while he played his games, but it always came back to him in his dreams.

9. Brady-Bear

BRADY'S head burst from the water, and he sucked in as much air as he possibly could in a great, drawing breath. He'd pushed himself hard on the final lap, and he was exhausted. He grabbed the edge with one tired, nearly limp arm while he slid his goggles up onto his forehead with the other. He looked up eagerly at his coach, who stood a few feet away holding a stopwatch.

"How you think you did?" his coach, a young, college-aged man, asked him.

"Arms like...noodles!" Brady whined while waving his arms about limply.

"Well, they should be. You shaved off a full second, Brady!"

"Yes!" Brady cheered as he raised his fist into the air in celebration before slamming it into the water.

"You'll be in good shape next weekend if you keep that up, kid." Coach Matterson looked pleased with Brady's accomplishment. He blew his whistle in three sharp bursts, signaling that practice was over and it was time for Brady and his teammates to head home.

Brady pulled himself from the water, high-fived his coach, and followed the other kids from his team into the locker room to change. As usual, he knew that he had to move fast, since his sister Abby was always on time, and his family had so much going on that being late was never an option. He dried off as quickly as he could and pulled his post-swimming clothes from his bag: a plain black zip-up hoodie and joggers he'd worn the day he'd placed second in a major meet. It had been the first time he'd done so well, and, being very superstitious, Brady had equated the outfit with good luck and had worn it to and from every practice and meet since.

But Brady soon lost his sense of urgency. He was thrilled at his accomplishment, already imagining winning the following weekend. He absentmindedly tried to pull his socks over his still-damp feet when his daydream was interrupted by the call of his name.

"Hey, Brady!" His coach yelled from locker room entrance of the local YMCA where he practiced. "Your sister is here. Better move it!"

Brady called it quits on his task and left his socks half off his feet as he slid into his sandals and ran through the lobby and out the front doors as quickly as he could. As usual, his sister was waiting right out front by the curb in the blue Honda she'd inherited from their dad, her face buried in her phone. When he saw she was distracted, Brady grinned, raced up to the car, and smashed his face and hands up against the window like a scene out of a cartoon. His sister looked startled for a moment, then stared at him with a look that to Brady seemed half annoyed and half amused. She pushed a button to roll down the window, but Brady kept his position like a mime, only moving his gaze to meet hers and smiling innocently. Though she tried to keep a straight face, she couldn't maintain her composure and laughed.

"Get in the car, you goober!" Abby ordered.

Brady finally broke his act, opened the door and flung himself into the car. He wanted to tell her about his accomplishment, but before he could get the words out, his sister grabbed him and pulled him into a bear hug. It was a daily ritual he wasn't much a fan of.

"Hi, Brady-Bear!" She beamed and squeezed her brother tight.

"No, you're evil!" Brady screamed as he tried to escape his sister's iron embrace. He was surprised at how quickly she let go.

"Oh my God, Brady!" Abby gasped. She pulled back, her sleeves soaked from Brady's pool-drenched hair that he'd neglected to dry again. Brady responded by running his hand through his hair vigorously, sending a fine mist of water droplets all over her.

"I'm going to kill you!" she shrieked, but her laughter told Brady otherwise. After Chase, Michael and Zack, she was his best friend and the only person who really understood him. If nothing else, she was one of only a handful of people who could put up with his weirdness and tolerate his pranks for more than a few minutes at a time. She'd joke and play with him, and he'd pretend not to like it. It had always been that way.

"I hate you," Abby said with a scornful expression that Brady knew was fake.

"I have a towel in my bag if you want it." Brady smirked, being irritating on purpose.

"You're such a turd." Abby finally laughed after a moment and shook her head.

"Your favorite turd!"

Abby just rolled her eyes and turned up the radio to their favorite station, and they started on their way home.

If a person could describe the pace of the McCormick family's life in one word, "full" would be a good choice. More so than his friends, Brady was involved in many different activities. He was never forced; he was just interested in a lot of different things. Of course, there was baseball with his friends, but he also participated in swimming, and his father had taught him how to cook and play the guitar. His sister was no less engaged in sports and music, while his father, when he wasn't working at the hospital being Dr. McCormick, had numerous hobbies he busied himself with. As if this weren't enough, his mother was a sales rep for a pharmaceutical company where she worked odd hours and often wasn't home in the evenings. Ultimately this was fine for Brady, who was fairly self-reliant and always had energy and curiosity to spare, even if that curiosity didn't always include the subjects taught in school. And unless that subject was gym, art, music, or science, he usually wasn't interested.

The siblings rolled into the driveway at nearly the same time as their father, who was still in his scrubs as he stepped out of his SUV. Brady leaped from the car, ignoring Abby's calls for him to carry his swim bag, and sprinted toward his father.

"Dad, can I cook tonight?" Brady asked hopefully.

"You mean I don't have to keep working and get to relax for a change?" Mr. McCormick asked. "Be my guest. Just don't catch anything on fire again."

"That wasn't my fault and you know it!" Brady insisted, leaning in close to his father like he was going to tell him a secret.

"I know Abby put that towel by the burner. I think she's trying to kill me!" Brady explained.

"If I was gonna kill you, I'd have done it already," Abby said dryly before hurling Brady's swim bag at his chest. Brady stumbled as he caught it but managed not to fall.

"See? She's out to get me, Dad!" Brady told his dad with wide, worried eyes.

"Enough with the stories, Brady, I'm hungry. Go get your chef on so we can eat," his father said, gently pushing Brady along through the front door, his story getting wilder by the second.

A half hour and an annihilated kitchen later, the three of them sat around the dinner table eating the meal Brady had prepared. It may have just been grilled ham and cheese sandwiches with tomato soup, but to him it was still an accomplishment, and Brady was proud to report that he hadn't caught anything on fire. Conversation shifted between Abby's softball and drama practices and Brady's barely-contained excitement about his faster swim time, but Mr. McCormick seemed distracted and checked his phone every handful of minutes.

"Dad, no phones at the table," Brady scolded his father jokingly.

"Hmm?" Mr. McCormick murmured as he looked up suddenly. It was as if he'd been snapped out of a deep thought.

"No phones at the table, Dad, you said!" Brady repeated with more authority, not about to see his dad doing something Brady knew he could never get away with.

"Oh, right. I'm sorry," his father stammered as he tossed it away onto the couch in the nearby living room.

"Is something wrong, Dad?" Abby asked.

"Well, your mother was supposed to be home by now, and I haven't heard anything back," he explained. "She's been getting home so late the last few weeks."

"She'll be home, Dad," Abby reassured him. "Maybe she's stuck with a client."

It was true that their mother would often get caught up with a potential customer and that meant getting home late, even on weeknights. Still, just because it made sense didn't make it any easier for Brady. He was starting to miss her and resented how late she'd been getting home.

"You're probably right," Mr. McCormick agreed. "I'm sure I'll hear from her in a bit.

In the meantime, let's enjoy this great feast from our very distinguished chef!" He ruffled Brady's hair. Brady grinned, enjoying the praise.

The trio finished, and Brady cleaned up and practiced his music for a time with his dad, then used up some of his screen time for the week before he went to bed around eight-thirty. As was usual for him, Brady lay quietly in bed for quite some time, trying to give his mind a chance to slow down, but tonight his brain was having none of it. He'd left a bowl of soup and a sandwich in the fridge for his mom, and he was hoping to have the opportunity to *accidentally* wake up when she got home so he could give it to her. And, of course, he also planned to use it as an excuse to stay up later. But no matter what stories he dreamed up or how much he played with the multitude of rubber bracelets he wore as fidgets, as nine o'clock rolled around, Brady's eyes grew heavy.

"Come on, Mom, where *are* you?" Brady asked while looking up at the ceiling fan spinning slowly above him.

Someone must have been listening, because no more than a minute later, he heard the front door open and shut, followed by the telltale *clip-clop* of his mother's shoes on the wooden floors. Brady's eyes shot open wide and alert as he hurled his blankets from him, swung his legs off his bed and darted to his door. Brady had every intention of running to the stairs and bounding the rest of the way down, but as he crept into the hallway, he froze when he heard the tone of his parents' hushed, yet undeniably heated conversation. He stopped, pulled the door closed until it was only open a crack, and listened to the angry whispers. He couldn't quite make out the words, but he knew what it was about, because it was always about the same things.

"Stop," Brady quietly prayed. "Please stop."

As the time crawled by, he hoped he'd hear one of them apologize, but the fight continued. Brady's eyes fell, and he softly pulled the door shut, sliding back onto his bed with a million thoughts running through his mind. He knew, just like every time his parents fought, that he wouldn't be getting much sleep that night. Going without enough sleep was something he was starting to get used to.

10 Practice

ZACK zeroed in on the grounder that sped toward him like a bullet, snatching it up in his well-worn mitt and zipping back to touch first base. Out!

"Nice job, Walden!" their coach called from home plate. "Keep it up!"

"Thanks, coach! Zack said, trying to catch his breath. This wasn't normal, wait-a-minute-or-two-between-plays practice; this was rapid-fire, coach-hits-a-ball-every-twenty-seconds practice. He basically hadn't stopped moving the entire time. It was exhausting!

Today was all about fielding, which was much more difficult to practice during the cold Ohio winters, and every kid was taking a turn at their starting and secondary position. Coach Nolan, Ander's dad, had started as their new head coach last year and had a different way of doing things than those they'd had when they were younger. One of those differences was ensuring his players could play at least two positions well enough to cover for a teammate in the case of an injury or other absence. Some of the boys and their parents loved it, some of them hated it, and Coach Nolan didn't seem to care what any of them thought.

This being the second week of 'threes' (what they called those weeks with three practices) and the boys were at their usual positions: Brady in left field, Chase at shortstop, and of course Zack at first. The obvious exception was Mikey, who wasn't even close to being able to pitch. He was on "light duty," as their coach put it, and it wasn't hard for Zack to tell that Mikey *hated* it.

"Coming your way, Chase!" Coach Nolan called to Chase at shortstop. "Plays are at second and first!"

All right, Chase, c'mon! Don't miss it this time!

With that warning, their coach tossed the white orb into the air. It spun rapidly as it rose and fell before the aluminum bat of their head coach connected with it. With an echoing *tink* of leather on metal, the ball sailed out toward Chase before dipping suddenly and speeding along the ground. But he was moving way slower than usual and didn't even get his mitt on the ground in time. The ball shot right under his mitt and between his legs before rolling into the outfield, where Brady was backing him up. He scooped up the ball and threw it to Ander at second base, who then hurled it to Zack at first, both making tags on their imaginary runners after they'd made their catches. Rookie mistake! How did Chase keep doing that today?

"Nice backup job, Brady!" Coach Nolan yelled out to left field. "Ander, Zack, good job getting your tags!"

That's the third easy play he's missed today. What's up with him? Zack thought.

It wasn't just Zack who noticed. Chase threw his head to the sky and growled. Made sense that he seemed mad; any one of those errors could have easily cost them a real game!

"Chase, you okay?" Zack called, but Chase didn't seem to hear him. Or maybe he just pretended her hadn't.

"You alive out there, Talbert?" Coach Nolan called to Chase.

"I'm fine, Coach," Chase yelled back, but he didn't sound too convincing when he said it.

"Why don't you go get a drink and a breather?" their coach suggested, pointing to the benches where their water and gear was stored. That was definitely an order, not a suggestion. Chase complied and dragged himself off the field, his gaze never leaving the dirt every step of the way there. Zack couldn't help but wonder if he was okay. He sure didn't look it...

"Michael, think you can throw it easy to third or second?" Zack heard his coach ask as Chase shuffled his way to the benches.

"Yeah!" Mikey answered excitedly, zipping onto the field and passing Chase along the way, who glared at him.

Come on, Mikey, don't poke the bear!

"Back in business!" their coach said before another *crack* rang out, bringing Zack back to reality just in time to see Brady chasing down the ball at mach speed, diving with his mitt outstretched. When he hopped to his feet, he was covered in grass stains and dirt, but he hadn't dropped the ball!

"I got it! I got it!" he happily yelled as he held it aloft and half-ran, half-hopped toward the infield, stopping to do his trademark victory dance.

"Brady, we're trying to make a play here! Runner is on the way to third!" Coach Nolan said with not even a hint of amusement.

"Sorry, Coach!" Brady apologized before sending the ball streaking into the mitt of their third baseman.

Chase probably wouldn't admit to it, but to Zack, it sure looked like he needed a break. Chase was a great friend and usually a nice kid, but sometimes he'd just get really mad or frustrated with himself, like he seemed to be today. Maybe he was tired since--uh oh.

"Oh crap, is he asleep?" Zack said to himself.

It sure seemed like he might be. He leaned against the dugout fencing and had his hat pulled down over his eyes. Coach would be so mad if he caught him sleeping! Zack had trouble keeping his focus for the next few minutes, and when their coach finally called time, he sprinted to the dugout as quickly as he could.

"Chase! Chase, hey!" Zack nudged his friend gently, but enough to wake him up.

"Zack?" Chase questioned, blinking the sleep from his eyes.

"You fell asleep on the bench, dude. Practice is over!"

"What? Oh no!" Chase looked around frantically, and his face turned white as a sheet when Coach Nolan entered the dugout.

"I'm sorry, Coach!" Chase stammered. "I didn't mean to fall asleep! I'm just really tired and…"

"Hey, it's *okay,* Chase. We all have our off days," he replied. "Get some sleep though, okay? You definitely didn't get enough last night."

"I will," Chase said, sounding relieved.

"Are you okay?" Zack asked. "You've never fallen asleep at

practice before."

"I'm fine, Zack!"

"Okay…" Zack said, shrinking back. Why'd he say it like that? He was just trying to help.

"Wait, I'm sorry," Chase began. "I stayed up real late waiting for my dad to call about the trip."

"Did he?" Zack asked.

"No." Chase's shoulders slumped.

"I'm sorry, dude." Zack said awkwardly. It was hard to find the right words when stuff like this happened. Chase's dad never seemed to want to talk to him or see him anymore.

"It's fine. Let's just get packed up, okay?" Chase tried to reassure him, even though Zack was certain he wasn't okay at all. Then Mikey came over, and that was probably the last thing Chase needed right now. He'd probably say something about playing Chase's position. But this time he managed to keep his mouth shut, which Zack thought was a real miracle, and he even helped gather their gear just as Zack's dad's van pulled into the muddy parking lot.

Unless it was a day when Brady's father wasn't working, Scott Walden and his wife Hannah were always the first off of work. "One of the perks of being a teacher," he would say. He and Zack's mother had volunteered over the years to be the main ferriers of the boys to and from their practices. If it hadn't been for them, it likely wouldn't have been possible for the boys to play together for so long.

Zack, Michael, and Chase each said goodbye to Brady as he

caught a ride home with his sister. They slid the van door open, tossed their gear into the back, and took their seats together in the front row.

"Hi boys! Good practice today?" Zack's dad asked.

"Hey Dad!" Zack greeted his father as he lifted himself into the van and slammed the door shut. "Yeah, practice was really good. I'm still at first!"

"Good job, Zack. Keep working hard!" his dad replied. "Think you guys are ready to tear it up this year?"

"Uh, yeah!" Zack insisted. "We're going to wreck everyone this year!"

"That's the spirit," his father said. "Chase, Mikey, what about you two?"

"Coach let me try shortstop today!" Mikey chirped excitedly.

"Even though your wrist isn't all healed up?" Mr. Walden questioned.

"Yeah! He let me throw easy to second and third," Mikey explained before Chase could get a word in. "And Chase missed a few easy plays, so Coach gave him a break and he fell asleep on the bench," he continued until Zack jabbed him in the ribs with his elbow. "Ow!" Mikey complained.

"Mikey!" Zack hissed, glaring at his friend, who had, as often happened, said something mean without intending to.

Zack turned to Chase, who looked back at him only briefly with hurt eyes before turning and resting his head on the window, staring silently at the road.

"Chase, are you okay, buddy?" Zack's dad asked, his eyes

reflecting in the rear-view mirror.

"I'm fine, Mr. Scott," Chase answered quietly. "I'm just really tired."

"Gotcha. Well, I'll drop you off first then, so you can get some rest.".

"Okay. Thanks," Chase replied with the same near-whisper voice, never taking his eyes from the road.

· · · · ·

A GOOD twenty minutes later, when both Chase and Mikey had been dropped off, Zack moved up into the front seat next to his dad. For the last leg of the journey home, Zack was quiet and deep in thought. It was some time before he finally spoke.

"Dad, do you think something's wrong with Chase?" he asked.

"I think he definitely looked tired," Mr. Walden replied.

"I think he looked sad," Zack said thoughtfully after a brief moment of silence.

"Why do you say that?" his father asked.

"I just do," Zack said, shrugging. "I dunno, I guess it's that Chase usually gets mad when Mikey says something dumb or mean to him, but today he didn't."

"Maybe he's just getting better at ignoring Mikey's big mouth," his father said jokingly. "But if you're worried about him, you should ask him what's wrong."

"That's weird, Dad." Zack looked skeptically at his father.

"How's that weird?" he asked.

"Because. Boy's don't ask things like that."

"Don't you ask Carter and Drew what's wrong when you see them hurt or upset?" he prodded, giving Zack a knowing look.

"Well, yeah. But that's different. They're my brothers."

"Zachary, you've known Chase ever since you were in little. I'd say he's just as much your brother as Drew or Carter. At least in all the ways that really count. You always look out for your brothers; don't you think you should look out for Chase too?"

Zack glanced at his father thoughtfully for a moment before turning to look out the windshield and considering what his father had said. He hadn't decided what he was going to do by the time they pulled into their driveway, but he was starting to get an idea.

11 Snap

CHASE slouched in the passenger's seat with his hat pulled low over his eyes. His arms were crossed, his posture making it clear he didn't want to be there and wasn't in the mood to talk.

"Chase?" his mother said. "It's time to go."

"Do I have to go today?" Chase murmured, hoping against hope that she'd cave and just take him back home. No part of him wanted to go to school today, but he was running out of ways to try to get out of it.

"Yes, you have to go. You're not running a fever, and you seemed fine last night," she replied.

"But my stomach still feels weird," Chase whined. "And I'm so tired!"

"I know you're not sick, Chase. Why don't you want to be at school with your friends? Is there something going on I don't know about?" Chase sat in silence for a long moment before he finally spoke.

"I sucked at practice, Mom. I sucked!" Chase ranted.

"Everyone saw. and Coach put Mikey at shortstop instead of me. He's going to say something about it today. I know he will!"

"I'm sure he won't, Chase. He's your friend," she insisted. "He probably forgot anyway."

"Mikey's like the most popular kid in our class, Mom! He definitely has the biggest mouth. He probably told everyone in class yesterday."

"Chase, that's ridiculous. He's your friend; he wouldn't do that." She reached over and pulled Chase's hat up and was startled when he glared at her with an angry, tear-filled stare.

"Chase, what's...?" she whispered.

"Nothing's wrong!" he raged, yanking his backpack from the ground and throwing the door open.

"Chase!" she yelled after him just as he slammed the car door shut, storming up the walkway and through the front doors of the school.

Chase dragged himself through the hall all the way to the office, wishing he hadn't snapped at his mom. She hadn't deserved it, which made him feel even worse than he already did. After he dropped off the note explaining the reason for his absence the day before, he tried to vent some of his frustration before he made it to class so he didn't say anything else stupid.

"I hate it here!" Chase swore under his breath, slamming the bottom of his fist against the wall as he made his way through the halls.

"Great, now my hand hurts too!" he growled, hating the pain and hating even more having to fight the urge to cry. He could feel it welling up, and it was all he could do to shove it down.

He looked for any possible excuse to slow his trip to class so he could calm down: a drink of water here, picking up a piece of paper there, and unpacking his backpack much more carefully than normal when he finally reached his locker. Only when the third bell rang did he reluctantly cross the threshold into Mrs. Meister's classroom, where he fully expected the rest of the day to be as horrible as the last few had been.

He dawdled to where Mrs. Meister sat, handed her his admittance slip, and walked listlessly over to his seat. Chase looked over to the area of the classroom Mrs. Meister called the "Reader's Corner," where a large, plush rug covered the whole corner. The first ten feet of the walls in either direction were lined with pillows and comfortable chairs, and it was usually reserved for the kids who got the best grades or those who helped the elder teacher with classroom chores. More like for the teacher's pets, so no surprise Mikey was there. Everyone else had to work hard to be allowed into that area, but Mikey was there almost daily because he was Mrs. Meister's "favorite helper." Biggest kiss-up was more like it. Mikey looked up from his book and greeted Chase, but he pretended not to hear. The last thing he wanted to do was talk to Mikey.

He dropped into his seat, pulled out his notebook, and pretended to work on the rough draft of the story he was supposed to be writing for class. If he could just make it through Language Arts with Mrs. Meister, his least favorite subject and teacher, he might make it through the day and get to the weekend.

He coasted through the first half of class easily enough, but then silent reading time came along. Chase rested his book in his lap and laid his head between his arms on the table so he could look down at it, and it wasn't long before he let his eyes close.

He couldn't have known how long he'd been out for, but it was long enough. The next thing he knew, he was pulled from a deep, dreamless sleep by a harsh tapping on his shoulder. He moaned tiredly as his eyes cracked open, barely able to squint in the harsh light. He felt a wet sensation on the side of his mouth from a thin line of spittle that had begun to fall down and stuck to his chin as he rose and turned his head. Mrs. Meister was standing over him like an angry statue, her arms crossed and her eyes anything but forgiving.

"Mr. Talbert, my desks aren't beds, and I don't appreciate you drooling on my books," Mrs. Meister said dryly.

"I'm sorry, Mrs. Meister!" was all Chase could manage. His eyes went wide with sudden panic, and his heart thundered when he realized he'd fallen asleep in class for the first time ever. "I'm just so tired!"

"I guessed that," the elder teacher said. "Don't let it happen again or I'll be giving your mother a call."

"Okay…" Chase whispered back. He slumped his shoulders and drew his arms in close to himself in an effort to seem smaller.

Though Mrs. Meister hadn't spoken overly loud to him, Chase was certain the class had watched the scene unfold. They wouldn't dare laugh out loud in the room of "Mean Ol' Meister," but he'd seen the grins and heard the whispering. The damage was already done. He pulled the bill of his hat down low to try to hide his red-hot face from his classmates. In that moment, he wanted nothing more than to disappear.

The rest of the morning was about as rough as the start had been. Chase wasn't able to finish his book questions for Mrs. Meister, he spilled paint on himself in art, and he was fairly certain he failed the science quiz in Mr. Dunlap's class. The thought of lunch and recess was all that got him through, and the moment they were told it was time to go, Chase was the first one out the door, nearly knocking over several of his classmates in his rush to leave. He moved at something between a jog and a fast walk and reached the cafeteria right on the heels of Mr. Dunlap's class, who always seemed to go before his. He sighed in relief when he saw Zack and Brady at their usual spot, unpacking their lunches, and he slumped into the seat next to Zack with a groan. He tossed his lunch bag on the table with a loud *thump*. Chase couldn't have put it into words, but he knew he needed his friends today.

"Hey Chase!" Brady greeted him through a mouthful of sandwich.

"Hey, guys." Chase sighed as he overturned his lunch bag and spilled its contents haphazardly over the table.

"What's up?" Zack asked cautiously.

"This whole day's been terrible!" Chase fumed. "Everything sucked!"

"What happened?" Zack inquired with genuine concern. "You didn't text me back or anything yesterday. Were you okay?"

"I played so crappy on Wednesday," Chase lamented. "My dad said if we make it to finals he'd come visit, but…"

Chase stopped when the gaggle of kids from his class a few tables away started telling a very animated story. The three who were listening turned and looked in his direction but quickly spun back around and huddled together when they noticed he'd seen. Chase shrank down as the embarrassment he'd felt earlier flooded back again.

"Just ignore them, Chase. They're being turds," Zack said reassuringly.

"Easy for you to say. No one ever makes fun of *you*…" Chase muttered.

"People laugh at me all the time. I don't care," Brady said absently.

"But I do, Brady!" Chase snapped, and Brady looked away.

"I'm sorry, guys. It's just…" Chase began. "It's just I'm supposed to see my dad over spring break and he hasn't called me yet. And with me sucking at practice…"

Chase tried desperately to find the words and get what had been weighing him down off his chest, but he never got the chance.

"I can't believe you fell asleep in class!" Mikey laughed as he slid into the empty seat next to Brady. "Mean Ol' Meister was so mad! You were so funny, dude, you drooled and everything!" Mikey wheezed, falling forward onto the table in a laughing fit.

"Shut up!" Chase hissed, trying to keep his voice as low as he could, but any attempt at not attracting any more attention was foiled by Mikey's gasping laughter.

"Mikey, stop!" Brady pleaded, pushing on his shoulder in a vain effort to get his attention.

"Seriously, dude, quit it!" Zack insisted.

Chase growled and clenched his teeth, his face growing hot.

That was it! He grabbed his sandwich in an iron grip, wound up, and hurled it into Mikey's face. The bread smashed into his cheek, lunch meat and toppings exploding out both sides. Brady flinched and only just got his eyes closed in time to prevent a glob of mustard from flying straight into them.

"What the heck, Chase!" Mikey demanded.

"I said shut up!" Chase screamed as he stood and slammed his hands down on the table.

"About what, you psycho?" Mikey yelled back definitely.

Chase nearly roared and started to lunge across the table, but Zack was up in a flash and got his hands on the sides of his shirt just in time.

"Chase, stop!" Zack yelled as he pulled his friend back. He was taller than Chase, and older too, but Chase was mad. He was strong when he was mad.

Chase twisted and ducked out of Zack's hold before driving his arms into his friend's chest. Zack clearly hadn't been ready to take the hit and stumbled backward, lost his balance, and fell, cracking his head on the corner of the table on his way down.

"Big surprise, Zack takes Mikey's side just like *every time!*" Chase thundered down at his friend, who had curled into a ball and was clutching his head with both hands. It took a moment for the anger to fade, but when it did, he saw Zack shaking and squeezing his eyes shut to try to hide his tears. Thick blood oozed from between his fingers from an unseen wound and dyed his sandy hair a deep crimson.

His classmates had all shot up and moved away from Chase and Zack and formed a circle around them. Brady and Michael ran to kneel by Zack, and a split second later, Evelyn smashed her way through the crowd and slid down on her knees next to Zack, medical gloves already pulled on.

"Get me towels, Brady!" she ordered.

"What towels?" Brady stuttered anxiously, looking around frantically.

"The ones we use for the tables! But unused ones!" Evelyn explained as she pried Zack's hands away from the wound and slapped a gauze pad on top of it. Still Brady didn't budge.

"From the lunch lady! Move it!" she bellowed, slapping his arm repeatedly until he got the point.

"Okay, okay!" Brady said hurriedly before turning on his heel and darting through the crowd to follow Evelyn's orders.

Chase took short, ragged breaths as he stood frozen in place. How could he have done that?

"Zack! Oh no! No, no, no!" he said quietly as he kneeled down to try to help, only to be shoved back by Mikey.

"Get away!" Mikey yelled as he knelt protectively over Zack. "What's wrong with you?"

Chase felt like he was in a dream. As Mrs. Meister and the custodian burst through the crowd to help Zack, he felt himself lifted upright, and a firm press on his shoulder led him away. He was only dimly aware of Mr. Dunlap, who must have heard the commotion from the hallway.

"Let's go, Chase. Right now!" Mr. Dunlap commanded.

"Zack, I'm sorry! I'm sorry, Zack! I'm sorry!" Chase tried to yell over the noise of the crowd as he was moved out of the cafeteria, never once taking his eyes off his injured friend and wishing he could take it all back. He'd ruined it. He'd ruined everything.

12 A Losing Day

ALWAYS first. Never second. Never third. Never, ever last. Michael's dad had taught him that. "Life is a competition," his father would say. "There's winners and there's losers, and Dzierwas aren't losers."

Days like today made Michael feel like anything but a winner, like his father's motto didn't apply to him. Sometimes even when he won, it still felt like losing. Michael hated losing. It scared him to lose.

Today was definitely a losing day. His face was bright red and stung almost like he'd gotten slapped, and Zack was in bad shape. The custodian had moved the gaggle of curious kids as far from the scene as they could go while Mrs. Meister knelt down next to Zack with Evelyn. Brady reappeared with the towels Evelyn requested and she pressed them tightly up against Zack's head, but Michael refused to budge from his side no matter how many times his teacher told him to move or Evelyn threatened to smack him.

"You're gonna be okay, Zack, I promise!" Michael frantically tried to reassure his friend, even though Zack seemed not to hear him. How had everything gone wrong so fast?

"Michael, you need to get back," Mrs. Meister said firmly while Evelyn kept pressure on Zack's cut, which seemed to be a never-ending fountain of red.

"Mmm-mmm!" Michael shook his head defiantly.

"Michael..."

"No!" Michael interrupted.

"Coming through!" Mr. Dunlap bellowed as he returned with the school nurse.

"Michael," Mr. Dunlap began as he and the nurse knelt down around Zack, "I know you want to help, but you have to move so we can."

Michael's gaze was a stone as he glared at his teacher and felt a hand rest on his shoulder.

"Mikey, let them help," Brady chanced, gently pulling him back toward the rest of the crowd.

In the end, he conceded a few feet so they could get in closer to help Zack. The nurse and Mr. Dunlap managed to sit Zack up, and after some coaxing, Evelyn was convinced to let them take over. Zack's head was bleeding profusely, and small streams of blood ran down his face and neck, staining his shirt. Mrs. Meister tried to calm him, but if it had worked at all, every trace of it disappeared the moment Zack looked down at his bloody hands.

Michael had never seen anyone hurt like this before, but especially not Zack. He'd seen him take a wild pitch straight to the eye, plowed over playing ball against kids twice his size, and take spills off his scooter and skateboard that left him with all kinds of scrapes, bruises, and even a broken finger. No matter the injury, each time he'd barely cried and gotten right back up, but this was different.

As Zack stared down at his hands, Michael saw real fear on his face, but it wasn't until Zack whimpered and began to yell that Michael realized it wasn't fear, it was panic. He was terrified, and it took liberal reassurances and coaxing from Mrs. Meister and the nurse to get him on his feet, holding the towel on his own head while Mr. Dunlap helped him make his wobbly way to the nurse's office.

"Come on!" Michael beckoned Brady as he made to follow.

"Wait, boys!" Mrs. Meister commanded them, holding out her hands and creating an invisible wall Michael knew would be foolish to try to pass. "I know you want to help, but you'll only get in the way."

"But!" Michael tried to think of a way to argue but couldn't find the words.

"I know you're worried about him, but he's going to be just fine, I promise," she assured them.

"Okay. C'mon, Brady," Michael conceded after a moment and made to return to his seat.

The cafeteria slowly became louder as the hushed crowds of kids took their seats once more and gossiped about what had just transpired. Michael and Brady sat in silence for the rest of the period, picking at their lunches with disinterest. Michael didn't feel like eating anyway, and he was pretty sure Brady didn't either. Besides, Michael could feel the eyes of the whole cafeteria burning into him, eyes he had no intention of meeting. He usually liked being the center of attention, but not like this. When the time came to be dismissed for recess, Michael and Brady left the cafeteria together, but Michael turned the opposite way down the hall, heading in the direction of the office instead of toward the doors to the playground.

"Hey, where are you going?" Brady called after him.

"I'm going to see if Zack's okay. You coming or not?" Michael responded impatiently.

"I dunno if that's a good idea, Mikey," Brady replied hesitantly.

"Well, I'm going. Come if you want to," Michael said and walked quickly down the hall.

"Hey, wait!" Brady called after him as Michael knew he would, his sneakers squeaking on the floor as he ran to catch up.

It didn't take long for the pair to reach the nurse's room. The outer door in the hallway was closed, which wasn't all that surprising, so they moved around the corner to go into the main office to try the inside entrance. But as they rounded the corner and looked through the glass windows, Brady nearly ran into Michael, who had stopped dead in his tracks.

Chase sat in one of the chairs inside. He hugged his knees to his chest, and his whole body shook with great, choking sobs. Chase noticed them looking through the window, and his mouth opened as if he were trying to think of something to say, but Michael beat him to it. He didn't care what Brady thought; he was hurt, Zack was hurt, and his hopes for the end of the season were slipping away.

"This was your fault, Chase! Zack's hurt and it's your fault!" Michael screamed. "What are we going to do now, huh?" he raged, slamming his palms up against the window. "I hate you! I *hate* you!"

Though it was surely muffled by the glass, Michael's body language and gestures were more than enough to get the message across. The secretary saw what was happening, stood up from her desk, and advanced toward the boys as Chase buried his face behind his arms and knees.

"Go!" Brady shouted, pushing and pulling Michael until the two of them were sprinting down the hall and out the doors to the playground. They came to rest near one of the benches next to the blacktop area and panted heavily from the exertion.

"Mikey, that was so mean. You didn't need to do that!" Brady snapped.

"I don't care," Michael retorted. "He hurt Zack!"

"Only because you made him mad!" Brady fumed. "You made fun of him."

"No I didn't! All I did was say he was funny."

"No you didn't, you were just laughing at him!"

"I was not!" Michael roared back.

"Whatever, Mikey, that was wrong," Brady said, shaking his head and backing away. "I'm gonna go play with Logan and Ander. I don't wanna get in trouble."

"Brady, wait!" Michael yelled after his friend as he ran off. When Brady didn't bother to look back, Michael threw his arms up in defeat and sat down on the bench to fume. Everything was falling apart! He was losing, and that scared him, a fear that only increased when he found himself staring up at Mr. Dunlap, who did not appear the least bit happy. The sight of his teacher made Michael nervous enough, but Mr. Dunlap hadn't lost his muscles from when he played college football, and that frayed Michael's nerves even more.

"Michael, I think you and I need to have a chat," Mr. Dunlap said.

Michael gulped down the lump in his throat and didn't dare say no, though he certainly wanted to. Mr. Dunlap took him just inside the recess doors and looked hard at Michael, who backed up against the wall. That was the only thing he could think of to keep from falling down.

"Michael, I can't even describe how disappointed I am in you," Mr. Dunlap stated.

"But I didn't do anything!" Michael insisted.

"Is that a fact? So you didn't walk through the halls to the office, scream at Chase that you hated him, and then run out here?" Mr. Dunlap questioned.

Michael opened his mouth to respond, but no words came out. His face flushed.

"Listen, Michael, from what I gathered, you didn't intend to be mean to Chase in the lunchroom, so I won't punish you for that," his teacher began. "But what you said to him in the office, that was just cruel, and I won't tolerate that any more than I would a fight. Zack getting hurt today was enough without you adding to it."

"Yes, sir," Michael responded quietly, never once looking up from the ground.

"I'm glad you understand. And I know you'll understand why you'll have detention after school next week too."

"De...detention?" Michael choked. "But I didn't hurt anyone like Chase did!"

"Maybe not with a punch, but if you had listened when you were asked to stop, none of this would have ever happened," Mr. Dunlap explained. "Chase is being punished too. I'm not singling you out."

"No, you don't understand," Michael began. "My dad will kill me if I get a detention! He'll kill me!"

"It's only for one day, Michael. I'm sure he'll understand the reason for it."

"No, please, Mr. Dunlap!" Michael begged frantically. "He really will! Please!"

"I'm not changing my mind on this, Michael. Now go outside and take what's left of your recess, and I'll see you back in class."

"Can I just stay here?" Michael asked insistently. When Mr. Dunlap nodded and made his way to his classroom, Michael sat against the wall, feeling like a boulder was on his chest. He could hardly breathe, and he spent the remainder of the day thinking about what was coming. He could think of nothing else. He thought about it through the entire math test in Mr. Dunlap's class, and as he rode the bus home, Michael knew he'd lost. Michael hated losing. It scared him to lose. Today, it terrified him.

13 Swim Meets and Soda

"**MOM**, they're not done yet! Just a few more minutes, please!" Brady whined from inside the laundry room.

"We should have been on the road five minutes ago!" his mother yelled back.

He knew that! So they'd be a little late, big deal. It was a small price to pay for victory. It may not have made any sense to her, but today was an important day for him, and he needed every advantage he could get. Brady slid out of the laundry room wearing only his swimsuit, with his swim cap and goggles already on his head. He held up one finger to argue as sternly as he could.

"One more minute, Mom!" Brady insisted. "I need them!"

"Brady, for heaven's sake, they're just clothes! They don't make you a better swimmer!"

"Yah-huh!" Brady argued. "I placed second last time, Mom! Second! I never even got close before. They're good luck."

"That's one minute," his mom said flatly.

"But!" Brady protested.

"Nope, you said one minute, and it's been one minute. Let's go!" she said with finality.

"Fine!" Brady groaned. "But if they're still wet and I get the seat all soaked it's not my fault."

He ducked back into the laundry room, yanked the dryer door open and pulled out his lucky sweats from among the tangle of his other clothes while the rest landed on the floor. He'd get those later. Trying to move as quickly as he could so his mom wouldn't get mad, he ran out of the laundry room with his sweatshirt still covering his head while he hopped up and down, trying to yank his pants up to his waist as he made his way through the kitchen.

"Ready!" he announced when he could finally see, running out the door to the garage.

"Brady, shoes!" his mother shouted after him.

"Oh yeah!" Brady exclaimed, sprinting back into the house to retrieve his sandals before leaping back out the door. His mom rolled her eyes at him as he left. Nothing new there.

The ride was uneventful and quick, but the long wait before his heat frayed his nerves. Brady always tried to hide when he was disappointed, but it was hard today. He wanted to show off his new speed record and hopefully snag a win, but he didn't have anyone to show off to. What was winning if he couldn't show off? Abby was working her weekend job, his dad was out of town for a convention, and he couldn't get ahold of Chase or Mikey. That wasn't a huge surprise; they were definitely grounded. Probably *super* grounded. But the worst of all was that his mom wouldn't stop texting. Brady didn't know who it was, but he figured it must have been important, with how absorbed with her phone she seemed. Whatever it was, she didn't look happy.

When his time came, Brady hoped onto the diving block and looked hopefully over to the bleachers. His mother glanced over just before he prepared to take the leap, and minutes of hard work later, Brady finished a respectable third. It wasn't second, but it was still pretty good! He rejoiced at his accomplishment and looked up into the stands, but his mother was gone. His face fell as he climbed out of the pool. He wrapped his towel around himself, pulled off his swim cap and goggles, and waited on a bench for his other teammates to finish their heats. He enjoyed the attention he received for his good performance, but each time he looked back to the bleachers, he found them just as empty. When the meet ended, Brady got dressed and roamed around the facility looking for his mom. After several minutes of wandering, he finally found her standing alone in the lobby, talking on her phone. Her back was to him, so Brady decided to be nosey and eavesdrop on her conversation. He strode up to her, quiet as a mouse, to listen.

"Yes, Brett, it has to be tonight!" his mother said fiercely to his father. "Do you know anyone who can watch Brady?"

The last line piqued Brady's curiosity, and he stopped dead in his tracks.

"No, Abby's friend has a party tonight. I couldn't bribe her if I tried!" She paused.

"Are you kidding?" She laughed. "Brett, there's no chance. He'd burn the house down if we left him alone!"

"I would not!" Brady interrupted.

"Fine, I guess I'll figure it out somehow!" she said quickly before ending the call. She was frustrated. Mad, even. That wasn't rare after she'd been on a heated phone call with his dad.

"I'm sorry, Brady. How'd you do?" she asked, obviously trying to change the subject.

"Why didn't you watch me, Mom?"

"I'm sorry, Brady. I've been trying to land an appointment with this guy for weeks, and he can only meet tonight. It's a huge opportunity."

"Are you going to go see them?" Brady asked.

"Yes, this is too important to let it slip by," she said, clearly trying to end the conversation. "But how about we go get something quick to celebrate, okay, Brady-Bear?"

"I guess." The two of them walked out of the building into the damp, cloudy day outside.

"Mom, I would not burn the house down. That's rude." he scolded.

"Okay, Brady, I apologize." She laughed. "Maybe I can try letting you stay home by yourself for a few hours tonight."

"Can I get pizza? And pop?" Brady grinned. "I can't burn the house down if I'm not cooking!"

"Yes to pizza, no to pop. No caffeine for you."

"Mom, you're leaving me home all alone for *hours*, you didn't watch me swim, and you won't even let me have pop?" Brady argued, striving to look as sad as possible. It worked.

"Fine, you can have pop," his mother caved, and Brady gave a silent cheer. Maybe today wasn't so bad after all.

. . . . .

"**MIKEY**, go A! Go A!" Brady yelled into his headset. He wouldn't have dared to be so loud this late if his parents were home, but he had the whole house to himself and didn't care even a little bit. He leaned in close to the television, tilted his head to the side and shot out his tongue to reach for the straw sticking out of pop can number three.

"I'm trying! There's too many swarming, B, I can't get around!" Mikey's angry voice boomed in his ears.

"Ok, jeez! I'll meet you there, just hurry!" Brady commanded. He hid himself behind a bush in his game, hurriedly guzzled the remnants of his pop, and stuffed half a slice of pizza into his mouth while he waited for backup. He'd finished half the pizza by himself already and was glad Abby wasn't there to ask him for the billionth time how he stayed so skinny when he ate so much. She knew the answer anyway; it was his "meta-lab-olism." At least that's what he called it. He knew it was really "metabolism," but it bugged his sister when he said it incorrectly, so now he did it on purpose. His fingers moved by memory alone, and once he entered the bunker, he swiftly took down two of the enemy players, having taken them completely by surprise. He reloaded and hid himself as best as he could while he waited impatiently for the countdown bar to show he'd captured the point. Once it was full, they would win.

"C'mon, c'mon, c'mon!" Brady fired off impatiently, bouncing up and down on the couch. Suddenly the bar froze, indicating that an enemy player was near. Brady looked around frantically for them, but the crack of gunfire and a metallic *ptang* put an end to his hopes. Brady could only watch in shock as his assassin took his hiding spot.

"No!" Brady screamed in fury, a cry that soon turned to joy when he saw a grenade bounce and explode. Mikey leapt in and, within a few agonizing seconds, finished capturing the point. They'd finally won.

"Yes!" Brady hollered in triumph, shooting up from his seat and dropping his controller in celebration.

"Get wrecked!" Mikey roared over the mic.

"Go again?" Brady asked hopefully. They'd been going at it for well over an hour already, but Brady knew he'd be bored without a friend to play with.

"Sure. I might need to get off for a few minutes when my parents leave, but I'll get back on after." Just what Brady wanted to hear! They waited in the lobby for another game to begin and were talking about nothing in particular when an idea sparked in Brady's head.

"So I was thinking we should all start practicing during recess. You know, all bring our gloves and stuff," Brady suggested.

"Sure, as long as Chase isn't there," Mikey replied angrily. "Besides, he got suspended, so he'll probably be kicked off anyway."

"But we promised each other, dude! Chase is our best shortstop and our fastest base runner. We can't win without him!"

"Whatever, yes we can," Mikey said coldly.

"Just say you're sorry and talk to Zack. He'll listen to you!" Brady begged. When Mikey didn't reply right away, he went right on with his argument.

"He was crying, dude, you know he's sorry," Brady insisted. "He was already mad before you even came to the table. Something's wrong!"

"I don't care. He hurt Zack! Friends don't do that," Mikey retorted.

"But…"

"I gotta go," Mikey said suddenly, cutting Brady off.

"Mikey, wait!" Brady yelled into his mic, but the notification that Mikey had left his party popped up on the screen, and he was talking to dead air. Brady ripped off his headset and put his chin in his hands. He stared aimlessly at the screen trying to think of something that would fix things. The plan he decided on wasn't great, and he didn't have too much hope it would actually work, but it was the best he had. Better that than nothing!

14 Never Good Enough

"**I GOTTA** go," Michael said quickly and quietly, cutting Brady off and immediately powering down his console. Brady probably thought he just didn't want to talk about Chase, which was true, and he'd done a good job of planting a seed of doubt in Michael's head about whether they really could win without Chase. However, this was the moment he'd been waiting for all day, the moment that would decide the rest of his school year and his survival. He heard the telltale clip-clop of his mother's high heels on the kitchen tile and knew it was time. He'd brought his gaming console downstairs for this exact reason, and it was time to put his plan into motion.

It seemed like every other Saturday his parents went to some expensive dinner to help raise money for someone Michael didn't know and didn't care about. Wherever they were heading, all that mattered was that they were running late, as usual. He'd be alone tonight, an increasingly common occurrence, and wished he could just ride his bike to Zack's house, where he'd sometimes show up unannounced even though it was several miles away. Of course, he'd never told his parents he'd ridden that far, but strangely he'd never needed to. They'd always just believe that he'd been picked up, and Zack's parents never said anything about it. But he had a feeling today wouldn't be a good day to try that. He knew the Waldens; they'd make Zack take it easy at home because of his injury, so Michael was stuck. Feeling trapped made what he was about to do even riskier.

As the echo of his mother's shoes grew closer, Michael reached into his backpack, pulled out his school planner, and opened to the section from the previous week. Stapled inside was the detention form awaiting a parent signature, but all that was visible was the line his mother needed to sign. The rest was covered by other positive notes his teachers had sent home, which he hoped would keep her from noticing what she was really signing. If she was distracted, as she was now, Michael thought his idea just might work. He hopped off the couch and ran to the kitchen to put his plan into motion. He hated lying to his mother, but it wasn't a simply a matter of getting out of detention; that was the least of his worries. The alternative was much, much worse. Michael slid into the kitchen, trying to look as hurried as possible, and skidded over to the kitchen island, where his mother was talking to someone on speaker while she fiddled with a gold earning with her hands.

"Yes, we're about to leave, Linda," Mrs. Dzierwa said urgently into her phone.

"Mom?" Michael ventured timidly, still unsure about what he

was going to do.

"Five minutes at most. Don't worry, the table is reserved," she continued, either not noticing him or purposely ignoring him.

"Mom, can you sign this please?" Michael asked, placing his open planner on the counter in front of her. When she continued to talk, he decided to get a bit more insistent.

"Mom!" Michael shouted.

"Hold on…" his mother said into her phone, irritated. "What is it, Michael? I'm on the phone!"

"I need this signed so I can stay after school for extra math help next week," he lied without missing a step.

"Aren't you doing well in math?" she questioned.

"Yeah, but I don't get this new stuff we're learning," Michael explained, keeping up the charade. "Zack's going too, so Mr. Scott can take me to practice and bring me home after."

Stop asking so many questions! Michael's mind yelled silently, but his plan was saved when his mother's attention was again divided by whomever she was talking to.

As she listened, she gave Michael a sideways glance and gestured for a pen, which Michael quickly gave her. She signed the form absentmindedly and pushed it back to him without bothering to look over it any further.

Michael mouthed 'thanks' and quickly turned to leave so his mother wouldn't see the huge grin rapidly spreading across his face. He couldn't believe it had worked! Still, he had to be sure he didn't show his excitement, so he quickened his pace to retreat from the kitchen, nearly skipping when he ran through the doorway, where he immediately collided with the stone wall that was his father, sending him stumbling into the doorframe.

"Michael, damn it, what's wrong with you!" his father swore as he regained his balance and lost his grip on the tie he'd been attempting to straighten.

"I'm sorry, Dad! I'm sorry!" As confident as Michael normally appeared, it all melted away in the presence of his father. He towered over Michael like a giant, and if that weren't enough, his booming voice and hard features made him even more intimidating.

" Just... slow down in the house." Mr. Dzierwa sighed heavily. "What are you so happy about?"

"Huh?" Michael replied. Then it came to him. Of course couldn't tell him the truth, but luckily he had something he did actually want to show his father. He opened his planner and took out a quiz and a test he'd gotten back Thursday and held them up.

"I got two A's!" he said proudly as he presented them to his father, who took them in his hand and studied them briefly while Michael waited hopefully.

"Hmm, an A-minus, huh?" he said as if he were disappointed, focusing on the Social Studies quiz instead of the 38/40 Michael earned on the science test. And just like that, Michael's smile disappeared.

"Yeah, but it's a 9/10. That's an automatic A-minus unless I get them all right," Michael explained, hoping his father would understand.

"Then get that hundred-percent. Only A's in this house, Michael. *Real* A's. You know that." Michael's gaze dropped to the floor, and his shoulders slumped.

"Yes sir," he answered, dispirited, while a familiar feeling washed over him: not good enough.

"What happened to your face?" his father asked suspiciously. Michael had forgotten the slight bruise Chase's sandwich missile had left.

"Oh, basketball at school. Someone ran into me," Michael fibbed. His father nodded, accepting his excuse.

"By the way, I was thinking next year you might try out for another team. Maybe one that actually wins," he said.

"We *do* win," Michael said quietly.

"Oh yeah? Then why have you choked in the finals the last two years?" You'd better get as good as your brother real fast if you want to make it."

"I am as good as him," Michael insisted, sure that now, with his cast finally off, he'd be able to catch up this year.

"Sure you are," his father dismissed him. "Anything else?"

"Oh yeah!" Michael cried, his enthusiasm quickly returning. He ran to retrieve his backpack and sprinted back to his father, who was looking impatiently at his watch.

"We're in a hurry here, Michael, come on," Mr. Dzierwa said bluntly.

"Hang on!" Michael dug through his backpack and pulled out a picture. He'd spent three entire periods of art class finishing it, not stopping until it was perfect. It was done only in pencil, but by anyone's account, including his art teacher's, it was very good. This was something he was definitely better at than Jason.

"I made this for you!" Michael beamed as he handed it to his father. "Could you hang it in your office, maybe?"

"You haven't been drawing in class again instead of listening to your teachers, have you?" his father asked while holding the picture loosely in one hand. He was referring to a note that had been sent home last year, when Michael had gotten in trouble for doodling in class instead of doing his work one day. But that was over a year ago.

"No, in art class," Michael said timidly.

"Good. Grades before art," his father replied sternly before more closely examining the picture.

"I don't even know why they have art anymore, but I suppose it's pretty good," he admitted after taking the time to look it over. "Maybe I can get a frame for it tomorrow."

"Yeah, can you?" Michael asked enthusiastically.

"I'll see if I have time after I'm done golfing tomorrow," Mr. Dzierwa replied.

"Okay." Michael tried to sound excited, but he knew what "I'll see" usually meant.

"Shoot," his father said, checking his watch again. "Allison, we're late, let's go!"

Michael followed his father into the kitchen, where his dad lay the drawing on the counter as he and Michael's mother donned their coats.

"Dad, aren't you going to put it in your office?" Michael inquired.

"We have to go. I'll do it when we get home," his father replied hurriedly.

"I can do it..." Michael began.

"No, that's off limits, and you know that, Michael!" his father yelled suddenly, causing Michael to flinch.

"I'm sorry. I just don't want anyone to ruin it," Michael finished quietly.

"I said I'll get to it when we get home," Mr. Dzierwa said, no room for argument present as he waved his hand impatiently for his wife to head out the door. She only had a moment to quickly kiss Michael good-night before she stepped out.

"In bed by ten," his father ordered as he slammed the door shut before Michael even have a chance to say goodbye.

Undaunted, Michael went over to pick up his drawing, and then walked over to the cabinet where his parents kept the alcohol and gently placed the picture on the countertop beneath it.

"He won't forget if I leave it here," Michael said glumly. "He's always here."

Michael returned to the couch and picked up his controller. He considered turning it back on but instead returned it to the floor and put on a movie instead, deciding he didn't want to keep talking to Brady about yesterday. Instead, he groaned and spread himself out on the couch.

"I am as good as Jason. I'm going to win," Michael said aloud, but when his own father was sure he wasn't, how could he believe it? *Not good enough. Never good enough.*

15 Seventy Times Seven

ZACK woke from a deep, dreamless sleep and squinted into the painfully bright light streaming in through a crack in his curtains. Pain washed over him, first from his cut, second from a throbbing headache that wasn't helped at all by the morning sunlight. He sucked in a breath and tried to prop himself up into a sitting position but quickly thought better of it. A sharp pain struck him behind his eye, like a knife was stabbing him. No, not stabbing. *Digging!*

"Oow…" he groaned, putting his hand over his eye as if it would somehow help. He lay his head back down onto his pillow slowly and closed his eyes against the relentless assault of the light.

He was glad he was in his room; he always felt better here. It wasn't huge by any means, but it was more than large enough for him. Both the walls and the checkered quilt on his bed shared the same blue-and-white color scheme: their team colors. A bedside table held his clock, a reading lamp and a few books, while a large dresser held his clothes. On top of that sat his many trophies and awards from baseball, lacrosse, school and scouts. The closet was well-organized save for the hamper with a few dirty clothes scattered around it, and a bookshelf held his favorite books, his toys, and his treasures. It was usually a fun place, a peaceful place, but not today.

Zack couldn't help but keep running the events of yesterday through his head. Evelyn and the school nurse had slowed the bleeding from the oozing gash, though it had taken uncounted gauze pads to do so. Zack didn't remember much of the time he spent in the nurse's office besides holding a clean towel to his head so long his arm went numb, leaving with his mom to go to the hospital, feeling scared and being very, very dizzy. He remembered getting the stitches (all ten of them), and when the doctor finally spoke to him and his mom about what to do about his concussion and gave him some medicine, and then he finally got to go home.

Everything was pretty blurry after that. He was exhausted when he got home, and all he wanted to do was sleep. Beyond that all he really remembered was feeling dizzy all day, having an awful headache, his brothers wanting to see his stitches and bothering him, and throwing up his dinner all over his comforter.

After a few minutes, the stabbing sensation behind his eye finally lessened, and Zack risked opening his eyes again, but what was this? Zack had no idea when they might have snuck in, but Drew was asleep right next to him, while Carter was curled up at the foot of his bed, covered by his blanket. How did they get in without waking him up, and why were they here? Zack decided he didn't feel much like moving anyway and just lay in quiet for a few minutes until the door opened slowly and his mother peeked in. Zack quickly shoved Baxter, the teddy bear he'd slept with since he was two, back under the covers, hoping his mom hadn't noticed. He just had a hard time sleeping without him, that was all, And he was hurt, so it was definitely okay!

"Aww, it looks like your brothers were worried about you," she whispered with a soft smile, placing her hand over her heart.

"I didn't even notice them until I work up," Zack said. "Why are they here?"

"Well, they were very worried about you yesterday. Maybe they wanted to keep you safe. You're their favorite big brother, after all."

"C'mon, Mom." Zack smirked.

"You are! They love you very much, and don't you forget it."

"Even when Drew's being a giant butt?" Zack asked.

"Yes, even when Drew's being a giant butt." Mrs. Walden laughed.

Zack's parents had told him that he had to spend the day at home taking it easy, and the order didn't bother him even a little bit. In fact, there were a lot of upsides to it: getting to lie on the couch all day watching whatever he wanted, being brought food and drinks, forcing his brothers to leave him alone, and getting to stay home by himself while his mother went shopping and dragged his complaining siblings along with her.

But for all those good things, Zack still didn't feel all that great and often found his mind drifting to how angry he was at his friends. Mikey being hurt was bad enough, but now he had at least a week of no baseball ahead of him, doctor's orders. He was in the middle of reenacting Friday's events in his head for the third time or so when he heard the garage door open and his father walk in. The accompanying swish of plastic bags told Zack that his father had brought home something.

"Hey Dad!" Zack called from the couch. "You want some help?"

"I've got it buddy, but thank you!" his father called back. "You keep resting and I'll be right there."

Zack had hoped that was what he'd say. He really didn't feel like getting up anyway and was afraid if he did he might feel dizzy and get sick again. He flipped listlessly through the channels until his dad walked into the family room and over to the couch and tapped the bottom of Zack's foot.

"Make room, squirt!" he commanded. Zack, always a couch-hog, gave an over-exaggerated groan and pulled in his legs, allowing his father to plop down with him. Zack gave him an irritated stare as his father studied him.

"Didn't even bother to change out of your PJ's, huh?" he teased. Zack just yawned and stretched his legs back over his dad's.

"Too much work!" he replied.

"Right, how silly of me!" Mr. Walden laughed. He looked back and forth as if suddenly suspicious. "Your brothers are with Mom, right?"

"Yeah, they're both getting haircuts, then Mom's taking them shopping."

"Good. I'm not supposed to have these," he said and produced a small blue, red, and yellow polka-dotted tube from behind his back. He pushed on a small red plastic stick, and frozen orange glory was squeezed out the other end.

"Push-ups!" Zack exclaimed. "I want one!"

"Nope, these are Dad's secret stash. No kids allowed," his father replied nonchalantly.

"No fair! Gimme!" Zack insisted and lunged to try to steal it from his dad.

His father stiff-armed his chest, easily holding him back as Zack grasped for the push-up. He kept up the fight for all of five seconds but had to give up when the dull throbbing returned to his head and he had to sit back down, defeated for the moment. But soon his look of disappointment was replaced by a sly smile.

"I'll tell Mom," Zack threatened. "Drew and Carter too. Then you won't have *any* left."

"You *wouldn't*."

"I *would*," Zack swore as he crossed his arms. "Unless you give me one."

Mr. Walden narrowed his eyes and studied Zack carefully. He was definitely going to cave. Zack could feel it. Finally, after what seemed like an eternity, his father reached behind his back and produced a second frozen treat and tossed it lightly over to him.

"Here you go, Zack-Attack. I was just messing with you."

"I know," Zack said confidently. "You always do that when I'm sick."

"Am I really that predictable?" Mr. Walden questioned, feigning shock.

"Yeah." Zack laughed. "But it's still fun. I like when you play with me."

"I'm glad to hear you're not too old for that yet," his father said honestly. "And I haven't had the chance to ask yet, but how are you feeling?"

"The stitches itch *really* bad and I still kinda have a headache, but it's okay I guess," Zack answered.

"That's great, but I really meant how are you feeling about what happened yesterday?"

"Fine," Zack said quickly, trying to sound as convincing as possible. He was caught off guard and squeezed himself into the corner of the couch, bringing his knees up to his chest almost like he was making himself into a fortress. He didn't want to talk about it, even with his dad, and he usually told him everything.

"The way you're sitting tells me otherwise," Mr. Walden said, observing Zack with a knowing glance, which Zack tried hard to avoid.

"I know it seems like everything went wrong yesterday, but you did the right thing," his father explained. "You saw Chase ready to hurt Michael, and you stepped in and tried to help. Not many people would have done that, Zack."

"I know…" Zack said honestly, his posture relaxing as he listened more intently.

"I know you do," his father said with certainty. "The question is, what are you going to do now?"

"Sleep! Good night!" Zack declared, closing his eyes and laying his head on the armrest.

"That's not what I meant." his father said, kindly but firmly.

Zack wasn't getting off the hook so easily.

"I know…" Zack groaned, sitting back up.

"I'd be willing to bet that Chase is really beating himself up over this," Mr. Walden stated. "You know he always feels bad after he does something wrong. You're one of his best friends. I'm sure he feels terrible."

"I know, Dad." Zack sighed. "But, I mean, he hurt me *really* bad! And I didn't even do anything to him! I guess… I just don't know if I really want to be friends with him anymore."

"I'm not going to tell you what to do here, Zachary," his father began. "It's your choice whether to stay friends with Chase or not. But I'll say this: Chase has had a temper ever since his dad left, but he's never done anything like this, especially not to you. Didn't you tell me something about how he was after practice the other day?"

"Yeah. I thought he looked sad. It was worse when I saw him Friday in the lunchroom, though. He was definitely really mad about something, and he looked like he was about to cry."

His father nodded. "I know how bad you want to win this year, Zack. Don't you think it'll be a lot harder without Chase?"

"But how can we even win now?" Zack demanded. "Mikey's hurt, I'm hurt, and Coach Nolan will probably boot Chase off the team since he got suspended!"

"So how can you fix it?" his dad prodded.

"I can't fix it!" Zack insisted. "I can't make Mikey's wrist better or make my concussion go away!"

"I think there's one thing you can do. I want to tell you a story, and then I promise I'll drop the subject." Mr. Walden began, "A man once asked his friend, who he respected deeply, how often he should forgive his brother when he did wrong to him. He asked him if up to seven times was enough."

"What did his friend tell him?"

"He said not to forgive him just seven times, but seventy times seven times," his father finished.

"That's a lot," Zack thought aloud, not exactly sure what it all meant.

"It is a lot," his father replied. "What he was really saying is that when someone hurts you or does something bad to you, you should always forgive them, no matter how many times they've hurt you."

"Where did you hear that story, Dad?" Zack inquired.

"Oh, I read it once in a book somewhere," his father replied nonchalantly.

"What book?"

His father smiled, leaned over toward him, and tapped the silver cross that hung from the necklace Zack hardly ever took off.

"You know, Zack, you can usually tell if something's right, because it's usually difficult. It's a hard lesson to learn, but part of growing up is learning to forgive. But you're a young man now, and you can make your own choices. Just do what you think is right, son. That's all I'll ever ask of you."

With that, the subject was dropped as promised, and his father never brought it up again. They sat watching a college basketball game together, but it didn't take long for Zack to start fading again. He closed his eyes, and though he barely felt his father cover him with a blanket, he clearly heard his words.

CHAPTER 15

"You'll do the right thing, son," he said. "I know you will."

Zack kept his composure at first, but he couldn't stop a few tears from falling when he heard his father's footsteps heading upstairs. His dad had called him a young man, but he didn't feel like one; his dad said he'd do the right thing, but he didn't want to. He should have been happy, proud even, but he wasn't. He was only eleven, and felt eleven. Still just a kid after all, who had no idea what to do.

16 Lonely nights

THEY hate me.

The thought wormed its way through Chase's mind for the dozenth time that day, distracting him from the schoolwork he was supposed to be completing so he wouldn't fall behind during his suspension that started the next day. He'd been sitting at the kitchen table for over an hour and hadn't been able to focus long enough to write more than one sentence. When his mother had brought him home Friday afternoon, he'd felt the disappointment and anger radiating off her like summer heat from the blacktop, so he'd barely said a word. Not that he'd wanted to anyway. He still hadn't told her. Not really. She knew, but she didn't know everything. Now she sat in the living room on the couch doing homework of her own far more successfully than he was.

Not going, Zack bleeding, they hate me, you should quit...

The list kept growing and growing. Chase gripped his pencil tighter; his heart felt like a stone in his chest, and two heavy droplets fell down and soaked into his paper.

"God, stop crying, you baby!" Chase scolded himself wrathfully, but he couldn't help it.

Dad won't come now…

He slammed his pencil onto the desk, and he couldn't hold it back any longer. He buried his head in his hands and cried. He tried to stop before his mother noticed, but she was too close for that and was walking over to him before he had a chance to stop.

"Chase, what's wrong?" she asked, slipping into the chair next to him and holding his shoulder reassuringly.

"They hate me now, Mom, all my friends!" Chase sobbed.

"I'm sure they don't, Chase. They're just upset," she tried to reassure him.

"Yeah they do. Mikey said so. Zack was bleeding so bad, there's no way he doesn't!"

"Chase, what's going on?" she asked. "You were so happy a few days ago. Aren't you excited to go see your father next week?"

"I'm not going," Chase replied sharply and suddenly.

"Why not?"

"I'm too scared to fly alone," Chase stuttered.

"I thought maybe something had happened when you didn't say anything else. Why didn't you tell me?" his mother soothed.

Chase gave a shaky shrug of his shoulder.

"I'm so sorry, Chase. I know how much that trip meant to you."

"I'm not even going to see him this year, again!" Chase cried. "And Mikey and Zack are hurt, so there's no way we'll make it to finals, so Dad won't come watch me. It probably doesn't even matter; Coach Nolan'll probably kick me off for getting suspended anyway!"

"I'll talk to your coach. Mr. Scott, too. I bet he'll help," his mother reassured him.

"Even if Coach lets me stay, Mikey and Zack won't want me there. Probably not Brady either," Chase sniffled.

"Things will work out, just give it time. You know, how would you like it if I called your uncle to see if he'd hang out with you sometime?" she asked. "Maybe you two can do something fun and get your mind off all this. What do you think?"

Chase thought for a moment and nodded. Uncle Mark was pretty cool. Chase didn't see him too often, but he'd always play with him on holidays and let him help out when he'd come over and fix things around the house. Maybe he'd take him somewhere fun. Anything was better than how things had been lately.

"Why don't you go get ready for bed? I think you've done enough for tonight," his mother suggested. Chase couldn't argue with that; he was tired and completely worn out. He brushed his teeth, retreated to his room and hopped into bed. When he'd buried himself under the cover Chase stuck his hand out and dragged his phone under with him and unlocked it.

Don't look at it again…

He told himself that same thing every time, and every time he did it anyway. He knew he shouldn't--it only made him feel worse--but he couldn't help it. He clicked on his texts and was preparing to read them yet again when his mother slowly entered. He hurriedly turned it off and left it under the sheets so she couldn't see and poked his head out.

CHAPTER 16

"Hey, sweetie. You didn't even wait for me to say goodnight, huh?"

"Sorry, Mom. I'm just really tired." It was the truth, mostly.

"I just wanted to tell you Uncle Mark said he'd love to hang out with you sometime," she said. "We'll see him next weekend on Easter, and you two can plan something fun to do together."

"Thanks, Mom," Chase said, trying hard to sound excited. He knew he should be, but it was hard to be excited about anything now.

"You two will have a lot of fun, I know it," she assured him, bending down and kissing his forehead. "I love you, Chase."

"Love you too, Mom," he replied quietly. She turned off the light, and as soon as the door shut he brought his phone back out.

His screen flickered on, and he went to the longest message by far. It hurt him each time he read it, but he just couldn't bring himself to destroy it. Chase let his phone drop over the edge of his bed onto the carpeted floor below, pulled a pillow over his head and tried to go to sleep. He didn't want his mom to know, but what about his friends? What about their promise? How would he see his dad now? The night was long and lonely, the first of many to come.

17. Beauty and the Zack

"**OH** my gosh she sounds like your mom!" Brady giggled uncontrollably. He couldn't help it; this was one of the funniest things ever! With everything that had happened the week before, Brady hadn't had high hopes for the week before spring break, but this morning had been pure joy. The moment Zack had entered the classroom, he'd immediately been inspected by Evelyn, who'd found an issue with basically everything he did. An argument soon broke out, and it didn't take long for a horde of curious classmates to come over and watch the spectacle.

"Zack, stop scratching at it!" Evelyn scolded. "You'll just open it up again and it'll get infected!"

"But it itches *so bad*!" Zack complained loudly.

"That's normal when something's healing, but you can't scratch it,"

"That doesn't even make sense! How does healing itch?" Zack argued. Brady could tell he was starting to get annoyed with Evelyn's know-it-all attitude.

"And yet it's true, Zack-A-Roo," Evelyn said in her sing-song voice. Whether she looked happy because she enjoyed showing off or because she liked to see Zack squirm, Brady couldn't tell.

"Do you have annoying nicknames for everyone?" Zack asked roughly.

"Nope. Just the ones that are cute."

Brady couldn't believe what he'd just heard. His classmates all *Oooed* when Zack's face flushed deep red, while Brady couldn't help but scrunch his face. Zack leaned closer to him, probably trying to put some distance between himself and Evelyn, and it was then that Brady saw them: the tiny black stitches standing up hard and straight from Zack's head. He knew he probably shouldn't, but he wanted to know what they felt like so bad! So, with great care, he reached out and gently dropped his index finger onto them.

"Ugh, they're all pokey!" Brady exclaimed, pulling back his hand as if he'd touched something disgusting and gagging.

"Get away from me!" Zack yelled, flailing his arms around and covering his head like a helmet.

"Okay, kids, time to leave Zack alone, he's not an exhibit," Mr. Dunlap said dryly, shooing everyone who wasn't a part of Zack's pod away.

"Thanks a lot, Evelyn…" Zack groaned.

"Whatever, get an infection if you want!" Evelyn shot back.

"That was mean, Zack. You shouldn't treat your girlfriend like that," Brady teased, laughing maniacally at his own antics.

"Shut up, Brady!" Zack and Evelyn yelled in unison.

Brady listened for a moment. He usually did, but he had an

idea that was too great not to act on. He stared at Zack until he got his attention and mouthed words so quietly that he knew Zack could barely hear them.

"Oh, Zack, you're so cute. I love you. Let's have doctor babies!" Brady recited dramatically in the best girly voice he could muster, trying his hardest to not fall into a giggling fit again.

"Kiss me, my love!" Brady said as he shoved his hands together and made loud, wet kissing sounds. Zack leaned down under his desk and tried to kick Brady's leg, but as usual Brady had his legs pulled up onto his chair.

"Hah-hah-you-missed!" Brady sang.

"Brady!" Mr. Dunlap warned. Brady snapped to attention. He sat up straight as a board, folded his hands in front of him, and smiled politely.

"Yes, Mr. Dunlap, sir?" he asked. "Is there a problem?"

"I saw what you did. Don't be cute," Mr. Dunlap scolded.

"I'm not cute. I'm Brady!" he replied as if he were mildly insulted. Mr. Dunlap opened his mouth to respond but seemed to think better of it and instead pointed to the math problems on the board.

"Yes sir, Mr. Dunlap," Brady replied with perfect, almost creepy politeness.

"And no more presentations for Zack," he told Brady as he walked away.

"It's a play actually. It's gonna be a huge hit! It's called *Beauty and the Zack*!" Brady called after his teacher.

Mr. Dunlap didn't even look up from the worksheet he was

helping one of Brady's classmates with. He just pointed in Brady's direction and said, "You owe me five of your recess."

"Dang it!" Brady groaned. Bummer, but worth it! Whatever, time to change the subject.

"Evil-lyn, I need your help," he announced.

"Oh no…" She sighed.

"I'm serious, really! Is Zack gonna die from what Chase did?"

"No!" she answered like it was the dumbest question she'd ever heard.

"See, Zack?" Brady said. "You're gonna be fine, so you should still be friends with him."

"I don't think it's that simple, Brady…" Evelyn explained.

"It should be!" Brady argued, leaning far over his desk. "Zack, you *know* he's sorry! I'm telling you something's up. He *never* would have done that on purpose!"

Zack glared at him for only a moment before getting back to his math work. It was like he was pretending he hadn't heard anything Brady just said! Brady opened his mouth to continue the argument but froze when he felt the calm weight of a hand atop his; it was Evelyn's. She looked sad and shook her head ever so slightly. He got it: not the time yet. But maybe in a few more days it would be…

• • • • •

IT was difficult for Brady to keep his focus throughout a normal day, but the two days left of Chase's suspension saw him gain an uncharacteristic focus. However, no matter how hard he tried, he just couldn't get Zack or Mikey to talk about it. Zack was avoiding it, but Mikey was being a total turd burglar and shut down the conversation every time Brady tried to bring it up. Typical, stubborn Mikey.

When Chase returned from his suspension, no one seemed to know what to do about it. Chase hadn't met Brady by his locker like used to every morning, and that wasn't like him.

He doesn't think I'm mad at him too, does he?

Everyone was mad, really, but he'd kept his thoughts to himself the last few days, hoping Zack and Mikey would come around. Maybe Chase would come sit with them at lunch or play with them on the playground and things would go back to normal. When they were released for lunch that day, Brady, Zack, and Mikey all walked together to the cafeteria, and Mikey shared the news he'd heard from Ander that morning.

"I can't believe our first scrimmage is against the Mavericks!" Brady exclaimed as they moved through the lunch line. "They kicked the crap out of us last year!"

"Only because I was hurt," Mikey bragged. "If I was pitching, we would've won."

"I dunno, Mikey, they were a lot better at bat than us," Zack said.

"No way they'll hit my curver. I practiced all winter!"

"Maybe, but can you even pitch yet?" Brady inquired.

Mikey wiggled his fingers, closed a fist, and moved his wrist in a circle several times, which produced several snapping sounds.

"It clicks now, but it's fine," Mikey said. "I'll make sure we win."

"You're so full of yourself sometimes," Zack said with a roll of his eyes as the trio walked to their usual table.

"What about Chase though?" Brady asked as they took their seats.

"What about him?" Mikey said.

"If he quits, or if Coach Nolan won't let him play, we'll be down our best shortstop," Brady argued.

Mikey shrugged. "Whatever. Braden or David can do it."

Brady looked apprehensively at Mikey, then turned to Zack, who didn't seem to be as hostile toward the subject. However, he did look like he was trying to avoid entering the conversation altogether. Brady could believe Mikey taking a while to forgive Chase, but not Zack. This was starting to get a lot harder than he'd thought it would be.

"Come on Zack! You're not really going to let this happen, are you?" Brady prodded. "We can't be *The Quad Squad* with just the three of us!"

Zack looked Brady in the eye briefly, then averted his gaze. Though he didn't say a word, his silence spoke volumes.

"Seriously, Zack, you too? Wow, you guys really suck, you know that?" Brady declared. "I'm gonna go find Chase and sit with him. He's still *my* friend. Come find us when you're done being stupid." He stood with his lunch.

"Brady, hey!" Mikey called after him, but Brady paid him no mind.

It took Brady quite a while to find Chase in the packed lunchroom. He sat alone at a table in the corner of the cafeteria, facing the wall with his back to the rest of room. If he was trying to avoid everyone on purpose, it was definitely working. Everyone else seemed to be avoiding him too; the memory of the Friday before was probably still very fresh in their minds. But Brady had never been everyone else.

"Hey!" Brady greeted in his usual friendly way as he slid into the seat next to Chase and began stuffing his face.

"Umm, hey Brady," Chase said, looking surprised. "What are you doing?"

"Eating lunch," Brady replied through a mouthful of half-chewed chicken nuggets. This wasn't anything special, he was just sitting with his friend the same way he always did and always would.

"No, I mean, you don't have to sit with me. You guys said you hated me..." Chase muttered.

"No, Mikey said that, not me!" Brady said firmly. "He and Zack are just being turd muffins. I'm still your friend."

"Thanks, Brady," Chase said gratefully as a faint smile found its way to his face.

Brady responded with crossed eyes and an open mouth full of chewed-up food, getting a laugh from Chase. That was easier than he'd thought it would be, and he was glad for it. He'd fix things, somehow.

18 What a Man Always Keeps

THE rest of the week before spring break was easy enough at school for Zack, but at home it was anything but. He had made way too many promises and wished he hadn't. Wednesday night he'd volunteered to babysit his brothers while his parents went on a date night, and they got home much later than he'd expected. When he woke the next morning for school, it seemed to him like he'd only just set his head on his pillow, and he didn't feel very rested at all. But even though he'd already saved close to half the amount he needed, he was starting to get a little discouraged. And tired. *Really* tired. The following afternoon he'd promised to mow the lawn, help with the laundry, and clean the bathroom. Anything to earn his new mitt!

But by Friday evening, Zack was running on fumes and hadn't talked to his dad more than five minutes in the van on the way home from picking up some mulch and plants at the store before he'd fallen asleep.

"Zack? Zachary? Wake up, kiddo." Zack heard the voice of

his father say from far off. It took a hand shaking his knee to finally jog him awake.

He stretched, yawned, and helped his father unload everything into the garage. That was work! When they finally finished, Zack sauntered into the kitchen. The moment his foot hit the tile, Carter, who was sitting at the kitchen table doing his reading homework, shot up and ran to greet him.

"Zack!" Carter cheered, his blue eyes brightening as he grinned. "I got my mitt! Can we go play now?"

It dawned on Zack then that he'd promised Carter that morning that he'd play catch with him that afternoon. He had forgotten, but Carter certainly hadn't.

"Can we play Sunday instead?" Zack asked. "Our first scrimmage is tomorrow and I don't want to be tired."

His brother's smile fell, and the twinkle left his eyes as he looked away from Zack.

"Fine..." Carter muttered in disappointment, and in that moment Zack knew he'd used the wrong words.

"I'm sorry, Carter. I promise we can do it Sunday, okay?" Zack said. "After my game, I swear."

"Okay..." Carter mumbled, walking back to his book at the table and tossing his mitt on the ground while Zack headed for the stairs.

"Dad, I'm taking a shower before dinner, okay?" Zack called as he ascended. He'd nearly reached the top when his father called him from the bottom of the staircase.

"Zachary, would you come here, please?" Zack walked back down slowly and guessed from his father's tone that he was about to be in trouble.

"Yeah, Dad?" Zack asked.

"Come here for a second. I want you to see something." His dad led Zack through the living room to a point where they could see into the kitchen. Mr. Walden pointed to the table, where Carter sat sniffling and wiping his eyes as he tried to read his book. His dad waited until Zack had taken it all in, then put a hand on his back and led him back to the stairs.

"Your brother has been looking forward to playing with you since this morning," Mr. Walden said. "Mom said he's been at the table waiting almost an hour for us to get home. Did you know that?"

"No." Zack was starting to feel guilty. His father was too good at making him realize his mistakes sometimes, even though Zack didn't always like to admit when he was wrong.

"Did you promise your brother you'd play with him today?" his dad asked, looking him square in the eyes but not showing even a hint of anger.

"But Dad, I'm so tired!" Zack protested. His father pointed in the direction of the kitchen. "I'm gonna do terrible at our game tomorrow if I'm tired!"

"Did you promise him, Zachary?" his father asked again.

"Yes," Zack admitted.

"What does a man always keep?" Mr. Walden asked firmly, and there was a long moment of silence before Zack finally responded.

"His promises," he said. "He does what he says he'll do, even when it hurts."

"I'm glad you remember that," his father said. "So, what are you going to do?"

Zack stared up at his father, who he looked up to more than anyone in the world. He didn't want to play poorly tomorrow, but he wanted to disappoint his dad even less. He was exhausted, but in the end it wasn't much of a choice.

"I'm gonna keep my promise," Zack said firmly. He walked to the kitchen, his eyes full of purpose. He snuck in as best he could and picked up Carter's mitt.

"Hey Carter, catch!" Zack warned his little brother. When Carter turned, Zack lightly tossed his mitt to him. He looked down at it, then up at Zack, and his expression instantly changed from downcast to thrilled.

"Are we gonna play?" Carter asked excitedly.

"If you can catch me!" Zack teased, pulling his hat from his own head and stuffing it onto Carter's so it covered his eyes.

"Hey!" his brother yelled, pulling it up so he could see and chasing Zack, who made a face at him as he ran out the sliding door from the kitchen to the backyard. They played catch until it was time for dinner, and after that Zack finally went upstairs with every intention of going to sleep early. But when he got to his room and flicked the light switch, he saw something he hadn't expected: a small, brown box sitting on top of his bed.

"What's that?" he wondered as he stepped over to it and found a small, handwritten note on an index card on top of it. Zack picked it up, and his chest swelled when he read the words that made him feel like a young man, not just a boy.

Zachary,

I'm proud of you for what you did today. You've worked hard and been a great big brother. You've earned this. Keep earning it every day.

-Love, Dad

No way this could be it, could it? Zack tore open the box with excited fervor and found a new glove, exactly the one he'd wanted. Now sleep was the last thing on his mind! He sailed down the stairs, ran to his father, hugged him without a word, then sped off again to the family room where Carter was. He wanted to say thank you, but in way only his dad would understand. Zack knew he'd probably be tired again tomorrow and hoped it wouldn't hurt his team, but it had been worth it. He'd made his brother happy and his father proud. He couldn't have asked for much more than that.

"Hey Carter!" he called. "Want to learn how to break in a mitt?"

19. The Scrimmage

"**YOU** ready, Zack?" Michael asked with a mischievous grin. He loved messing with Zack; he could be too serious sometimes!

"Stop, I don't have a catcher's mitt!" Zack protested, holding his new mitt up defensively; ready to catch the ball should Michael throw it.

"Come on, you need to break it in!" Michael called back while taking his stance. Zack started to say something, but Michael didn't let him finish. He wound up and loosed a fastball as hard as he could. Zack caught it with no problems, but he'd definitely felt the heat on the ball.

"Ahhh!" Zack cried out, pulling his hand out of his glove and shaking it. "Dude, what the heck!" He held his bright red hand palm-out toward Michael, who just laughed.

"Dzierwa, don't waste your arm on Zack!" Coach Nolan ordered from mid-field.

"Sorry, Coach!" Michael called back, barely catching a revenge throw from Zack.

Today was finally the day: their first game! It was only a scrimmage, but it was against the Mavericks, the team who'd knocked them out of contention last year. Michael hadn't been there for that game and had always been convinced that if he had, it would have made the difference. Today, with his dad coming to watch and his hand finally free of its cast, he was ready to prove he was right.

Michael wished it was warmer, but it was otherwise the perfect day. Though the sun shone brightly and a few wispy clouds streaked the air, a constant breeze carried a noticeable chill. Even with the cobalt blue compression shirts sticking out from their short-sleeved white uniforms, Michael and his teammates were cold. Even in late April, mornings in Ohio could still be quite chilly. At least they were playing at Derring Fields, so they had the home field advantage. The grass was green and freshly cut on each of the four ballfields and the dirt dry but not too dusty. The perfect day to start their winning season!

"Bring it in, boys!" Coach Nolan's booming voice echoed across the field. Michael hurled one last ball Zack's way and took off toward the dugout before he could retaliate. Brady, late as usual, sprinted full-tilt down Derring Field's central walkway with an overstuffed bag of gear and Chase ran along beside him.

"Whatever. As long as we win," Michael thought. All that mattered was that they won.

"Wow, I forgot how chilly these early season games could be!" Coach Nolan commented when everyone had entered the dugout. "Not too cold to play, are you boys?"

"No, Coach!" Michael yelled along with his teammates.

"That's what I like to hear!" their coach said. "Okay, here's your assignments…"

Michael didn't pay much attention as his coach read off the positions. He knew he'd be the closer; he always was. He'd be put in the last few innings to make sure any lead the Mavericks had was stopped cold, probably sitting bench or being put in the outfield until then. His gaze wandered toward the bleachers, and his heart quickened when he saw the bright red folding chair his father always brought being set up. Michael chewed on his bottom lip, a nervous habit he'd never kicked, and hoped he was ready.

"Michael, are you cleared for duty?"

"Huh?" Michael exclaimed, snapped back into reality by the mention of his name.

"Did the doctor clear you? Can you pitch?" Coach Nolan asked.

"Yeah, Coach, I'm ready!" Michael twisted his wrist this way and that to prove that it was in working order.

"I know you're used to closing games out, but I want to test you today and make sure you're at one hundred percent before I push you too hard. So you'll be in the first two innings, okay?"

"Okay, Coach," Michael replied. Maybe this was okay just this once. After all, the last thing he wanted to do was lose them the game! He adjusted his cap and jogged out to the pitcher's mound, determined to put on a good show.

"Let's go, Mikey-Man!" Zack called encouragingly from first base when the first of the Maverick's players walked up to the plate.

Michael sized up the boy, readied himself, wound up and hurled the ball with a near perfect extension of his arm. It streaked across the plate right into Logan's mitt.

"Strike!" the umpire called as he held up one finger.

The second pitch did the same, while the third held the same trajectory before dipping suddenly the last few feet to the plate. The batter swung, missed, and the Rangers' side cheered at the first strike-out.

"Yes!" Michael cheered, pumping his fist in celebration.

"Woo, great job, Michael!" Zack's mom called from the bleachers.

"Two more, Mikey-Man! Two more!" Zack yelled as the next batter trotted into the batter's box.

Michael got in one strike and a ball before the boy's bat connected and sent the ball flying in a line drive to Michael's right. He couldn't get to it, but luckily Chase, always quick on his feet, covered three steps in a second before he leapt out on reflex alone. The ball sank into his glove and stayed there until both his feet found the ground again. He turned, and though he'd been wearing a grin only a moment before, it changed to a more neutral expression as he threw the ball back to Michael like it was simply business.

The final batter hit Michael's first pitch and sent a bouncing grounder straight at him. He moved his body in front of the ball and reacted quickly to a sudden bounce that sent it into his chest. He got it under control and whipped it to Zack, who didn't have any trouble catching it. Three outs in a row, and the Rangers ran back to their dugout to prepare for their first turn at bat, where they had a productive inning. Zack hit a double that sent their teammate Bryson home, and Zack himself crossed home plate after Brady clocked one into right field. But that was the end of it. A pop fly and two strikeouts in a row sent the Rangers into the field once more.

Michael's second inning on the mound definitely didn't go as smoothly as his first. He still managed a strikeout, but it came with two balls. After that it continued to be a steady mix of balls and strikes. A walk and one single later, Michael was finding it more and more difficult to ignore the dull ache in his wrist. He grit his teeth and powered through, managing another strike out and a full count on the next Maverick, a stocky, thick-limbed boy.

Michael moved his wrist about, hoping to stretch it out before he loosed his curver. The stocky boy swung and connected, sending the ball flying just to Michael's left. Michael dove after it, but it came too fast and sailed just out of his reach. As it shot between first and second base, Michael, not thinking, put down his throwing hand to cushion his fall. The stabbing needles returned as his wrist instantly buckled under his weight, and he landed hard in the reddish dirt. By the time he'd recovered, the boy had slid into second, barely beating a tag from Ander.

Michael's wrist felt like it was on fire, but he bit back the pain as best he could and tried to shake it off. It seemed to help, at least at first. The next up to bat was a taller, lankier boy, and Michael wound up and threw a fastball. But no sooner had he released it than the pain returned and threw off his aim. Two more balls followed, and then another after he'd managed one strike that was more due to the overeager batter than a good pitch. It was the second time Michael had walked someone that day.

"Michael, what are you doing!" his father yelled from his seat. "Get it together!"

Michael glanced quickly in his father's direction. He'd left his chair and now stood behind the chain-link fence, and that was never a good sign. Michael snapped his attention back to home plate as another boy moved up. He puffed out his cheeks and let out a slow breath to focus, just as his pitching coach had taught him. His fingers rotated the ball behind his back and found the right placement on the laces. He wound up and threw, but it went wide. He threw again. Too low that time. The next pitch flew too high, while the fourth nearly beaned the batter in the arm. Now the bases were now loaded, and Michael's confidence was sinking lower with each pitch. The next batter came, and Michael threw a ball, a second ball, then the batter hit a foul.

"Damn it, Michael, strike this kid out!" Mr. Dzierwa roared. If he was trying to motivate him, it definitely wasn't working. Michael flinched at every word and was doing his best to blink back the beginnings of frustrated tears, which he knew would only make his dad angrier.

"You got this, Mikey!" Zack yelled from first base. Michael guessed he could see something was wrong. Somehow, Zack could always tell. Michael didn't want to let him down, so he gritted his teeth and hurled a fastball right down the center of the plate, finally managing a strike. That's when he felt it. Michael grimaced and pulled his arm in close to his chest.

"Coach!" Zack called to the dugout, but Michael could see Coach Nolan had already noticed. He called a time out and jogged onto the field.

"He's fine, Nolan, keep him in!" his father called from the fence. Michael was grateful Coach Nolan ignored him.

"What's going on, Michael? Is your wrist starting to hurt?" he asked.

Michael didn't want to admit it, but he knew he couldn't keep going. He wiped his eyes before looking at his coach and nodding.

"Okay, it's all right, Mikey. I'll bring Cole in, and we'll get that on ice before it starts swelling up." Coach Nolan walked Michael back to the dugout. "Better safe than sorry, right? We'll need you when the season really starts."

"Don't you take him out, Coach!" Mr. Dzierwa fumed as he followed them to the dugout. "Suck it up and get back out there, Michael!"

Luckily for Michael, any further progress his father made toward entering the dugout was halted by Zack's dad, who had moved to intercept him.

"John, you need to calm down," Mr. Scott implored, but Mr. Dzierwa ignored him and again tried pushing forward through the entrance. Mr. Scott moved in front of him and held him back forcefully with an outstretched hand.

"Get it together! You've had too much already. You're embarrassing yourself and your family!" Michael heard Mr. Scott whisper threateningly.

"The only thing embarrassing me today is my son," Mr.

Dzierwa retorted. "All that money on that pitching coach, and this is what you do, Michael?"

"But Dad, it's my wrist! It's not right yet!" Michael argued, the jab from his father cutting deep.

"The doctor said you were fine!" his father growled, looking at Michael with something more than just disappointment.

"But it's not, I swear!" Michael cried, no longer able to keep his emotions in check.

"I can't believe this. You know, Michael, you really were one hell of a mistake." Michael gasped and felt like he'd been punched straight in the gut. He slowly collapsed onto the bench.

"John, what's wrong with you!" Mr. Scott interjected.

"Fine, Scott, I'm done!" his father ranted. "I came to watch my son win a game, not sit on the bench and cry. I think I'll just go tee off early."

"Dad! Dad, wait!" Michael frantically called after him, but not once did his father look back. He turned, grabbed his chair, and marched to the parking lot, leaving a distraught Michael behind. Mr. Scott followed him for a few yards, then turned and jogged back to where Michael sat, crushed by his father's words.

"Mikey? Hey, buddy, are you okay?" Mr. Scott asked quietly as he entered the dugout and knelt down in front of Michael, who tried to nod convincingly but knew he wasn't doing a good job.

"He didn't mean any of that, Michael. It's not your fault. He'll cool off," he explained.

"It's fine, Mr. Scott," Michael sniffed. "I'll be okay."

"All right," Mr. Scott said. "We'll be up in the stands if

you need us, okay? But Michael..." He reached up, grasped Michael's hand and held it tight. "You are not a mistake. You hear me?" he said insistently. "No matter what he says, you are *not* a mistake."

Michael nodded and squeezed Mr. Scott's hand for a long moment. How he wished he had a dad like Zack's...

"Thanks, Mr. Scott," he stuttered after he'd recovered enough to speak.

"You bet, Mikey-Man. Keep your head up, okay? You'll be back at one hundred percent before you know it."

Michael nodded, pulled the bill of his hat low over his eyes, and hoped his returning teammates wouldn't say anything about what had happened. Cole had managed to only let in one run that inning, and the Rangers kept the game tied up when they went to bat. Coach Nolan skipped Michael in the batting order so he could keep the ice pack on his wrist a bit longer. When the Rangers took to the field again, their coach rotated a few positions, and Michael found himself in the dugout alone with the last person he wanted to be with. The two sat at opposite ends of the bench at first, both doing their best to ignore one another, but as time dragged on in the particularly slow inning, and Michael saw Chase slide down the bench out of the corner of his eye. To his surprise, Chase chanced a greeting.

"Hey, Mikey, you want my Gatorade?" Chase asked, holding out a chilled bottle of pale blue sports drink.

"No thanks," Michael responded suspiciously as he fiddled with his ice pack. Chase pulled back his peace offering and set it on the ground between his cleats.

"I'm sorry your dad did that to you," Chase remarked. To his surprise, Michael could tell that he really meant it.

"He's such an ass!" Michael fumed.

"Yeah, my dad is too," Chase agreed.

"What do you mean? Aren't you going to see him in California?" As far as Michael knew, Chase idolized his father, even if Michael never understood why.

"Not anymore," Chase answered somberly.

"Oh. Sorry, I didn't know." Chase shrugged it off like it didn't really matter to him at all, though Michael could tell that it did.

"Our dads both kinda suck, huh?" Michael chanced.

"Yeah. Hey, I'm sorry for hitting you with my sandwich last week."

"I had mustard in my hair for two days!" Michael said jokingly.

"You didn't wash it out? That's pretty gross!" Chase teased.

"Shut up!" Michael said, shoving Chase lightly on the shoulder and cracking a smile despite himself. A moment of quiet passed, but Michael couldn't stand it any longer. He had to know.

"Why'd you do it, Chase? I swear I didn't mean to make fun of you," Michael said.

"I know. I don't really even remember doing it. I was just... I was just so mad! I can't see my dad over break now, and if we don't make it to finals, I won't see him at all!"

"Why can't you?"

"I mean won't," Chase quickly corrected himself. "I'm too scared to fly alone."

Somehow Chase could always tell when Michael was lying,

and it drove Michael crazy, but Chase wasn't a very good liar himself. Michael saw the way Chase clenched his fists slowly after he'd changed his story and knew something was wrong.

"But he'll come if we get to finals, right?" Michael asked.

"He said he would, but I don't know. He lies a lot." Chase sighed.

"He'll have to come when we crush everyone this year!" Michael encouraged him. "Don't worry, man, we're gonna make it. I know it."

"Friends?" Michael asked, extending his good hand to Chase, who regarded it for a moment, smiled, and took hold.

"Friends," Chase confirmed gladly.

"Talbert, you're at short next inning!" their coach barked through the fencing as he and their team jogged back into the dugout after a painfully long inning. Brady squeezed his way through to get to his bat, looked back and forth curiously between Michael and Chase, and grew excited to a level only Brady could achieve so quickly.

"Oh my gosh, are you guys friend's again?" Brady shouted.

"Umm, yeah?" Chase shrugged.

"Coach, it actually worked!" Brady yelled, putting his arms above his head in celebration and hopping up and down before Michael or Chase could get a word out.

"What worked?" Chase asked suspiciously.

"Uhh, the power of friendship," Brady explained with a nervous grin.

"Wait, what?" Michael began, but he didn't get a chance to finish before Brady stuffed himself on the bench between him and Chase.

"The power of friendship!" Brady insisted, putting his arms around Michael and Chase and pulling them into a group hug.

"Brady, you are so weird!" Chase gasped as he strained to pull away.

"Zack! Zack, come here, the squad's back together!" Brady called frantically, waving him over. When Zack walked up to them Brady held his fingers out to complete his corner. No one followed suit, so he looked back and forth impatiently between all of them and sighed.

"Oh, come on! Seriously, can we *please* just be friends again? I'm tired of things being all awkward!" Brady complained.

"I'm really sorry, Zack. Really," Chase said earnestly. Michael watched Zack thinking hard, unsure of what he'd do.

"It's cool. We can't be the Quad Squad with just three of us anyway, right?" Zack said, smirking. He added his corner to the square, and soon the sounds of explosions filled the dugout. Logan, who had just pulled on his helmet while waiting for his turn at bat, rolled his eyes.

"You guys are so weird," he groaned.

"Quiet, Logan, we're having a bro-ment!" Brady shot back.

With that, their friendship was repaired just as suddenly as it had ended. Michael wouldn't admit it to any of them, but he was glad things were back to normal, maybe even better than normal. He needed his friends, now more than ever.

The game carried on for a good while longer, with the score going back and forth the entire time, but when it finally came to an end, the Rangers had lost by a single run. Michael's pitching had indeed been missed.

Soon the boys and their families prepared to leave. Bags were stuffed with equipment, empty water bottles were forgotten, then remembered, and siblings were rounded up from the playground. The four of them strode down the main walkway together, and as they neared the parking lot, they noticed a group of four players from the Mavericks crowded around some large wooden posts that kept cars from driving down the walkway. Their ringleader, who Michael recognized as the same stocky boy who hit a double off him in the second inning, looked straight at him and held his wrist as if he were in agony.

"Oww, my wrist! It hurts so much!" he jeered and pretended to sob. "Don't yell at me, Daddy! Don't yell at me!"

Michael slowed, and his face flushed hot as the quartet erupted in laughter. He didn't know what to do, but luckily Brady did.

"Hey, Mikey, do you hear something?" Brady questioned in his best Australian accent. Michael could tell by Brady's tone that he was about to engage in some theatrics, so he, Chase and Zack all played along.

"Yeah, Brady, I do. What is it, though?" Michael asked.

"Yeah, I can't tell," Chase said.

"Look! Over there!" Brady exclaimed in mock excitement, pointing at the group of Mavericks players. "It's a group of rare Derper Monkeys! Look at those big, stupid faces and the long arms, perfect for flinging their poo at each other!"

"Are those related to Derp-O-Potomuses?" Zack questioned.

"Only that one!" Brady explained, pointing to the stocky boy who'd started it. "I'll see if I can communicate with them!"

Brady threw his arms up above his head and walked around in a half squat like orangutans do at the zoo, screeching as loudly and obnoxiously as he could. Michael, Chase, and Zack roared with laughter, and now it was the Mavericks' turn to be embarrassed. They glared hatefully at Brady but didn't make any further moves.

"Oh no, they're territorial!" Brady yelled. "Run! Run before they throw their crap at us!"

Brady broke into a full sprint, screaming as if he were being chased by a monster, or maybe a kid that was about to beat him up. Michael couldn't believe Brady had managed to insult the Mavericks players and give them a way to escape the situation all in one. They took off after his lead, yelling as they ran after him, while the Mavericks players stood frozen in utter confusion.

When they reached the cars, Michael could tell by the looks on their parents' faces that they were glad they'd made up. Brady's father, Mr. Brett, invited them all out to ice cream at D-Freeze, the local ice cream shack, to celebrate. The last thing Michael wanted to do was go home after what his father had done, but his family was having company that evening, and his mother had politely declined for him. Despite his protests, he got in the car. She'd been all apologies ever since.

"Why do you let him say those things to me, Mom?" Michael argued. "Just let me stay with Zack tonight, please! He's just gonna drink more, and you know what he's like when he's drunk!"

"He didn't mean it, Michael, I know he didn't. He's been under so much stress at work."

"Yeah, he did," Michael mumbled.

"Michael…" his mother tried to interject.

"He meant it, Mom! He always means it!" Michael turned away, making it clear he had no intention of continuing the conversation

He hates me... Michael thought as he rolled his wrist around, listening to it tick and pop and trying to work out the soreness that had set in. He didn't say another word until they'd pulled into the garage of their home. Michael flung his bag down and followed his mother in through the laundry room door.

"Hey, Mom," Jason greeted as she walked into the kitchen. Michael following behind after he'd kicked off his cleats.

"Hello, Jason. Did you finish what your father asked you to do?"

"Yeah, everything's done except the kitchen, but I'll get to it soon," he replied as Michael stormed past him, stopping only for a moment when he saw the picture he'd given his father a week earlier, still in the same spot he'd left it on the counter. He snatched it up, crushed it between his hands and stuffed it into the trash before taking off down the hall and bounding up the stairs.

"Mikey, hey!" Jason yelled after him, but the only response Michael gave him was the sound of his bedroom door slamming shut.

Michael flung himself onto his bed and lay there, still in his uniform, staring up at the ceiling and letting his mind create pictures out of the swirls of plaster above him. He'd hoped to have some time to himself, but as usual on days when his parents were having company, someone smashed that dream.

Knock knock knock.

Michael turned his head toward his door but said nothing and hoped whoever it was would just go away. He received no further greeting as his door opened and Jason stepped in.

"Get out of my room!" Michael yelled as he sat up quickly in his bed. Jason stared at him a moment, and walked toward Michael's bed.

"I said get out!" Michael growled. He was showing a fair bit of bravado, but that was before Jason closed the distance between them in quick, purposeful strides. Michael panicked and put his arms up in front of him, expecting the usual slap or two.

"Jason, don't. Please don't," Michael pleaded as Jason took hold of his right arm.

"Loosen your arm up," Jason commanded firmly, but without any anger.

"Huh?" Michael allowed himself to look at his brother's face.

"Mom told me what happened. Now loosen up your arm," Jason ordered.

Michael let his guard down and did as he was told. It wasn't like he really had much of a choice anyway. He still expected Jason to do something to hurt him and was surprised when he took out a compression bandage instead and gently wrapped it around his hand and wrist.

"What are you doing?" Michael asked, looking quizzically at his brother.

"Stabilizing your wrist. You need to keep it straight and not wobbling around for a few more days so it can finish healing," Jason explained. "We'll ice it too so it doesn't swell up again."

Michael stared at his brother, still unsure of what to do or say. "Why…?" was all he got out.

"I hurt myself like this when I was around your age and in middle school. Just listen to me, okay?" Jason instructed as he finished his work.

"Okay," Michael said.

"And you have to learn not to talk back to Dad when he gets like that," Jason said sternly. "And don't cry either; he hates that. He *really* hates that."

"Okay, I'll try," Michael replied.

"Don't try, Mikey. You just have to, okay?" Jason insisted. "If you don't, it'll just get harder."

Michael nodded, not fully understanding what he meant.

"Good. Now get changed. You have to help me clean the kitchen before Mom and Dad's friends get here." Jason flicked Michael between his eyes.

"Ow!" Michael yelped, rubbing the new welt on his forehead. Yep, things were definitely back to normal.

20. The Admission

THE first scrimmage was over, Chase had his friends back, and Easter had come and gone. Chase spent two days with Brady, who had re-invited him to the indoor water park when he learned Chase wasn't going to San Diego after all. He'd let Brady know what he'd told Michael at their game, and Michael had told Zack so they were all on the same page. He never would have believed he'd have his friends back so quickly after what he'd done. It had been an amazing week, but today was the day Chase most looked forward to: the day his uncle was going to hang out with him! He was even more excited when he learned what they were going to do.

"Keep your hands up, Chase. Don't drop your guard," Mark instructed.

"Like this?" Chase asked. He moved his clenched hands to either side of his head close to his face and thought he understood, but was still very unsure of himself.

He wasn't the only boy at the boxing gym, but he was

definitely the youngest and the smallest, standing out like a sore thumb amongst the men and older boys sparing and practicing around them. His uncle had come here for years, and the owner had tried his best to make Chase feel comfortable, but even with all that, it was hard for Chase not to be nervous.

"Yeah, just like that. Good," Mark praised. "Now widen your stance and bend at your knees a little bit."

Chase wasn't quite sure what his uncle meant, so he took the same stance he would have taken while in the batter's box. "Is this good?"

His uncle smiled. "Not quite. Here, let me help you." He knelt down and pushed on Chase's ankles until he had guided them into the correct position. "There we go!"

"Why's that so important?" Chase questioned.

"Because if you have a weak stance, someone can knock you over," Mark explained. "And if you're on the ground, you lose. Okay, next lesson. Watch me first." He took his stance and slowly demonstrated a punch. He repeated the motion a few more times as Chase watched intently.

"Now, follow along with me," Mark said. "Take it slow. Form before speed."

Chase didn't understand the last thing his uncle said, but he did his best to mirror his movements. Mark taught him how to throw a selection of punches: jabs, crosses, hooks, and uppercuts. Chase always learned new physical skills quickly, and this was no exception. Before long, after his uncle had taught him how to wrap his hands and found gloves that fit him, he was practicing on a sparring dummy. Chase threw a string of hesitant punches at the dummy while his uncle watched, but he was holding back.

"You can go a little harder if you want to," Mark said. "You won't hurt it."

"I know, but what if I hurt my hand?"

"If you do it like I taught you, that won't happen. I promise. Give it your best, okay? You see that dummy's face?"

Chase nodded.

"I want you to pretend it's someone you don't like or are really angry at," Mark said. "Take it all out on it, and I promise you'll feel better."

"Okay, I'll try."

Chase practiced once again while his uncle watched him. He started slowly at first, but soon his eyes became focused; he set his jaw, clenched his teeth and steadily hurled his fists at the dummy as hard and as fast as he could.

"Chase?" Mark said, concern rising in his voice, but Chase barely heard him. His demeanor continued to change, and he drove his right fist into the dummy's stomach over and over and over again with every ounce of strength he had.

"Hey, I think you should stop," Mark said worriedly. But Chase didn't stop. If anything, he redoubled his efforts. Soon his face felt hot and angry tears welled up in his eyes. With the way he was recklessly throwing his punches, he might hurt himself, but he didn't care.

"Chase, hey..." Mark said gently. He put his hands between Chase and the dummy, but Chase continued his attack, ignoring the new obstacle and going around them instead.

"Chase, stop." Mark grabbed Chase's arms tightly.

"Let go." Chase tried to pull away.

"You need to stop."

"Let me go!" Chase screamed as he strained against his uncle's hold with every ounce of his strength.

Cautiously, Mark released Chase's arms, and he stumbled a few steps back, his breathing quick and shallow as he glared hatefully at his uncle. His hands were still raised and ready for a fight, but then, as if a switch had been flipped, his hands fell, his shoulders slumped, and he was Chase again.

"I'm... I'm sorry, Uncle Mark..." Chase began to choke up. "I'm sorry..."

"It's okay, Chase, it's okay..." Mark said gently, kneeling. "It's all..."

Mark didn't finish his last reassurance. Chase fell forward, wrapped his arms tightly around his uncle's neck, and buried his head into his shoulder.

"Can we go, Uncle Mark?" Chase sniffled. "Please?"

"Yeah, buddy, we can go." Mark patted Chase's back reassuringly. "We can go..."

• • • • •

"**DID** you tell my mom?" Chase asked fearfully as they pulled into his driveway in his uncle's SUV.

"I had to, Chase. She needed to know," his uncle replied. "Are you going to be okay? You sure you don't want me to walk you inside?"

"No, it's okay," Chase muttered. "Thanks for taking me. I'm

sorry I screwed up the day."

"You didn't screw up anything, Chase. Everyone has off days. How about we try doing something else next time?"

"You still wanna do stuff with me?" Chase asked, surprised. "Even after today?"

"I still owe you, since we didn't even finish," Mark said. Chase managed a small smile and opened his door.

"Chase?" Mark asked when he stepped out onto the driveway. Chase turned and looked at his uncle apprehensively.

"Your mom loves you more than anything. I don't know what's really going on, but you should tell her. Or you can tell me, if you'd feel more comfortable," Mark explained. "Just remember you're not alone."

Chase nodded, closed the door, waved to his uncle half-heartedly, and shambled up to the front door. He fumbled with his keys, not really wanting to go inside but not wanting to stand outside looking like an idiot either. He didn't notice his mother at first. He hung his keys on his hook and laid his backpack down next to where he'd taken off his shoes. He turned to head to his room, and his eyes locked with hers.

"Chase, come sit with me." She patted the spot on the couch next to her.

Chase barely looked up but did as she requested.

"Am I in trouble?" he asked nervously. "I'm sorry I messed up today."

"No, you're not in trouble." Chase could see the pain in her eyes as she slowly held out his phone.

4/01/2019

6:42 PM	Hey dad! Can you call tonight? =)
7:35 PM	I fell asleep before you did last night!
8:14 PM	Dad can you? Mom says bed soon.
9:03 PM	Tmrw plz? I gtg. Night dad.

4/4/2019

Sorry Chase I got stuck at work
the last two nights.
I'll call you tonight.
12:26 AM

7:41 AM	Ok!
6:03 PM	Ttys dad.
9:39 PM	wru?

Chase I'm sorry I didn't have time to call.
Let's shoot for Saturday ok?
Then we won't have to talk late at night.
11:01 PM

4/05/2019

7:26 AM	Ok luv u dad.

4/6/2019

11:40 AM	morning dad!
11:41 AM	When u calling?
12:07 PM	moms taking me to get a new swimsuit. BBL.
2:08 PM	back! had to go grocery shopping too

2:58 PM   WYD?

6:28 PM   u promised ud call dad

Hey Chase I'll call you now.

10:13 PM

Sorry I missed you buddy.

You must have been asleep.

I'll try again tomorrow at noon. Your time.

10:15 PM

4/09/2019

Morning Chase.

Before I call let me look

at ticket prices ok?

11:45 AM

11:46   ok

4/10/2019

5:40 PM   did you find a ticket dad?

5:55 PM   baseball is starting btw.

I'm starting shortstop again this year

5:59 PM   and mikey hurt his wrist!!!!

So might be down our best pitcher

6:03 PM   BBL dinner and HW.

9:16 PM   nite dad. Luv u

4/11/2019

7:52 AM   can u call 2nite plz?

7:53 AM	spring break in less than 2 weeks!

3/21/2019

I know you're at school
but so u know I'm calling
tonight at 8 your time.
11:33 AM

8:14 PM	dad can we plz???
8:16 PM	i rly miss u!!!
8:19 PM	plz dad!

"Why didn't you tell me?" his mother asked tearfully as Chase's face fell. He couldn't keep it in anymore, and the tears he'd held for weeks finally began to fall.

"He said he was too busy," he wailed. "He's always too busy! He never wants to see me. Why doesn't he want me, Mom?"

Chase fell onto his mother and asked the question he'd wanted the answer to for two years. A question his mom didn't have an answer for no matter how many times he asked.

"Why doesn't he want me?"

"Why doesn't he want me…"

21 Black and Blue

"IT'S great you guys are all friends again," Evelyn commented as she exited *The Big Cheese* with Michael on their first day back from break. "I mean, you guys fight constantly, but I was actually worried this time. What made you and Zack change your minds?"

"I dunno. Chase said he was sorry, and now I know why he was so mad," Michael replied.

"What was it that made him lose it?"

"Sorry, Ev, that info's Quad Squad only. What happens at Bro-Time stays at Bro-Time."

"Oh, come on!" Evelyn blurted. "You guys and your stupid bro-code!"

Michael looked at Evelyn with a confused expression, but she quickly regained her composure and changed the subject.

"That's a really good wrap job," Evelyn commented, referring to the bandage on Michael's wrist. "Who did it? It definitely wasn't *you*."

"I can wrap my own wrist, Evelyn. I'm not stupid!" Michael snapped back.

Evelyn raised an eyebrow, and Michael could tell he'd just have to be honest. She'd just keep at it until he told her anyway.

"Fine, Jason's been helping me," Michael finally admitted.

"Jason? The same Jason who torments you daily?"

"Yes, that Jason. He told me he's hurt himself before like I did a few times, so he knows what to do."

"Well, I guess it's nice to know he has some human left in him," Evelyn said with a hint of sarcasm.

"Maybe a little bit. He still flicks me every time he finishes though, so maybe not too human." Michael narrowed his eyes when Evelyn studied him again. "What now?" Michael groaned.

"How are you wearing a hoodie today?" she asked. "I know you hate short sleeves, but seriously, it's gonna be like seventy today!"

"I'm not hot, and it's always cold in Mrs. Meister's room."

"Whatever you say," Evelyn said sarcastically, elbowing him in the side.

"Umph!" Michael grunted, clenching his teeth and bringing his arm in defensively.

Oh man, please don't say anything...

"Jeez, Mikey, isn't that a little dramatic?" Evelyn laughed.

Crap, how does she notice everything!

"Just messing with you, Ev." Michael smirked, hoping she'd buy it.

What's her elbow made of, steel?

"Hmm..." Evelyn hummed as she studied Michael with

narrowed eyes. Finally she held up her index finger and, before Michael could react, jabbed it into his back and straight into a pressure point.

"Don't, ahh!" Michael yelped, arching his back and lurching forward to get away from Evelyn's iron finger. "What'd you do that for!" Michael complained as he waited for the feeling to return in his throwing arm.

"To see if you were faking or not. Pretty sure you're not, but I'd better be sure." Evelyn stalked toward Michael, who didn't stick around to test if she was joking or not.

Spring break had been great and all, but Michael was glad to be back at school. He and Chase were way better friends now, and that definitely came as a surprise to Mrs. Meister and Mr. Dunlap. He wished Chase could have seen their faces when he asked to sit near him in class: totally confused! It hadn't been hard to convince them either. Michael just promised he'd help Chase in class where he'd been struggling lately.

"Chase!" Michael whispered harshly. He didn't think he'd have to help him this soon. Was he sleeping or what? This was the second time today!

Michael received no response from Chase, whose eyes were barely slivers. He lay his head on his hands with that same glassy-eyed look as when he was daydreaming. Michael bet it was a good one where he wasn't stuck in math class! He probably couldn't hear him off in la-la land, so Michael resorted to the last tactic he could think of. He slid down in his chair a few inches and kicked Chase's knee. That did it! Michael scooted up to sit straight in his chair before his teacher could notice.

"Mikey, what…!" Chase whispered harshly across the table to Michael, who guessed he was ready to retaliate, but before he could, Mr. Dunlap called his name.

"Chase, you're up next," Mr. Dunlap said. "What do you think the product is for this equation?"

"Uhh…" Chase muttered. His eyes went wide in panic, and Michael stared dead at him to get his attention. Looked like he was up to bat…

"Twenty-four," Michael mouthed slowly. Hopefully Chase would understand him.

"Twenty-four?" Chase answered hopefully.

"That's right, good job!" Mr. Dunlap replied. "Now let's get someone from table five to try this one."

"Thanks!" Chase whispered across the table.

"Sure, but now you owe me," Michael replied. "I need you to do me a favor, okay?"

"Sure, what is it?" Chase asked.

"At recess, can you go to the nurse's office and get me an ice pack?" Michael inquired. "Just say you fell or something."

"Why can't you?" A look of uncertainty formed on his face.

"Because the nurse always thinks I just go there so I can mess around in the halls," Michael explained. Chase was asking too many questions. Why couldn't he just say yes?

"Oh, okay. I guess I can."

May rain fell outside of Frasier Elementary and guaranteed an inside recess. That was something Michael normally didn't like, but today he made an exception. As the chaos of twenty-three fifth graders jostling over games and seats began, Chase and Michael made their way toward the classroom door.

"Hey, can you bring it to me in the bathroom?" Michael asked.

"Okay, but..." Chase said hesitantly.

"Just do it, okay? Please!" Michael begged. "You promised you would."

Chase put up his hands as if to say "peace" and left. Michael headed to the boy's bathroom and waited impatiently. He was tired; he'd had trouble sleeping the evening before and felt a yawn coming. That was the last thing he needed. *Don't be a big one!*

"Oww!" Michael hissed when he inhaled too much and fire arched from his side. Getting elbowed by Evelyn had been bad enough, but when he'd leaned under the table to get Chase's attention, something happened, something moved, and now it hurt a little to breathe.

Michael stopped to listen for anyone coming and heard nothing. Good, now he could check to see if it had gotten any worse. He stood in front of a mirror, reached down and pulled up his sweatshirt.

"Oh no..." Michael gasped when he saw his left side. It was bad, but he hadn't thought it was this bad. And it hurt; it really hurt!

"Mikey, I've got it!" Chase called out as he entered the restroom. Michael swore under his breath and pulled his sweatshirt back down just in time. Chase couldn't see this. No one could.

"What do you need it for, anyway? You didn't get hurt again, did you?" Chase asked, offering Michael the ice pack, which he accepted gratefully.

"No. Well, yeah. Kinda. I wasn't paying attention this weekend using my pitching machine, and I got beaned. So yeah, it kinda hurts, I guess."

"Well, get better soon, okay, bro?" Chase said, offering Michael a warm smile as he turned to leave.

"Chase, wait!"

"Yeah?" Chase asked, stopping just before he reached the exit.

"Why do you keep zoning out in class?" Michael inquired curiously. "You used to only do that in Mean Ol' Meister's class."

"I dunno, I guess I just haven't been sleeping good lately." Chase shrugged. But there had to be more to it than that, and Michael wanted to know what.

"Is something wrong?" Michael pressed, trying to dig it out of him. Chase swallowed heavily, like what he wanted to say was going to be difficult.

"I wasn't afraid to fly. That's not why I didn't go to California," Chase said quietly.

"Then why didn't you?" Michael asked. He really had no idea what to think, but Chase was being honest, he could tell. No way Chase would've been scared to fly on a plane!

"Because my dad said he was too busy." Chase hung his head and didn't bring his eyes from the floor. "He didn't want me to come... That why I can't sleep. I just keep thinking about it."

Michael knew exactly what Chase felt then. Sure, Michael's dad lived with him, but he was pretty sure he'd never wanted him around either.

"Why do you still want him to come visit, then?" Michael

asked. "You know, if we make it to finals like you said."

"Because he's my dad." Chase shrugged. "I still miss him, even if he doesn't miss me..."

"Well, then I'm gonna talk to Brady and Zack. We'll practice together at recess every day to get better so we'll make it to finals. Then your dad will *have* to come see you."

"Really?" Chase said.

"Yeah, bro, we're gonna make it. I promise."

"Thanks, Mikey," he replied, a smile of pure thankfulness spreading across his face. "I'll see you back in class, okay?"

"Yeah. I'll be back in a few minutes," Michael replied. Chase started to the exit, but stopped suddenly and turned back.

"Mikey?" he asked, and Michael turned back to his friend questioningly.

"Thanks for staying my friend," Chase said. He didn't stay around long enough for Michael to respond, but Michael could tell that hadn't been easy for him to say. But he'd been brave enough to, and Michael wasn't, so he waved and watched Chase leave, making sure he didn't come back in.

That was close, way too close. Michael quickly moved into the stall farthest from the entrance and locked the door behind him. He'd meant what he'd said to Chase, but he needed him gone and thinking about something else, too. Michael stuffed the frosty bag inside his shirt and onto the dark contusion on his skin that was now much bigger than the baseball that had hit him. Michael leaned against the wall but soon found himself sliding down toward the ground. He was relieved no one else was around. He didn't want anyone to hear him cry.

22 Scary Stories

"**JAKE** and Jenna walked slowly through the dark woods. They could hear nothing except for the sound of snow crunching under their feet."

Zack sat with Mikey and his brothers in complete silence, enthralled by his father's story. It was Friday night, and they sat outside huddled around their fire pit, the dancing flames illuminating their anxious faces. Popcorn and other snacks were scattered about the blankets and towels they'd brought with them to ward off the cold, while drinks sat forgotten on the grass.

Zack had heard this story before, but he still enjoyed the way his heart beat quickly with the suspense of it all, even though he knew what was coming. Mikey and his brothers were an altogether different story, though. Carter sat crisscross on the grass with unblinking eyes and a gaping mouth. He pulled on the grass absently and slowly tore each piece apart as if trying to calm himself. Drew didn't do well with scary stories, and it showed. He sat with his legs pulled tightly to his chest, one hand wrapped around them tightly while the other was raised to his mouth. He chewed nervously on his fingernails, a habit their dad disliked but was probably ignoring for the sake of the story.

"Wow, they're really into it!" Zack thought, trying not to let an evil smile spread across his face. He loved it when his dad let him help out with the stories. He wasn't as good at telling them yet, but he would be someday. For now, he took his part seriously. Mikey lay on his stomach on a beach towel, enthralled by every word, his feet kicking up and down slowly, and Zack couldn't wait to scare him. He screamed like a girl each time but still came back every story night he could! Maybe it was because his own family never did anything like this....

"The frozen wind shook the branches and rustled the dead leaves of the trees that surrounded them like prison bars, getting closer and closer with each passing moment.

"'I'm cold...' they heard the wind answer."

The boys quietly gasped and leaned in closer.

"'Who is it?,' Jake demanded. 'Who's out there?'

"'I'm cold...' answered the faint voice, much closer this time.

"Jenna shone her flashlight all around but saw only snow and ice.

"'What do you want?' Jenna yelled.

"'I'm cold...' the voice said, closer still.

"Jake spun around, frantically searching for the source of the voice.

"'Leave us alone!' he screamed.

"An icy breath blew gently in his ear, and a hand, cold as death, clasped his neck.

"'I'm cold…'"

The boys sucked in a collective breath of suspense. That was the moment Zack was waiting for. He let go of the ice cubes from his drink he'd been holding. He reached out, brushed the back of Drew's neck, clasped Mikey's ankle, which was bare from where the cuff of his joggers had ridden up, and pulled roughly.

Drew screamed and flailed his arms wildly, while Mikey shrieked in a pitch that could have shattered glass as his leg was yanked back. Carter, despite not having been touched, jumped what seemed like several feet into the air and ran screeching to their father and hid behind him.

That was so great! Zack's part in the story had gone even better than he'd hoped, and he loved every second of it. Of course, his brothers and Mikey weren't nearly as amused as he was. Mikey still looked half-panicked and struggled to catch his breath, while Carter peeked out nervously from behind his father. Drew's reaction was predictable and made Zack howl even louder.

"Oh, how rude!" Drew yelled before slamming his fist down into Zack's leg just above his knee.

"Ow!" Zack yelped in between laughs as his brother barreled into him and knocked him back onto the damp grass.

"Drew, hey!" Mr. Walden interjected, quickly pulling him off Zack and setting him down next to his own chair.

"Daddy, that was so mean!" Drew complained as he sat and scowled at Zack.

"It was, wasn't it?" Mr. Walden agreed, looking at Zack and

raising his eyebrows. Zack thought he was in big trouble for a moment, but that was before his father winked at him.

"What do you think, Mikey?" Mr. Walden asked next. Mikey groaned loudly and let his face fall into the grass.

"You okay, Mikey-Man?" Zack teased.

"I hate you so much right now! *So much!*" Mikey mumbled into the ground.

"So, who's ready for bed?" Mr. Walden piped up and clapped his hands together.

"No!" Drew and Carter yelled in unison.

"I'm probably not gonna sleep at all tonight now, Mr. Scott," Mikey said.

"Good thing you're sleeping in the basement tonight then, huh?" Mr. Walden replied.

"What? No way!" Mikey panicked.

"Mikey's scared of the dark! Mikey's scared of the dark!" Drew sang obnoxiously.

"Be quiet, Drew, I am not!" Mikey shot back.

"Woah, let's take it down a notch. I was just kidding," Mr. Walden intervened. "Seriously though, boys, it's getting late, and I only promised one more story."

"But you didn't even finish it!" Drew whined.

"It was almost done anyway, Drew. Besides, I think your brother gave it the perfect finishing touch. Now come on, guys, let's clean up and head inside."

With that, blankets were folded, towels were rolled up and cups were collected before they all passed through the sliding door that connected their porch to the house.

"Done already?" Mrs. Walden inquired as they all stuffed their way through the door.

"Well, you know, the boys got a good scare tonight." Mr. Walden laughed.

"Oh, I heard. Pretty sure the whole neighborhood did too."

"That was Mikey. He screams like a girl." Zack chuckled, and Mikey immediately whacked him over the head with his towel.

"I thought some time to cool off before bedtime would be a good idea," Mr. Walden explained.

"You mean time for Carter and Drew to not be scared so they won't come sleep in your bed and hog the blankets again?" Zack asked.

"More or less," his father agreed, which earned him a pair of upward glares from Zack's brothers.

"C'mon, Mikey, let's go to my room," Zack suggested, wanting some time away from his brothers.

"Need me to check for monsters under the bed when I come up?" his father teased.

"Be quiet, Dad!" Zack playfully punched his dad's stomach.

"You know, Hannah, it's weird, but I just got really hungry for potatoes," Mr. Walden said with an evil grin.

"No, not Zack of Potatoes!" Zack yelled as he bolted for the stairs, Mikey right behind him with his father giving a slow, zombie-like pursuit.

"Come back, I'm so hungry!" Mr. Walden called after them from the bottom of the stairs, panting like he was exhausted.

"Too slow!" Zack mocked, even though he knew his dad could probably have caught them if he'd wanted to.

"Yeah, yeah. Try not to stay up all night, okay? You know your brothers get jealous when you get to stay up later than them."

"Okay, we absolutely will not stay up all night. Just until three," Zack swore, crossing his heart.

"Midnight at the absolute most. I mean it," his father said seriously.

"*Fine.*" Zack sighed.

"All right. Good night, Zachary. I love you, son," his father said. "Night to you too, Mikey-Man."

"Night, Dad! I mean, Mr. Scott," Mikey said, quickly correcting himself.

That wasn't the first time Mikey had slipped, but Zack let it go like he always did. To keep Mikey from getting too embarrassed, Zack quickly wished his father a good night and shoved Mikey along to his bedroom, which was on the far right side of the hall, farthest away from his parents' bedroom and separated from his brothers' by their bathroom.

"Zack, you seriously have the best dad in the world," Mikey declared, lying down on a large bean bag pulled close to Zack's bed that he'd sleep on when he stayed the night.

"Why's that?" Zack asked, honestly curious why Mikey would say that.

"Because he plays with you, and you can joke with him and stuff. And he tells you he loves you a lot," Mikey muttered, which Zack thought sounded a little jealous.

"Your dad doesn't?" Zack inquired, but when Mikey slowly shook his head, Zack wasn't surprised. He hadn't ever really considered that other dads weren't like his, but the memory of what Mikey's father said to him at their scrimmage quickly reminded Zack of how lucky he really was.

"So, what do you wanna do?" Zack asked, hurriedly trying to change the subject. At first his only reply was a thoughtful "hmm" from down below on the beanbag.

"Hey, Zack?" Mikey called excitedly.

"Yeah?" Zack expected there to be an idea to follow, but instead Zack's field of vision was filled with a descending pillow. A muffled *flump* filled his ears as it slammed down on his face with enough force that it stung. Zack rolled out of the way of the second strike and hoisted his pillow-club into a fighting position in a single motion.

"Cheap shot!" Zack declared. He wound up and swung at Mikey, who deftly ducked under it.

The two traded a few shots, and Zack wasn't about to give Mikey time to strategize. He raised his weapon above his head to deliver a heavy blow but saw his mistake too late when Mikey swung his pillow at his knees. Unable to keep his balance, Zack tumbled down onto the bed with a heavy *thump*, trying his best to defend himself against the barrage of attacks that filled his vision. Zack waited for an opening, and when it came, he slammed his pillow into Mikey's left side. Much to Zack's surprise, Mikey went down hard.

"Yes! Walden wins again!" Zack cheered as he stood triumphantly over his friend, but it only took a moment for him to realize that something wasn't quite right. Mikey lay on the ground, clutching his side and fighting for breath like the wind had been knocked out of him.

"Are you okay?" Zack asked cautiously. He didn't know what was wrong or how he could have hurt Mikey so badly with just a pillow, but whatever it was, he wasn't faking it.

"Wait here, okay? I'll go get my dad!" Zack reassured Mikey, but when he stood, a hand grabbed hold of his ankle.

"No, don't! I'm fine," Mikey wheezed, wincing as he sat up and leaned against the bean bag.

"You don't look fine." Zack knelt down next to him.

"I'm *fine!*" Mikey replied sharply, his eyes fierce and angry.

Zack shrank back, unsure what to think of his friend's response. Why would Mikey talk to him like that when all he was trying to do was help? Something wasn't right. He could feel it.

"Mikey, what's going on?" Mikey wouldn't look him in the eyes. Zack could tell from years of experience that he was trying to come up with a story. He seemed nervous, but after a deep breath and what seemed like an eternity, he reached down and pulled up his shirt. Zack's mouth dropped when he saw it: a ring of putrid yellow surrounded a black bruise larger than a baseball on Mikey's ribs.

"What happened?" Zack asked frightfully.

"I just got beaned by my pitching machine," Mikey explained mechanically.

"But didn't your pitching machine break a while ago?" The story sounded too planned. It didn't feel right.

"We got it fixed over spring break."

"Dude, I know you're lying. What's wrong?" Zack demanded. Why was he lying? What was there to hide?

"I can't tell you!" Mikey insisted. "I can't! I... I..."

Mikey shook his head slowly, but soon his eyes watered. He squeezed them shut, his head falling forward into Zack's chest, and he shook with heavy, breathless sobs.

"I was just trying to practice to get better, that's it! He was so drunk, Zack! He gets so mad when he's like that!" Mikey rambled.

"What do you mean? Who?"

"My dad! He said I was a mistake. He says it all the time! I just said I wasn't, and he... he just threw the ball at me!" Mikey cried. "Then he walked away like he didn't even care!"

Zack was at a complete loss for words. He knew Mikey's father was hard on him, but this? How could his dad even call him a mistake? Mikey did better in school than Zack did, excelled in every sport he played, and was a great friend; there wasn't anything about him that was a mistake. Zack didn't know how long Mikey had held this in, but he'd chosen to tell him. Now his best friend needed him, and Zack did the only thing that made any sense to him, the same thing he'd have done for his brothers if they were hurt: he hugged him tight and didn't let go. The minutes ticked away, and Mikey didn't say a word. Finally he pulled away from Zack and asked something Zack never would have expected.

"Zack, promise you won't tell anyone. Please," Mikey asked in barely a whisper.

"But he hurts you, Mikey. My Mom and Dad can help. I can help!" Zack exclaimed. How could Mikey even suggest such a thing?

"No! I don't wanna lose my family! He only does it when he drinks too much. He'll stop if I do better, Zack, I know it," Mikey insisted.

"Please don't make me. I can't!"

"Promise me, Zack," Mikey demanded a final time, and Zack couldn't fight it. Even though no part of him wanted to give his answer, somehow he choked out the words.

"Okay, I promise," Zack swore. His father's words echoed in his mind: "A man always keeps his promise. Even when it hurts." Zack had a feeling this would hurt, but though he'd given his word and meant to keep it, he wasn't going to let things stay as they were either. He could help. He could fix it!

"What else did he do to you?" Zack chanced.

Mikey took a deep breath before pulling up the sleeve of his sweatshirt and showing Zack the bruising on his forearm where fingers had gripped him far too tightly.

"That's why you never wear short sleeves..." Zack said, finally understanding. How many times had he made fun of Mikey for that? How many times had Mikey been hurt and not told anyone?

"It was my fault. I shouldn't have talked back,"

"No, Mikey, that's wrong! He shouldn't ever do that to you," Zack said. "Did he ever do stuff like that to Jason?"

"I don't think so, but Jason had always been so good at everything. I'm the loser," Mikey replied miserably.

"Stop it, you're not!" Zack insisted. He knew that wouldn't probably convince Mikey, but then it hit him. Yeah, it just might work...

"Wait, that's it," Zack shouted. "Jason always won, so your dad didn't do anything to him. Maybe if you win, he'll stop."

"What do you mean?" Mikey asked.

"I mean like if we win regionals! That'll show him you're better than Jason, and he'll stop hurting you!" Zack explained.

"But I'm not as good as he is. I keep trying, but I'm not!" Mikey argued, but no way Zack was backing down.

"Maybe not on your own, but you and me are. You, me, Brady and Chase definitely are," Zack exclaimed. This was it! This would work!

"But you swore you wouldn't tell anyone," Mikey insisted.

"I won't. Jason goes to Saint Joseph's, right? We'll tell everyone your dad is making you go there next year unless we win."

"But what will that even do?" Mikey asked, unconvinced.

"I'll tell the team that so we'll practice harder," Zack began. "We already planned to start anyway, to help get Chase's dad to come visit him. This'll just make everyone work even harder."

"It won't even matter, Zack. We only have like two weeks left of school before summer starts."

"Sure it will! You know Brady won't let anything break up the squad, and this'll just make Chase work even harder," Zack insisted. "Even if your dad doesn't care about you, we do. You're our brother, dude. No way we're gonna let anything happen to you!"

Mikey didn't say anything, but when the ghost of a thankful smile appeared on his face, Zack knew it had helped for him to hear that.

"But you have to promise me something, too." Zack said. "When your dad gets really mad like that, promise you'll tell me, and I'll ask my mom and dad if you can come over. They almost never say no."

Zack waited apprehensively as Mikey thought it over, but he soon looked up with a hopeful smile and nodded.

"Definitely. I promise. Thanks, Zack."

"We're gonna win, I swear. No matter what." Zack gave his word for the second time that night. It was a promise he wasn't sure if he could keep, but he wasn't going to let Mikey down, even if it hurt. Even if it would be one of the hardest things he'd ever have to do.

23 Taking the Long Way Home

"**ABBY**! Abbeeeeey!" Brady sang, frantically trying to get his sister's attention. Their parents' anniversary was tonight, so after his swim practice, Brady and Abby had gone to the mall to get presents for them. Brady had already picked out his gift: a box of his mom's favorite truffles from Chrissie's Candy, which he got because they were also *his* favorite and he hoped she'd share. Now Abby had dragged him along to a store where he knew she was shopping for herself and not their parents (probably because she was stuck watching him again) and his patience had ended within five minutes of entering. Probably less, actually. So while Abby browsed, he'd found a way to entertain himself.

"Abbers! Abbertron! Abbersaurus-Rex!" Brady pestered, hoping his sister would at least give him a look, but she continued to ignore him. She was good at that.

"Sissy!" he whined as obnoxiously as possible. No way she could ignore that!

"What, Brady? Oh my God..." Abby gasped.

In the few moments she'd been distracted, Brady had found himself a bright pink headband with a large, white horn adorning it, along with a multi-colored scarf and sparkly sequin gloves.

"I'm a rainbow unicorn!" Brady announced. He threw his arms jubilantly into the air and broke into a dance.

"Brady, take that off *now*!"

"Why? Am I too bea-utiful?" Brady asked innocently. Abby quickly dug through her pocket and produced a stack of dollar bills. She pulled a ten out and shoved it into Brady's chest.

"Take it off and go get something in the food court. Get a table close to here and I'll be out soon."

"Can I get whatever I want?" Brady asked enthusiastically.

"Yes, whatever, just go!"

Brady didn't wait any longer. He threw off his accessories and ran out of the store. He knew exactly what he wanted, and as soon as he had it, he found an empty table and unwrapped his feast.

"Hello, cookie," Brady said longingly before he lunged with an audible *nom* and bit off a huge piece that filled his mouth completely. He'd have to embarrass Abby more often!

"Hey, it is him! It's the monkey kid!" Brady heard a boy's voice say as he chewed.

Brady looked up, and his happy grin quickly turned into a frown. Before him stood two kids from the Mavericks, the same team they'd played a scrimmage against the month before. Worse yet, it was the same kids who'd made fun of Michael. The ones who looked like they'd wanted to beat Brady up when he'd insulted them.

"Uhh, hi. What's up?" Brady offered as the two boys took a seat at the table with him.

"Nothing. Just hanging out," the stocky boy with short brown hair said. "You remember us?"

"Yeah, we played you guys last month." In an effort to diffuse the tension, Brady decided on a hasty introduction. "I'm Brady."

"I'm Cameron, and this is Ryan," the boy answered, introducing himself and the tall boy next to him. "Who was the kid who was crying about his wrist being hurt?"

"Michael Dzierwa. And he really was hurt," Brady said defensively, already not liking the direction the conversation was going.

"Does he always cry when his dad yells at him too?" Ryan laughed.

"Dude, be quiet. You don't even know him!" Brady shot back. This wasn't going well.

"Geez, I'm sorry. I didn't mean to make fun of your boyfriend," Cameron mocked.

"Whatever. Just wait until we play you guys for real. We'll destroy you."

"Who? You and crybaby? Yeah right." Cameron laughed.

"I think you guys should go away," Brady suggested.

"Why?" Cameron asked.

"Cause' you're douchebags," Brady said flatly.

"Wow, that's rude!" Ryan said as he stood up. "You hurt my feelings, Brady. I think I need that cookie to make me feel better."

Brady jumped to his feet and held his treat tightly. Cameron stood as well, and Ryan moved in on Brady's side. Brady felt a little afraid, being both outnumbered and outsized. Ryan lunged to grab the cookie, but Brady slid back just out of range. He was quicker, but wasn't about to run away and let them win, and he *definitely* wasn't going to let them make fun of Mikey. No options left; time to get weird!

"Help, I'm being bullied!" Brady screamed at the top of his lungs. "They're trying to take my cookie and are touching me inappropriately!"

Cameron and Ryan froze, their faces confused and fearful. Brady stumbled to the ground like he'd been pushed, clutching his stomach like he'd been hit and being careful not to drop his cookie.

"Oww, stop!" he yelled again in mock panic. He now saw nearly everyone nearby looking their way, and the two Mavericks backed off.

"Hey, get away from my brother!" an enraged voice barked fiercely from behind Cameron and Ryan.

Abby rushed toward them like an angry bull, wrath and fury burning in her eyes, and Cameron and Ryan didn't stick around, turning only once as they fled. Brady flashed them a toothy smile and waved smugly.

Bye, I win again!

"Yeah, you better run!" Abby roared as they fled. Brady was so caught up in his victory he didn't realize his sister was staring daggers into him until it was too late.

"You did that to get my attention?" she yelled. "The whole mall saw you!"

"Oh shoot…" Brady croaked. He wasn't afraid of Cameron

and Ryan, but he was definitely afraid of Abby!

"Get up right now!" Abby yanked on his arm and hauled him up.

"But they were making fun of Mikey again!" Brady insisted as he got to his feet. "They were gonna take my cook--oww. Oww!"

"We're going home right now!" Abby growled, grabbing Brady by the scruff of his neck and leading him toward the exit.

Brady squirmed and tried to reason with her the entire way out into the parking lot, but Abby wasn't hearing any of it. He didn't try to make any more excuses after that, no matter how true they were. She was furious and wouldn't hear him out anyway, and he was smart enough to know it. He got in the front seat without complaint or further argument and kept his mouth shut, but it wasn't long before Brady got antsy when he noticed Abby taking what he considered to be the long way home through the old downtown. He liked the area, since it was full of restaurants, neat shops, and a splash pad that he would play in during the summer, but they hardly ever went this way because it took much longer to get home.

"Why are we going this way?" Brady asked, staring out the side window at the stores whizzing by.

"I don't feel like cooking, so I thought I'd pick us up a pizza from Don Vito's," Abby answered.

"Really?" Brady blurted excitedly. "Can I get a soda?"

"Not a chance. You're already too sugared up from your cookie!"

"*Please,* sissy?" Brady begged, leaning his head on Abby's shoulder and giving her his best sad puppy look, hoping it would work.

"No, and get off me." She shrugged his head off.

"Mom's been at work late a lot, Abby," Brady observed after in an effort to change the subject.

"She's just been with important clients, Brady, that's all."

"I know, but it's been for weeks!" Brady continued. "She's hardly ever home before I have to go to bed anymore."

"It's not like you need her to tuck you in," Abby said jokingly.

"No, I just miss her. And the way she tucks me in," Brady admitted with a shrug.

"I'm sure it'll be fine, Brady. She hasn't forgotten about you or anything."

"Sometimes it feels like it though…" Brady admitted.

"I know, Brady-Bear. It'll get better soon, I promise." Abby pulled into a parking space on the side of the street.

"Stay here, okay? It'll just be a minute," Abby instructed Brady as he moved to exit the car.

"Fine," Brady moped, choosing not to chance his luck after what he'd done earlier. He watched Abby disappear through the door of the pizza parlor and quickly got bored as the minute she'd told him to wait turned into two, then five, then nearly ten.

"Ugh, what's taking so long?" Brady wondered aloud as the clock moved to the eleventh minute. "Whatever, I'm going in."

Brady moved to open the door, but something caught his eye, and he lowered himself back into his seat. He stared out the windshield at two people who had just hurriedly exited a restaurant across the street: one his mother, the other his father. Though Brady couldn't make out the words, their gestures were wild and animated, more than enough to tell him it was serious.

Time slowed, the minute the argument lasted feeling like an hour, until his mother stormed to her vehicle, slammed the door, and sped away. His father ran his hand through his hair as he stood by the curb for a time before he too got in his car and left.

"Brady?" he heard a voice say from what seemed far off.

"Hey, Earth to Brady-Bear!" Abby's voice came through more clearly this time, and Brady snapped back to reality. The smell of the pizza made his mouth water and helped him shake himself back to reality.

"Huh?" Brady responded. It was all he could manage with his thoughts so scattered.

"I got you a soda," Abby replied, handing the bottle to him. "Sorry for making you wait so long, but a friend was inside and I wanted to say hi."

"Oh, thanks," Brady replied without the enthusiasm he could tell Abby had expected.

"How are you not excited about this?" Abby questioned. "Are you okay? You look like you did after I took you to that haunted house last Halloween."

"Hssssh!" Brady hissed, baring his teeth and lunging at his sister like a vampire. Abby stiff-armed his head and held him back.

"Okay, I get it! You're fine!" She laughed. Brady pulled back and smiled devilishly.

"Let's go!" he said, his voice dripping evil. "I need pizza blood!"

"You are so weird." Abby sighed, shook her head, and started up the car.

Brady watched the businesses and houses pass by as they drove back home. He tried to push what he'd seen from his mind and convince himself that he hadn't seen it. By the time they'd reached home, his mind was focused firmly on pizza, then a video game, then his guitar, then getting ready for bed. But the second his head hit the pillow, his mind, now absent something to keep it focused, went right back to the scene from hours before. He didn't know what to do, what to say, or who to tell. He wasn't even sure what it meant. As he ran through every time he'd gotten in trouble at school, forgotten his homework, been weird and annoying at home, or the multitude of other things, he came to a conclusion that it was somehow, in some way, his fault. So Brady lay in his bed for what seemed like an eternity, staring up into the darkness until the faint light of dawn broke on the horizon.

24 • Fort McTalwaden

CHASE grit his teeth and strained with effort as he struggled to push the log, his feet finding little traction in the damp earth that had swallowed some of it. Probably from the creek flooding, but he didn't know for sure. He wanted to get stronger so he could be a better boxer and had insisted on moving it himself, even though Brady had offered several times to help. Uncle Mark said he had potential, and he was gonna prove him right!

"You sure you don't want help?" Brady asked cautiously from his seat on a nearby rock.

"I said I got it!" Chase insisted, hurling himself once more at the immovable hunk of wood but having no more luck than the previous three tries. To make things worse, this time his foot slipped and he fell flat in the dirt, skinning his elbow on the bark as he went down. He hissed in pain as he sat himself up and looked down at the raw cuts.

"Okay, I don't got it," Chase admitted.

"Just wait for Zack and Mikey to get here. It took all four of us to move it last fall, remember?" Brady said encouragingly, and Chase was surprised to find it actually made him feel a little better. If the last two months had taught him anything, it was that he didn't have to do anything on his own anymore.

"Yeah, you're right," Chase said.

"Why'd you try so hard to do it alone?" Brady asked curiously. Chase lifted himself up onto the log, still breathing heavily from the exertion, and shrugged.

"I dunno. I really wish I was bigger!" Chase said. "My uncle says I'm getting pretty good at boxing, but I wanna get stronger so I can be really good!"

"That's cool he teaches you that stuff," Brady said jealously.

"Yeah, he shows me how to do all kinds of stuff," Chase agreed. "He's really cool."

"Sounds likes he's more like your dad than you actual dad." It was weird, but it was kinda true. He'd learned more from his uncle in the last month than from his dad in two years.

"Yeah, I still miss my dad, though." Chase admitted. "I really hope he comes if we make it to regionals."

"I bet he will. Oh, hey, you're not gonna use your boxing stuff on us, though, right? Like, if you get mad?"

"No way, I swear," Chase promised. "Uncle Mark says I can only use it if someone else starts it or to stick up for someone."

"Okay, good." Brady breathed a sigh of relief. Chase understood why Brady had asked, but he still wished he wouldn't have. Reminding him of that day just made it harder to not think about what his dad had done, and what he'd done to his friends.

"Well, guess I'll start cleaning up the inside while we wait for

Zack and Mikey to get here," Chase announced, pushing himself up from his seat.

"I'll go up top and try to fix the roof," Brady said, standing and pulling himself onto the trunk of the massive fallen tree that provided the foundation for the roof of their fort.

If there was one thing Chase didn't mind about having to move, it was that his new house was it was only a few blocks from a park. For the last two years, it had provided the Quad Squad a place to play when they went to Chase's house, and for when his mom banished them when they were getting too loud or she decided the time for video games had ended. While exploring one day, they'd followed the creek until they'd come across a large fallen tree that Brady had claimed was struck by lightning. It was here that Fort McTalwaden lay. Chase still thought the name should be Fort Talbert since he'd found it first, but Zack helped them all compromise on McTalwaden since it had a little of everyone's last name in it.

Over the years, they'd gathered as many logs and branches as they could, which they leaned against the fallen tree to make walls. Then they'd covered the top with vines, smaller sticks and leaves to make a roof of sorts and had made it mostly waterproof using a tarp Zack had brought from home. Thick logs served as seats, and they'd left the area where a fourth wall could have been open so they could look out on the stream that ran not ten feet from the fort. Brady had caught a frog in that stream the summer before and hid it under his sister's bed sheets, but she hadn't thought that was nearly as funny as he had.

"Well, this place looks like crap!" Chase declared upon

entering the fort and seeing the debris that had found its way inside. "I think the creek flooded or something!" he called up to Brady, who he could hear tossing branches and leaves into the woods around them.

Chase set upon clearing the floor and the area around their fire pit as best as he could. Things didn't need to be perfect, but they needed to be usable. Zack had sent him and Brady a message to meet here late the night before asking to meet them here. Chase wasn't sure what he and Mikey wanted to do, exactly, but it didn't really matter as long as they had fun. Whatever they did, at least it was still early enough in May that they could wear pants and not get too hot. They'd learned wearing shorts in the woods wasn't very smart the year before when they'd all come back with poison ivy all over their legs. That was a terrible week!

Drip. Drip. Drip.

Chase was snapped from that funny but uncomfortable memory by the rapid dripping of water from above him.

"Brady, what are you doing?" Chase called up anxiously as a stream cascaded down and blocked him inside the fort.

"Hold on, there's water in the tarp! I'm almost done!" Brady yelled down. Chase didn't like the sound of that, but he didn't want to risk getting soaked by running through Brady's waterfall. Then it happened: the sound of Brady straining against something heavy, followed by a ripping sound and a heavy slosh of water.

"Oh crap!" Brady yelled in alarm.

"Brady!" Chase screamed in panic, unable to escape as the roof gave way and dozens of gallons of water filled with sticks, leaves, and scum plummeted down. He only had time to crouch and cover his head in the split second before he was doused from head to toe in the frigid water.

Chase spat a mist of water and slowly stood, his arms dripping as he walked slowly from the fort, his soaked shirt clinging to him. Shivering, he looked up at Brady, who smiled nervously as if to say he was sorry.

"I... hate... you..." Chase stammered through his violently chattering teeth.

"You have leaves in your hair," Brady said matter-of-factly as he pointed at his head and grinned.

"I'm gonna kill you!" Chase roared, not at all amused by Brady's attempt at diffusing the situation. He bent down, grabbed two handfuls of mud, and hurled them up at him. Brady shielded his face with his hands as Chase's missiles impacted all over him, laughing through it all until a baseball-sized glob of mud flew toward his head. He dodged the mud ball, but lost his balance.

"No, no, no!" Brady sputtered as he slid off the log, unable to grab a branch in time, and down he fell into the newly-created puddle of frigid water, mud, leaves, and scum with a sickening *sploot*.

"Oh, oh God. Oh God, this is so gross!" Brady shuddered as he slowly pushed himself up, his entire front half soaked and dripping with goop. Now it was Chase's turn to laugh.

"You suck, Chase!" Brady yelled as he flung two handfuls of earth Chase's way. Chase didn't even try to block them, instead going on the offensive with his own bombardment until a sidearm throw from Brady found his face. Chase slowly squeegeed the grime from his face and glared at Brady.

"Umm, sorry?" Brady smiled nervously. Chase tackled him into the dirt a moment later. Neither gave any quarter as they wrestled, and only when Chase finally got Brady in a headlock did he gain the upper hand.

"Give up?" Chase yelled.

"Never!" Brady retorted.

"Guys? Guys!" a commanding voice rang out from behind them. Chase turned his head and saw Zack and Mikey, each looking beyond confused.

"Help, he's choking me!" Brady croaked, reaching out to Zack and letting his tongue roll out.

"Stop being dramatic, Brady, I'm not even!" Chase said, releasing his hold. "You are such a pain sometimes!"

"What did you guys do?" Mikey asked as he looked upon the devastation of what used to be their fort.

"His fault!" Chase fumed, pointing a finger accusingly at Brady. Mikey and Zack looked to him for some kind of explanation.

"We were working on the fort, and I kinda made the roof cave in. Sorry, guys," Brady said sheepishly.

"You two are worse than my brothers sometimes." Zack sighed, setting down a cooler that looked pretty heavy.

"What's in that?" Chase asked curiously.

"My mom made us some lunch. C'mon, let's move the bench near the creek so we can eat," Zack said.

The four of them set to rolling the log Chase had tried to

move on his own closer to the edge of the gully. When they were satisfied with its position, a gentle breeze caused the warm sunlight to occasionally flicker through the leaves of the maples and sycamores that lined the edges of the creek as they sat together. This was one of Chase's favorite places in the world; he loved coming here and dangling his feet off the edge and watching the water rush along five or six feet below. He told his friends he never came here without them, but the truth was he'd been spending a lot of time here lately. He was feeling a lot better than before, but sometimes when he felt himself getting upset, he'd come sit by the creek so his mom wouldn't see. He was tired of making her worry about him all the time and hated seeing her sad.

"Chase, you want lunch?" Zack asked, snapping Chase from his daydream.

"Sure!" Chase replied, accepting the sandwich Zack handed him, followed by a bag of chips, a bottle of water and a banana. The four of them sat quietly, watching the water and listening to the sounds of nature around them. It was peaceful, and Chase wasn't even a bit surprised that Brady couldn't stand it and had to say something.

"Ugh, I feel so gross," Brady groaned as he peeled a muddy leaf from his joggers.

"Your lucky pants not so lucky today, huh?" Zack asked jokingly.

"No..." Brady moped.

"At least they're black, right?" Zack said reassuringly.

"You could go swimming and wash it off!" Chase teased.

"And drown in poop water? Yeah, no thanks," Brady announced with a firm shake of his head.

"Are you kidding? There isn't any poop in the water, Brady!" Mikey said with a sigh.

"You don't know that! A whole herd of deer could've walked in and done their business in it this morning! Didn't think of *that,* did you?" Brady reasoned.

"No, because I'm not crazy!" Mikey laughed for a moment but soon winced and, it appeared to Chase, forced himself to stop.

"You alright?" Chase asked. "Does it still hurt from where you pitching machine beaned you?"

"Yeah, pretty bad too," Mikey admitted, grinning through it. Chase couldn't believe it. A few months ago, no way Mikey would have told him that. They really were better friends now.

"Can I see?" Chase pressed. Mikey seemed to think about it for a moment, nodded, and lifted up his shirt. Wow, that was even worse than he thought it would be!

"What the crap, dude, no wonder you needed ice!" Chase exclaimed.

"Yeah, but it'll take more than that to take me down!" Mikey bragged, flexing his arms.

"Where's the muscle again?" Zack questioned, inspecting Mikey's arms.

"Whatever." Mikey rolled his eyes.

The three of them had a laugh at Mikey's expense and went back to their lunches. Chase couldn't help but notice that besides the cooler, Zack and Mikey hadn't brought anything else out; no materials to work on the fort, no nerf guns for a war, no nothing. Weird. Maybe they just wanted to explore? That was always fun, but Chase had a feeling something else was up.

"So why'd you want to meet here, Zack?" Chase blurted, his curiosity finally getting the better of him. He couldn't help it, he needed to know! Zack pursed his lips nervously and looked to Mikey, who gave a faint nod as if to give him permission.

"Guys, we gotta tell you something," Zack began. "Mikey's dad told him he wants him on a better team next year, so he's going to send him to St. Joseph's with Jason."

"What? No way!" Brady yelled in shock.

"That's such bullcrap!" Chase exclaimed, slamming his hand onto the log.

"Hang on, guys. I have a plan, but we need your help. You in?" Zack asked them, as if he even needed to.

"Obviously!" Brady assured him.

"Yeah, no freaking way we're letting your dad send you away!" Chase agreed.

"Okay, my dad said he wanted me to go there, but he said if we won, like, really won, *everything*, then I wouldn't have to and I could go to Trace with you guys next year," Mikey explained.

"Oh..." Brady mumbled. That was about what Chase was thinking too. They all wanted to win, but could they really do it?

"I know it's gonna be hard, but I want to stay with you guys," Mikey said, leaning far forward from his end of the log. "We're already practicing extra at recess so your dad will come visit, Chase."

"Yeah, so we're gonna get Logan and Ander to practice with

us every day at school and let the whole team know so they can practice at their schools too," Zack explained. "My dad said he'd take us to the batting cages extra times if I keep helping him with chores and yard work."

"Then when we get to finals, Chase's dad will come, and I'll get to stay with you guys," Mikey finished.

"We barely have two weeks of school left, though. I mean, is that even gonna be enough to make a difference?" Chase questioned. He wanted to believe it could work so badly, but he had his doubts. What could a few weeks of extra practice really do?

"Better than nothing," Zack replied. "It's not like we won't still have practices, this is just extra."

"How do you know it'll work?" Brady asked. "We've never made it that far before."

"Because it has to work, Brady. If it doesn't, we probably won't ever see Mikey anymore, and Chase won't get to see his dad." Zack explained.

"So what do you guys think?" Mikey asked after a long pause. He looked nervous, maybe even a little scared. Chase knew what being afraid of losing friends felt like all too well.

"No way I'm letting your dad break up The Quad Squad!" Brady insisted. "I'm definitely in!"

"What about you, Chase?" Zack asked him. Chase just smiled, the memory of their fight long forgotten.

"We got this, Mikey-Man. I'll see my dad, and you'll go to Trace with us. No way we're losing!" Chase said with total confidence, holding his fingers out to complete his corner. The sound of explosions filled the woods, and the pact was made. They could do it, he knew they could! Now, it was time to prove it.

25. Charles

"**COME** on, Zack, you got this!" Brady encouraged, even though he honestly wasn't certain Zack did. Brady had stopped putting his helmet and batting gloves on to watch Zack at bat, feeling worse for him with each second. Zack had struck out each time he'd gone to bat in all four of their games this weekend. Something was definitely up. Worse yet, this game decided the Memorial weekend tournament winner. They already had one out and were two runs down. Talk about pressure!

"Good eye!" Brady affirmed when Zack let one go by, but his scowl and set jaw spoke to his frustration. A fastball right down the middle came next. Zack swung, missed, and slammed his bat on home plate before he began another trip back toward their dugout. That wasn't like him at all! Brady could see Chase doing that for sure, but Zack? No way!

"It's alright, bro, you'll get it next time!" Brady said, extending a hand as Zack slogged toward the dugout and returned his high-five half-heartedly at best. It sure seemed as if things were going fine for everyone but him. At least Mikey was up next, and he was usually good for a hit!

Brady took his place on deck as Mikey moved up to home plate. After one strike, followed by a ball, Mikey swung and sent a lightning-quick grounder that sped out to center field. Brady couldn't help but be nervous, but Mikey made it to first base without any problems. Just a single, but that was okay, except now he was up to bat with two runs down and one out left. Craptastic...

"Batter up!" the umpire ordered. Brady advanced toward home plate, hefting his scarlet Easton as he stepped into the batter's box.

"C'mon, Brady-Bear!" Michael called toward home, clapping as Brady made his way up to bat. Brady made a face and waved frantically at Michael, getting nothing but an eye-roll in return.

"Okay, don't choke! Don't choke! Don't choke!" he whispered to himself as he took his stance, licked his lips and waited. He wouldn't strike out. He couldn't! Not with his new good luck charm, the reason they'd made it to the fifth and final game of the tournament. He hadn't told the guys about it yet though; he didn't want to jinx it. And, if he was honest with himself, it *was* kinda gross. But whatever, things would be fine as long as Mikey, who was leading off first as far as he dared, didn't try what Brady thought he might.

"Don't try to steal, you derper!" Brady muttered. No way could they risk that with just one out left. Another fastball was definitely coming. He was pretty sure, anyway. Digging his left foot into the ground, Brady shifted his weight to his back foot and tightened his grip. The ball streaked toward him, and Brady swung with all his might.

"Steeeeee-rike one!" the umpire called.

"No way! That was way high!" Brady fumed. He'd thought he'd had that one for sure. He thought he had the next one too, but that just ended up being a foul. Two strikes now. Crap!

"Come on, Charles, don't fail me now!" Brady yelled to no one in particular as he stepped out of the batter's box for a moment to take a practice swing before nervously stepping back in and waiting. First the windup and then...

Crack!

"No way... No way!" Brady put his hands on his helmet and yelled, first in disbelief, then in jubilation as he watched the ball sail out far into left field. *Really* far into left field!

"Dinger!" Brady screamed at the top of his lungs, taking off around the bases with his arms in the air as if he were flying. He couldn't believe it. His first ever home run!

"Brady-Bear!' Michael ran to him when he neared home plate. The two leapt into each-other's sides before they were mobbed by their teammates, and Brady soon found himself at the bottom of a dogpile.

"Oww, my spleen!" Brady shrieked with laughter despite the huge weight on top of him and having to bear with it for what seemed like an eternity until their coaches pulled everyone apart.

Brady lay there with his tongue rolled out, acting as if he were dead until Zack and Chase hauled him to his feet. He couldn't stop smiling; the raw excitement was almost more than he could handle. He barely even noticed shaking hands with their opponents or receiving their medals, and he'd never been more proud of an award in his life. Things were finally going right! He'd done it, they'd done it, and they were definitely going to go all the way this year!

"All right boys, picture time!" Ander's mom said. "One, two, Brady!"

"Mhat?" his muffled voice answered. He'd hurriedly stuffed his medal into his mouth like an orange slice and crossed his eyes. She seemed a little mad, but his friends were laughing, and that made the pictures better anyway! Mrs. Nolan tried once or twice more to restore order, but ended up just taking them anyway. As soon as they were done his dad and Mr. Scott quickly wrangled them all into the van; Brady could tell they were ready to get going. It was a three-hour drive home, after all...

"Dad, can we stop for dinner? I'm starving!" Zack begged when they'd piled into their seats.

"Yeah, please, Mr. Scott?" Chase seconded.

"Don't worry, boys, we'll get you fed," Brady's dad said.

"I think we'll just swing through a drive-thru though, okay, guys? We've got a long drive back, and I'd like to get home before the sun sets," Mr. Scott explained.

That brought a collective groan from them all, but they accepted it. Brady liked their yearly ritual of stopping at a cool restaurant they all liked, but he understood. It was already nearly six o'clock, and they'd never had to leave at such a late hour before. Small price to pay for victory! They finally agreed on a place, and ten minutes of shouting orders, changing minds, and waiting later, they were on the road again with the smell of french fries, burgers, and Brady's favorite filling the van.

"I'm gonna smash me some nuggets, yo!" Brady declared, eagerly opening his bag and stuffing two into his mouth.

"Slow down, Brady," his dad pleaded. "I'd really prefer if you didn't choke in the car."

"Sorry, Dad." Brady opened a packet of ranch and slowed his pace.

"Well, we're both really proud of you boys!" Mr. Scott declared. "You all played great this weekend!"

"Thanks, Mr. Scott!" Michael said almost immediately.

That was Mikey, sucking up all the praise he could. Made sense though. His own dad sure never gave him any. *Ever.* Brady thought about it and couldn't recall even one time Mr. Dzierwa had even said "good job" to Mikey, much less saying he was proud of him. He was so mean!

"I was terrible again, though." Zack mumbled. "I suck now! I don't know what happened!"

"It's okay, Zack, everyone gets into a rut every once and a while," Brady's dad explained. "I bet you'll be back to normal next weekend."

"Doubt it." Zack sighed.

"I still can't believe I hit that dinger!" Brady recounted dreamily.

"Oh, sorry, Zack." Brady said, realizing that it might have sounded like he was bragging. Zack shrugged like it didn't matter, but his face said it all. It totally mattered.

"Yeah, that was big for you, Brady!" Mr. Scott said. Brady was a consistent hitter, but he'd never hit a home run before.

Until today he didn't even think he could, with how little he was.

"I couldn't have done it without Charles!" Brady said proudly.

"What? Who's Charles?" Mr. Brett asked.

"My lucky underwear."

"What!" Michael, Chase, Zack, and his dad all yelled at once, which was pretty much the reaction he'd expected.

"Yeah. I forgot to pack extra, so I wore him the whole tournament," Brady explained.

"Brady forgot something? Never!" Zack said in mock surprise.

"I have A-D-H-D," Brady spelled slowly. "I forget sometimes, okay?"

"That's disgusting!" Chase gagged. "You seriously didn't change your underwear the whole tournament?"

"Nope. I didn't want to make my dad spend money to get me some. So really I was doing him a favor!"

"I think we might need to burn them when we get home or they may come alive!" his dad said with a laugh.

Brady gasped. "No way! I'll never let you burn Charles!"

"I can't believe you named them." Zack exclaimed. "Who does that?"

"Brady!" Mikey laughed.

"Hey, we won, didn't we?" Brady asked defensively, shaking the medal around his neck. "Charles is good luck! I'm wearing him every game from now on!"

"I think you and Charles need a bath. You guys stink," Mikey teased, pulling his shirt up and covering his nose to further the point.

"Charles doesn't like your attitude, Mikey!" Brady said as if he were deeply offended. "But he's a gentleman, so he'll forgive you this time."

"You are so weird!" Michael proclaimed.

The argument and complex backstory of Charles that Brady had invented continued for miles after they'd finished their dinner, but eventually the exhaustion of the wild weekend caught up to them one by one. Zack was the first to go, passing out with his face up against the window only a few minutes after putting his headphones on. That sure didn't look very comfortable, but Zack could sleep anywhere; that was his superpower. Chase and Mikey didn't last much longer and lay against one another in the backseat, snoring softly. Brady fought it, but with no one left to talk to and it being too dark outside to watch the scenery go by, he popped his earbuds out, curled up in his seat and used his backpack as a pillow. He'd always had trouble sleeping in cars, and his dad's phone ringing just as he was starting to doze off definitely didn't help!

"Hey," his father answered quietly. "We stopped to get the boys some dinner, and we're on our way home now."

Good start to the conversation. Still early though.

"Kathy, this isn't the time; Brady's in the backseat!" his father whispered fiercely.

There we go…

"I said we'll talk, and we will, but when we're home and Brady's in bed. We'll see you in two hours," his dad said before ending the call and letting out a heavy sigh.

What were they going to talk about?

"Things still not going well, Brett?" Mr. Scott asked.

"No. I'll tell ya, Scott, I don't know if we're gonna make it. I really don't," his dad answered.

Not gonna make it? What did that mean?

"Be patient, brother. Keep trying and let the good Lord help you. He'll find a way for you and Kathy, just like He did for me and Hannah," Mr. Scott said.

"I hope so, Scott. I really do," Brady's father said. "For Brady's sake…"

What were they talking about? No, it couldn't be that. Definitely not that!

Brady stopped listening after that. He didn't want to hear any more. He slowly stuck his earbuds back in to drown it out, but it didn't work. Not really. It didn't drown it out when he got home either. It never did…

26 The Last Day

"**YES** sir, *Captain* Zack!" Chase confirmed with a quick salute, taking a readied stance as Zack tossed the ball up and clocked a bouncing grounder his way. Chase shifted his feet rapidly, kicking up a faint cloud of dust, and caught it one-handed on a bounce. He twisted to his side, hurled it to Ander at second, and made his fifth or so out that practice session. Well, imaginary out anyway.

"Nice play, guys!" Zack congratulated them. Chase had to admit, the extra practices were definitely helping, and Zack wasn't a bad coach either, even if he was relentless in making them practice. It was easy to see why Coach Nolan made him team captain, and even though the title didn't really mean much, Zack was definitely acting like it did. At first Chase was glad he got it, but Zack was as bossy as Mikey ever was! Chase couldn't put his finger on it, but lately Zack definitely wasn't acting like Zack. Chase just wished he knew why.

"Here it comes!" Zack yelled, his voice carrying into the

outfield. Chase turned around to see Brady *definitely* not paying attention. In fact, he was dancing, totally oblivious to the ball coming toward him.

"Heads up, Brady!" Chase yelled. Brady snapped out of it, watched the ball for a moment, then hurled his mitt into the air to try to knock it down when it soared above him. When the ball continued out a fair distance, Brady slowed, spun in a half circle and flopped down into the grass. Probably on purpose...

"Come on, Brady, go get it!" Zack ordered.

"Can we please take a break?" Brady moaned loudly.

"Yeah, can we? It's the last day of school!" Ander remarked.

"Yeah, shouldn't we play on the playground or something, since we won't get to again?" Logan added.

"We still have a lot of games to go, guys. Which we *need* to win, *remember*?" Zack not-so-gently reminded them.

"The last day of school is supposed to be fun, Zack! Baseball is supposed to be *fun*. We should just chill today," Brady said, sitting up in the grass.

"No, we can't. If we don't win, Chase's dad can't come and we might... we might lose Mikey." Zack stumbled over his words.

"You're not gonna lose me, Zack. We swore, remember?" Mikey reminded him.

"Yeah, but we don't know that for sure!" Zack retorted. "A promise doesn't mean anything if we don't get better!"

Zack's yelling at Mikey? That's weird...

"We only have a couple more minutes anyway. Let's just keep going!" Zack reminded them. "We can walk to the playground when you come to my house, remember? Now let's go!"

And that was that; no one fought it. Chase exchanged a glance with Mikey, who shrugged in reply. He looked as confused as Chase was. This *definitely* wasn't like Zack at all. Everyone took their positions, and they continued on.

It wasn't like it was the last time they'd have recess together, and they'd still remember everything that had happened on their playground, all the great memories: Zack running face-first into the soccer goal post in fourth grade chasing a ball, or when Mikey climbed *way* too high in a tree to get away from Evelyn after he'd hit her in the head with a kickball in second grade. And so they practiced together on the playground for one last time, until a wonderful and long-awaited sound carried across the field.

RIIIIIIIING!

That was it, it was finally time! Summer! Normally Chase would have to stay after school, but his uncle was picking him up to go to the gym and dinner until his mom got home from work. It was bittersweet. Frasier Elementary had been his second home for six years, but he was too excited to let it bother him much.

"Bye, Mrs. Meister! Bye, Mr. Dunlap!" Chase called behind him as he ran by, returning the waves they gave him as they wished him good luck in sixth grade. He saw Mikey and Evelyn boarding their bus, and Zack starting the last walk home he'd take with his brothers. Chase stopped for a moment on the cement, looking up and down the line of waiting vehicles, and a nervous pit formed in his stomach when he didn't see his uncle's truck. He hadn't forgotten, had he?

"Chase!" came a cry from way back in the line along with a

brief honk. Chase turned and saw his uncle waving him down out of the window of his silver truck. Chase sprinted down the sidewalk, leapt into the front seat and dropped his backpack at his feet. He felt so small inside this thing!

"You ready for a workout, little man?" his uncle asked.

"I'm always ready, Uncle Mark."

"I'll remind you that you said that when you complain about today being too hard." Mark laughed.

"What about dinner?" Chase asked eagerly.

"I have a good idea. I need an excuse to eat something bad for me. You in?"

Chase's head bobbed up and down vigorously. He was definitely in! When they arrived at their destination after a body-numbing sparring session, Chase flipped. They'd arrived somewhere his mom never, *ever* took him. The delicious, greasy smells of fried foods mixed with the sweetness of ice cream filled the air as Chase walked excitedly alongside his uncle up to a window to place their order. Nothing but junk food. It was *perfect*! They found a table outside with a bright red umbrella and enjoyed the warm sun and breeze. Chase wasted no time in stuffing his face.

Burp!

"Chase!" Mark scolded.

"Excuse me," Chase apologized, but he felt his smirk and knew it made it look like he thought it was funny. Which he did.

"So I take it you like the food, then?" Uncle Mark asked.

"Mmm hmm!" Chase nodded as he slurped more chocolate milkshake up his straw and held his second chili dog at the ready for when he finished taking his drink.

"I can't believe your mom's never taken you to Ruby's!" Mark exclaimed. "This place is Martin family tradition! Your grandpa used to take her and me here all the time when we were kids."

"Mom doesn't let me eat junk food much," Chase explained. "And she doesn't really like hot dogs either."

"Guess we must have had them too often back then. You know, Chase, I was thinking, you and I are a lot alike. I used to get in fights a lot and get into trouble all the time back then. Kinda like you!"

"Hey!"

"Let me finish. So your grandpa signed me up for boxing and *made* me do it. He said if I was gonna fight, I might as well get trophies for it!"

"Then what?" Chase pressed.

"Then I stopped doing bad stuff as much," Mark explained. "My grades went up, and I made some good friends. I got better, just like you did."

"I guess I've kinda been mad a lot." Chase smiled sheepishly.

"Nothing to be ashamed of. You had good reason to be upset."

"Yeah, 'cause of Dad," Chase said, looking away and not feeling as excited about his food anymore.

"Don't get yourself down. I know how you feel. I guess it's a little different, but my dad, your grandpa, passed away when I was only a little older than you."

"Do you still think about it?" Chase asked.

"Sure, sometimes it pops up again. It's kinda like ripping off a scab: things start to get better, then it comes off and the healing has to start all over again." That made a lot of sense to Chase, but understanding it didn't make things seem any easier for him.

"Uncle Mark, do you think my dad will come if we get to finals this year?" Chase asked hopefully.

"I don't know, buddy. All you can do is try your hardest and hope for the best, right?"

"I think he will. He *has* to if we make it, right?" Chase asked.

"I bet he'll come, Chase. Keep bugging him to come see you like you bug me and he definitely will!" Mark joked.

"Hey!" Chase exclaimed, throwing a french fry at his uncle's head for the second good-spirited jab he'd taken at him that day. Uncle Mark was right; his dad would definitely come. If they got to finals, he'd have to. He wouldn't break his promise twice, right?

27 The Storm

RUMBLE...BOOM!

Zack lay wide awake in bed, staring up at his ceiling with wide, anxious eyes as it was illuminated every few seconds with brilliant flashes of lightning. The wind howled, and rain sheeted against his window so loudly he couldn't even hear himself think. It almost sounded like being inside the van when they went through a car wash, if the car wash was trying to kill you with lightning and explosions. Zack wasn't scared of much, at least not much he'd admit to, but fierce thunderstorms were a definite exception. His brothers weren't big fans either, but they were lucky enough to be able to sleep through one. Zack couldn't. Some fearless big brother he was! Now every bad thought and every rumble of thunder, no matter how distant, made him dig his fingers deeper into Baxter and clutch him tighter to his chest.

Today had been fine until now; it was hard not to be when it was the first day of summer vacation! He had walked Drew and Carter home, and they played outside until they had barbequed chicken on the grill for dinner--his favorite, even if it did come with asparagus. Yuck! But now he was stuck in bed, and if the storm wasn't bad enough, it was so hard to sleep every night wondering if Mikey was hurt or not. What if his dad went too far? What if he didn't stop? Zack knew he was keeping his promise, but it was getting to be too much. Why was being responsible so hard?

"Please keep Mikey safe. Please," Zack prayed, gripping his necklace and hoping he'd be heard even over the thunder.

"I'm scared. I don't know what to do," he admitted. "I never should've promised him, should I?"

Zack listened intently, hoping against hope for an answer, but all he could hear was the storm get closer and closer.

"Please…"

CRACK-BOOM!

"Ahh!" Zack yelped at the latest explosion in the sky, and the air around him seemed to shudder. He pulled his covers up to block the light and took deep breaths to try to calm himself down. His door opened slowly a few moments later.

"Zachary?" his father said quietly.

Great, he was eleven, heading into sixth grade, and still afraid of thunder *and* still sleeping with a stuffed animal! Zack didn't say a word and slowly moved Baxter under the covers so his father wouldn't see and hoped he'd believe he was asleep. But Zack knew better than to think he'd fooled his dad. Somehow, someway, he always knew when something was wrong.

"It's okay to be scared, Zack," he said gently as he sat on the edge of the bed.

Zack tried to keep up his charade, but another clap of thunder and flash of lightning, even more violent than the last, was all the encouragement Zack needed. He gasped violently and squeezed in close, and when his dad wrapped his arm around him, Zack immediately felt more at ease.

"I'm sorry I woke you up, Dad," Zack whispered. "I know I'm too old to be scared of stupid storms."

"Don't worry about it. I was awake anyway."

"Yeah, because of me," Zack mumbled, disappointed in himself.

"Well, I was a little worried about you, but that's not why I'm awake."

"Then why?" Zack asked.

"Because storms scare me sometimes too," his father confessed.

"Don't lie, Dad, you're not afraid of anything."

"I swear! Even I'm afraid sometimes," his dad said. Zack felt his father's posture shift then, and when he looked up at his face, there was a sadness there that Zack hadn't seen before. It worried him.

"Why would you be afraid of storms, Dad?" Zack asked.

"Because sometimes they bring up old memories."

"Are they bad things?" Zack questioned. "From when you were in the war?"

"Sometimes they are," Mr. Walden admitted. "But don't you worry anymore, okay? We'll get through this one together just like all the others. How about we read a book or something while we wait for it to pass?"

Zack nodded and lay his head back down as his father turned the light on his bedside table on.

"Oh, and it's okay to still sleep with Baxter. You don't need to be embarrassed," Mr. Walden noted. "Lots of middle school kids still do, even though they won't admit it."

"You're just saying that, Dad."

"Zachary, I promise you I'm not lying. Do you believe me?" His tone showed no hint of a lie at all. Zack thought for a moment and nodded. Then, smiling sheepishly and still feeling a little childish, he brought Baxter back up from under the covers as his father searched through the pile of books.

"Hey, Dad? Can I ask you something?"

"Sure. What's on your mind?" his father asked, turning back to him with a paperback novel in hand.

"Is it ever okay to break a promise?" Zack asked, praying every second his dad would say yes.

"Well, I think if you give your word you should always keep it if you can," his father reasoned.

"But what if, like, you know something and someone made you promise not to tell?" Zack pressed. "But if you don't tell, they could get hurt?"

"Well, if someone could really get hurt, then I think keeping that person safe is more important than keeping the secret."

Zack nodded slowly and thoughtfully but said nothing more.

"Zack, is there something you want to tell me?" his father asked gently.

Zack froze. He wanted to tell so badly. But what if Mikey found out? There was no way he'd forgive Zack if he told! And what would Mr. Dzierwa do if he found out Mikey told? No, Zack couldn't say anything. It would only make things worse. He looked his father in the eyes and slowly shook his head.

"No, I was just curious," Zack answered. For once he was grateful it was storming; it helped hide the true reason he felt so scared.

"All right. Just remember I'll always be here if you need me, okay?" his father reminded him. "Now, should we read a little bit?"

"Can you just stay with me until I fall asleep?" Zack asked hopefully. He didn't really want to read anyway; he just wanted to his dad there. He *needed* him there.

"Sure." His father reached over to replace the book on his bedside table.

"Promise you won't leave?" Zack asked, needing to hear the answer.

"I promise," his dad swore.

Zack squeezed as close to him as he could and closed his eyes. He didn't feel all that grown up then, but at that moment he didn't care. He was glad his dad was there to make him feel safe. It was more than Mikey ever had...

28 Contention

IT was hot. *Really* hot. The kind of hot where Ohio goes from "Hey, it's June, let's warm up a little," to "Surprise, it's August now!" all in one weekend. But Michael suffered through it. It wasn't like he had a choice anyway. He was soaked, and no matter how many times he twisted his hat, sweat continuously dripped down from his drenched hair and stung his eyes, which were slivers in the glare of the intense sun. He took in a deep breath, stepped into the batter's box, twirled his bat in a circle, and waited. Everyone was counting on him. No way was he gonna strike out! No, he was gonna clock it, get Logan home, and win the game. Somehow.

The ball came faster than Michael was used to, and it was a strike. This kid was good, but not good enough to fool him twice. When the second pitch came, he swung his bat in a wide arc and heard it connect with a deafening metallic *crack*. He didn't watch to see where the ball went; there wasn't any time for that. He just bolted for first. Cheers arose behind him, but

Michael was only focused on his coach waving him on. He made for second and saw the center fielder scoop up the ball and turn to whip it in. No time. No time!

He gritted his teeth and slid hard into the base, kicking up a huge plume of dust that showered him like a cloud, turned his already-dingy uniform a light brown, and caked his sweaty face with dirt. He looked up hopefully at the umpire to see if he'd made it in time, but a backhand wave of his thumb informed him he was out.

"No!" Michael exclaimed, smacking his gloved hands down into the dirt and groaning in disbelief. That was the game; he'd lost it! He felt tears welling up, the losing ones, but he forced them down and pushed himself up, expecting to hear disappointment from his teammates. Instead, he heard cheers.

He heard Mr. Scott and Ms. Hannah's voice rise above the rest. "Way to go, Mikey!" Slowly he turned to the chain-link fence of the dugout, which the Rangers were shaking in celebration. Then he saw it: Logan had made it home before he'd been tagged! They'd still won!

Michael didn't say a word; he just sprinted to the dugout with his arms raised high in celebration. He passed through the gauntlet of his teammates smacking his helmet to the side where the rest of The Quad Squad stood.

"You did it!" Zack boomed while Brady leapt up and down joyfully.

"We're almost there, Chase!" Michael celebrated. "Just a few more!"

"Thank you, Mikey! Thank you *so* much!" Chase blubbered,

wrapping his arms around Michael and squeezing him way too tight.

"Chase, you're squishing me!" Michael squeaked as his friend crushed him, but he was thrilled despite the discomfort. They were in contention now! Just a few more games and they'd make it! They'd *finally* make it! Then he'd be safe from his father, and Chase would finally get to see his dad. His heart soared; everything was going right!

After they'd finished giving the other team handshakes, Michael was still riding high, but he wondered what he could do after the game. Zack's parents were supposed to take him home after, and while Michael wanted to tell his dad about how he'd helped win the game, he didn't want to just yet. It was Saturday, and that meant golf day, which meant his dad would be drinking...

"Zack, can you ask your parents if I can stay over?" Michael asked hopefully.

"But you don't have any other clothes or anything," Zack stated.

"I'll just borrow some of yours." It wouldn't have been the first time he'd done it.

"You mean Drew's?" Zack teased.

"Hur hur!" Michael laughed sarcastically. So what if Drew was almost the same size as him, even though they were two years apart. Zack was only like two or three inches taller than him, so they'd still fit.

"Great game, boys!" Mr. Scott congratulated. "Mikey, way to bring it home!"

CHAPTER 28

"Thanks, Mr. Scott!" Michael said, accepting his high-five.

"Dad, can Mikey stay the night?" Zack asked.

"Sorry, Zack, not tonight. Grandma and Grandpa are coming over for dinner, remember?"

"Come on, Dad, please?" Zack protested. "Mikey's family too!"

"Yes, he is, but tonight's just not a good night," Ms. Hannah said. "Maybe tomorrow, okay, boys?"

"Okay. Sorry, Mikey," Zack apologized. Michael shrugged and said it was fine, even though he wasn't sure it would be. But he could hope. He'd done well today; maybe that would be enough.

· · · · ·

THE Walden's van pulled up in front of Michael's home close to a half hour later. Jason was mowing the lawn with his headphones on, and their father's car was sitting in the driveway. Michael really wished getting back to his own home felt like it did when he pulled up to Zack's. Maybe it would, someday.

"Bye, Mikey!" Zack and his brothers called as Michael grabbed his gear and hopped to the edge of his driveway.

"I'll talk to your mom about you spending the night with us tomorrow, okay?" Ms. Hannah told him from out the window.

"Thanks, Ms. Hannah," Michael replied, waving as they drove off before turning to walk up the driveway. Jason had stopped the mower and gone to the garage. Michael walked in as Jason pulled two bottles of water from the mini fridge and cracked off the caps. Michael tried to slink by, but Jason stepped right into his path.

"Come on, Jason, leave me alone!" Michael said. Figures, he hadn't even been home a minute and already Jason was messing with him.

"Just drink this," Jason commanded. Michael looked at the bottle with a suspicious raised eyebrow.

"Why?" Michael asked.

"You look all pasty, Mikey. You're dehydrated. You never drink enough at your games, man. You'll get sick if you don't."

"Oh. Uhh, thanks," Michael managed, accepting the bottle from his brother and taking a sip.

"How'd you do? Beat my record yet?" Jason asked. As far as Michael could tell, he was asking honestly.

"I pitched good. Two no-hitter innings, and I hit the winning run." Jason appeared at least a little impressed.

"How'd you get so dirty?" Jason inquired.

"On that hit, I slid into second and it was really dusty. I got tagged, but Logan made it home," Michael recounted, unable to help smiling a little at his accomplishment.

"You guys just have to win a few more to make it to finals, right?"

"Yeah. Regionals, anyway. We've never made it that far."

"I never did either," Jason admitted.

"What? Yes, you did!" Michael retorted. Jason was lying. He'd definitely made it when he was younger.

"Not when I was your age. My team didn't make it until I was twelve. Just saying, you guys are pretty good."

"Thanks," Michael said earnestly. He didn't think Jason had ever told him anything like that before.

"Now, go get changed, but don't take a shower. Dad wants us to trim the bushes and weed the garden."

"Seriously?" Michael groaned.

"Don't whine, just do it." Jason turned with him to go into the house. "I'm gonna come in while you get changed. It's too freaking hot out here."

Michael strode through the kitchen and past the living room, where his dad sat watching golf with his laptop resting on the footstool and a drink in his hand. The usual. Probably working on his stocks or something for work. Michael slowed, his excitement to tell his dad about the game rising, and stepped into the room.

"Hey, Dad!" Michael chirped. "I--"

"Michael, get off the carpet. You're filthy!" his father boomed at him. Michael leapt back. His dad would kill him if he got dirt all over the white carpeting.

"Sorry, Dad, I forgot!" Michael stammered. "I just wanted to tell you we won. I got the winning hit, and no one got a hit off me in two innings!"

"Okay. Go get some different clothes on and help your brother," his father said absently, nodding his head but not saying anything else. And just like that, Michael felt all the gladness of the day sucked out of him, an all-too-familiar feeling. Not good enough...

"Just say good job..." Michael mumbled sadly under his breath.

"What did you say?" his father asked, looking up from his laptop.

"Nothing," Michael said shakily. He hadn't even meant to say that out loud.

"I asked you what you said, Michael," his father said again, rising from the couch and not once taking his gaze from him. Why? Why wasn't he brave enough to say it? Just say it!

"Why do you always do that, Dad?" Michael screamed. "I try so hard and you don't even care!"

Michael would have continued, in fact for a moment he didn't think he could stop, but that was before his father's cup exploded against the fireplace and the sound of shattering glass filled the room. Michael was paralyzed. He wanted his legs to move, but they wouldn't let him. The most he could do was fall back into the wall, and that moment was all it took for his dad to close the distance between them and seize Michael's mouth in a vice-like grip.

"Don't you *ever* raise your voice to me! *Ever!*" his father roared in his face. "Do you understand?"

"Yes!" Michael answered immediately, but that wasn't enough. It never was.

"Do you understand!" he yelled again, even louder than before.

"Yes!" Michael cried out.

"Dad! Dad, let him go, he's sorry!" Jason's voice pierced Michael's ears like a light in the fog. His father's grip loosened slightly, but only slightly, as his brother's hands found his dad's arm.

"He didn't mean it, Dad, he's just tired from the game!" Jason frantically explained, and his father released his grip at last. Michael realized then he'd been standing on his tiptoes, and his heels fell to the ground, having nearly been lifted off the floor by his father.

"Come on, you have to help me outside," his brother ordered. Michael tried to remember how to breathe again as his brother ferried him out the door and onto the driveway, where Michael's trembling legs finally gave out. He crashed to the cement, pushed himself up against the bricks of the house, and let himself break down.

"Don't talk back to him, Mikey. I told you never to do that," Jason said, his voice cracking as he sat next to him.

"I know! It's just, why? Why does he do that?" Michael sobbed. "Why isn't he ever proud of me?"

"I don't know. He's always been like that."

"Is he ever gonna stop?" Michael pleaded, hoping that somehow his brother knew. His brother, who he'd never seen cry until now. His brother, who hadn't come close to hugging him until now.

"When you're a winner," Jason said shakily. "Because life is a competition. There's winners and there's losers, and the Dzierwas aren't losers."

"Then I'm gonna win, Jason," he swore. "I'm gonna beat your record. Then I'll be a winner too, and he'll stop!"

"I hope so, Mikey," Jason said. "I really hope so..."

29. Pregame

UNIFORM, on! Charles, wearing! Cleats, check! Glove, check! Bat, check! Hat, check! Sunglasses, not check! Not check!

"Crap, where are they!" Brady dropped the checklist Abby had made for him to make sure he didn't forget anything, digging through his bag and searching frantically around his room. He'd been wired for days in anticipation of the game, but as Abby had commented on the night before, now he was full-on bonkers. It didn't help that in the weeks since they'd won their tournament over Memorial weekend, his parents' arguing had only gotten worse. If that was even possible. It was weeks like this he wished he still took his medicine or had a lifetime supply of earplugs.

But even that may not have helped, because it was today! It was finally today! The Big Game! *Their* big game! The regional finals. It had been close, razor close, but they'd made it. This was it, his chance to keep his friends together; the game that would fix everything. It was basically the most important day ever, and of course he couldn't find his *freaking sunglasses*!

"Abby!" Brady shouted. "Abby, I need you! Emergency!"

"What's wrong!" Abby yelled as she burst into his room.

"My sunglasses! I can't find my sunglasses!" Brady yelled, though it quickly changed to more of a whine. Today was starting off terrible; he knew he was getting too worked up, but he couldn't help it.

"Brady, they're right here," Abby said gently, reaching toward his head and presenting his sunglass to him.

"They were on your hat, Derpasaurus-Rex." Abby grinned. "Calm down, okay? You're making yourself all crazy!"

One crisis averted. He was going to thank his sister, but the second major issue that was ruining his morning decided to make itself known again.

"Ugh, they fell down *again*!" Brady growled, dropping onto the floor.

"What is it now?"

"These socks are *too big!*" Brady ranted, yanking up on the top with both hands until they were stretched above his knee. What was Mom thinking? They weren't even close to his size!

"Oh my gosh..." Abby sighed, rolling her eyes.

"Don't make fun of me," Brady snapped. That was the last thing he needed right now! Abby knelt in front of him, her face full of infinite patience.

"They don't fit because they aren't yours," she said calmly. "Dad must have accidently put those in your drawer. They're mine for softball."

"Oh..." Brady muttered, his face growing hot as Abby stood

and opened his dresser drawer. How did he not notice that? Stupid, stupid, stupid!

"Here's the right ones." Abby said gently, handing Brady the correct pair. He took them in hand but stared aimlessly at the fabric of the carpet.

"Hey, what's wrong?" Abby asked, sitting down next to him.

"They're arguing again. I don't wanna go down there."

"It'll be okay." Abby gave him the bear hug he usually hated, but he decided he didn't today.

"You've gotta eat some breakfast or you'll never make it through your game," she said. "Just go downstairs. They'll stop when they see you; they never fight around you."

"Okay. Thanks, Sissy." Brady sighed, pushing himself to his feet. "And thanks for the list. It really did help."

"No problem. Now go eat, quick. We've gotta leave in fifteen minutes!"

"Okay. I'll meet ya downstairs," Brady relayed, trudging past his sister and thumping his way down the stairs, his bag bouncing every which way. He reached the foyer and turned to head to the kitchen but slowed to a stop when he heard it. He still couldn't believe it. What could it possibly be this time? He listened for a moment, decided he didn't care what it was about, and strode in purposefully.

"Good morning!" Brady said as cheerfully as he could, attempting to diffuse whatever the heck it was they were going on about, but course it didn't work. Why would it? If anything, they got louder. They didn't even hear him!

That's it! This is my day, and they're not gonna ruin it.

"Stop!" Brady shouted at the top of his lungs. His parents looked over at him in shock. It was like they didn't even know he was there until that moment.

"Brady, don't yell at--" his dad began.

"No! All you two do is fight, and I'm tired of it!" Brady ranted. "You never stop, and it makes me sad! I always think about it, and I can't sleep!"

"Brady, we're--" his mother tried to interject apologetically.

"No, just stop! Figure it out or don't come!" Brady demanded. "If you don't, I'll just have Abby take me to my game. I don't even want you there!"

Yeah, that's right. I can be mad too!

"Now move! I'm *hangry* and need some *freaking Cheerios*!" Brady thundered, dumping his bag on the floor and storming between his parents to the pantry. Neither his mom nor dad said anything as he sat at the kitchen table, poured his bowl and sat down to eat his breakfast, glaring at them the entire time.

His parents stood completely dumbstruck. Neither one seemed to have any idea what to say, and Brady wouldn't really have cared if they did. He hardly ever got mad, but enough was enough! He'd probably dug himself a really deep hole, but something strange happened: his mom's hand slowly reached out and grasped his father's. Then, slowly, a strange grin formed on her face. She snorted, and she and his dad both started roaring with laughter.

"What?" Brady demanded, but he didn't get an answer.

"Your face!" she howled.

"I'm not trying to be funny, *Mom*!" Brady retorted, but they kept going. At first he thought they were making fun of him, but whatever it was, he supposed it didn't really matter. It was good to see them laughing together again, even if it was at him. Maybe he'd let them come to the game after all. Maybe.

· · · · ·

THE closer they got to Derring Fields, the more Brady had trouble sitting still. He was a coiled spring, ready to pop at any moment. Today he'd keep his friends together. That was the most important thing. The *only* important thing. His parents got stuck in a line of traffic leading to the rear parking lot, so Brady hopped out and ran full-tilt to their field. He had pre-game team meetings and rituals to do and couldn't be late! Luckily, Zack, Chase, and Mikey were all waiting for him at the end of the path at their designated meeting spot: a patch of grass alongside the right field fence.

"Hey guys!" Brady greeted as he skidded to a stop right before he ran into them.

"You ready, Brady?" Zack asked.

"Yes sir, Captain Zack! Got Charles on and everything!" Brady grinned. What followed was a mix of laughter and grossed-out noises.

"Don't laugh at Charles, guys! He's very sensitive, and you're being hurtful!" Brady scolded. They knew he was good luck; every game he'd forgot him, they'd lost! Chase seemed ready to argue the point, but Zack interjected before he had the chance.

"Brady, enough with the Charles stuff! It's gross!" Zack

ordered.

"*Fine*," Brady surrendered. "So, Chase, is your dad coming? Is he here?" he asked, trying to change the subject. And being nosey.

"Not yet, but he said he would be!" Chase chirped hopefully. "He told me he got a plane ticket last week."

"That's awesome, dude!" Brady hollered. At least Chase would get to see his dad, so at least one good thing would happen if they lost!

"What about you, Mikey? Is your dad here?" Zack inquired.

"Yeah, he is," Mikey answered uneasily. Chase looked worried too, but Mikey was a nervous wreck. Brady didn't think he'd seen him look this bad before.

"Good. He'll get to see us wipe the floor with the Mavericks!" Chase cheered.

"Yeah, we're gonna crush those Derper Monkeys!" Brady agreed, and when he held out his corner, everyone followed suit.

"*BOOM!*" they all shouted as the square burst apart. Brady prayed this wouldn't be the last game where they'd do that together. He was certain his friends felt the same.

"Hey, it's Brady the Monkey Kid!" an amused voice said from the other side of the path. They all turned, and there stood Cameron and Ryan, looking just as dumb as ever.

"Ooh ooh, ahh ahh!" Brady shot back.

"You guys seriously made it this far?" Cameron jabbed. "Wow, the other teams must have really sucked!"

"The only reason we didn't beat you the first time is because Mikey's wrist was still hurt!" Zack fired back.

"Is his dad here today?" Ryan asked, pointing to Mikey. "He can't strike us out if he's crying the whole time."

"Shut up! Leave him alone!" Chase took a step forward with his fists clenched.

"Need him to help you like your sister did?" Cameron asked Brady mockingly.

"You gonna run away from him like you ran away from her?" Brady jeered. That was it, he was done even faking being nice to these two.

"Oooh!" Zack and Mikey mocked. That definitely hit a nerve; their faces were so red!

Brady wasn't sure if Cameron would try something else, but he almost hoped he would so he could see Chase in action. Brady was *pretty* sure he was about to pop. He tried to find the good in everyone, but he was pretty sure there wasn't any to find in Cameron. At least, he didn't have the patience today to find it. Cameron was just a jerk, plain and simple. But whatever, it didn't matter anyway. Ryan prodded him a second later and pointed to their dugout, where their coach was waving them in. They glared at them, but in the end they hoisted their bags and left to join their team.

"Jerks," Chase said flatly.

"Whatever, they'll be crying when we win," Zack said, and with that they started walking down the rest of the dusty stretch to their dugout, where their coaches and the rest of their teammates were setting up.

"Hey, Coach, Captain Zack and the Cube Team are here!" Logan notified their coach with a good-natured grin.

"Shut up, Logan." Zack gave him a friendly shove on the shoulder as they stuffed themselves into the dugout.

"That's all of us, then!" Coach Nolan announced. "Okay, boys, take a seat."

The clatter of bats and the bonks of dropped water bottles rang through the dugout as the boys jostled for position on the bench.

"I'll be honest, guys, I didn't prepare a big speech or anything," their coach admitted. "I just want you all to know how proud of you guys I am. Play your hardest, be good sports, and win if you can. Sound good?"

"Yes, coach!" Brady and his teammates barked in unison.

"Okay, we're up first, so let's put some on the board quick. When we take the field, we'll start with the usual positions. I want everyone where they're strongest. Cole and Tyler will rotate first four innings pitching. Mikey, we'll need you to close us out today, got it?"

"Yes, Coach!" Michael answered.

"All right, then. Zack, get 'em fired up!"

"Bring it in, guys!" Zack shouted. He put his hand out, and Coach Nolan and the rest of the team joined the circle.

"One, two, three..."

"Rangers!" the boys yelled.

Brady kept a smile on his face as he took his spot in the lineup, the butterflies in his stomach going crazy. But he was sure everything would be okay. This was *their* day! The Quad Squad came in together, and that's the way they were leaving too. That's what they promised, so that's what was going to happen. And he had Charles, so that couldn't hurt either. This was it. No turning back. Game on!

PLAY BALL!

30 Late

WHERE *is he?*

Chase sat next to Brady and shifted back and forth nervously, unable to get comfortable. He saw his mom, but that was it. Why wasn't his dad here yet? He *promised* he'd be here! He said he got a ticket, so he'd be here, right?

"First three up: Jessing, Distel, Walden!" Coach Nolan barked, leading to a scramble for helmets, bats, and gloves.

"Crap…" Zack sighed, turning pale as a ghost. He looked like he was gonna puke.

"C'mon, Zack, you got this, bro!" Mikey encouraged him. "The rut ends today!"

"You want to high-five Charles for good luck?" Brady asked, reaching for his waistband.

"I will hit you. With this bat," Zack jokingly threatened, but Chase wasn't so certain he was really joking.

"Fine, just remember he believes in you, Zack!" Brady said.

"At least you probably won't be up with two outs already,"

Mikey chanced. "Well, probably."

"Right..." Zack replied, his head already hanging as he walked out of the dugout.

Chase hoped Zack would do okay; he'd been so hard on himself lately. But for now, Chase had a while until his spot in the rotation came up, so he walked to the exit of the dugout. He waved and jumped up and down to get his mom's attention, but she was too busy talking to Ms. Hannah and didn't even notice.

"Coach, can I ask my mom something?" Chase asked anxiously.

"Be quick!" his coach said. Chase thanked him and ran out to the edge of the bleachers.

"Mom, did he text you?" Chase asked eagerly, hanging onto the edge of his mom's seat.

"No, not yet, sweetie. But I'm sure he'll be here soon."

"Yeah, right..." Chase sighed, unable to hide the frown that instantly formed on his face. He probably wasn't even coming... "Is he really coming, Mom?" His mother took his hands in hers.

"I promise I'll let you know as soon as I do. I'll keep calling and calling until he picks up," his mother assured him. "You go play and let me handle it."

"Okay. Thanks," Chase put on a smile for his mother's sake. It probably wasn't very convincing, but it was the best he could manage.

He walked backward toward the dugout, looking out into the parking lot hopefully, but no one was coming yet, so he spun on his heel and plowed right into someone.

"Jeez, Chase, watch where you're going!" a familiar voice

scolded him.

"Evelyn? What are you doing here?" Chase asked. Talk about unexpected. She always said that it was "too much weird" when the Quad Squad was together.

"Brady invited me," she said with a warm smile.

"Really? But he drives you crazy!" Chase blabbed.

"He does, but I wanted to watch you guys. I think it was nice that he asked."

"Hi, Evil-lyn!" Brady yelled excitedly from the dugout.

"Hi, McMidget with Cheese!" Evelyn shot back without delay.

"At least I'm delicious!" Brady yelled back, and Chase finally had a laugh that day. Brady hated being reminded of how small he was.

"Talbert! McCormick! Back inside!" Coach Nolan boomed.

"Shoot, I gotta go," Chase said. "Bye, Ev! See you after?"

"Long as you guys don't suck." She smirked.

"Don't worry, we won't." He rushed back into the dugout, planning to drill Brady on why he'd really invited his arch-nemesis, but found him and Mikey up against the fence in complete silence. Why were they so quiet?

"Go, Zack!" Carter and Drew cheered from the sidelines. That was why; Zack was up. His record hadn't gotten any better since their tournament over Memorial Day weekend. What was going on with him? Why couldn't he hit anything anymore?

"Good cut!" Mr. Scott clapped from the bleachers even though it had been a strike.

"Come on, Zack, breaking ball next," Mikey muttered

anxiously. Chase watched as Mikey's prediction came true. Zack swung, and he actually connected! Up it went, but high. Way too high…

"Oh no…" Mikey moaned, letting his head fall into the chain-link.

"Dang it..." Chase grumbled as the descending ball was easily caught by the Mavericks shortstop, ending the inning. Zack turned from his trip to first and walked back, shaking his head all the while and blinking his eyes rapidly.

The Rangers shifted about, grabbing their mitts and preparing to head back out into the field as Zack came back in, receiving a pat on the back from Coach Nolan and encouragements from their teammates, but it didn't seem to be helping.

"Good try, Zack," Brady said as Zack hung up his bat and popped off his helmet. He nodded, wiped his eyes and tried to stifle a sniffle.

"I'm sorry, guys," Zack apologized. But why? He hadn't done anything wrong.

"It's fine, dude, you'll get it next time!" Brady reassured him.

"Yeah, definitely," Zack swore, regaining his composure and following Chase as they again took to the field, preparing themselves for another hard inning. The game sure wasn't going anywhere fast, but it was only the first inning, and things could change in an instant.

Chase ran out to take his position at shortstop and began passing a ball around with his teammates while they waited for Cole, their opening pitcher, to warm up. Chase caught a throw from Brady, then sent it to Zack at first, spitting sunflower seed shells while he checked the bleachers again. His mom was on her phone, talking to someone. She wasn't yelling, but it definitely looked like she was insisting. He couldn't read lips, but he was pretty sure she'd said "please" at least once. Was it Dad? She noticed him then and waved. He returned the greeting half-heartedly but he couldn't ignore the empty spot saved next to her.

"He'll be here. He promised," Chase said under his breath. He really wished he believed that.

"Batter up!"

Chase shook his head, gritted his teeth, and stood focused and alert. He was like a cat ready to pounce and hoped it would come to him. Cole was good. Not as good as Mikey was, but still good. He'd make it hard for the Mavericks. Man, they were really strong at bat, though. Their lead-off hitter started them with a single to right field, but Mikey fielded it and got it to Zack at first, stopping the runner.

"Next one's yours, Cole!" Chase called, swaying back and forth and waiting for prey to come his way. Strike one, two, three! Yes! It was a quick reply to the early single, and Chase hoped they could keep it up. Cole did, striking out the next batter as well.

"Come on, come to me. Come to me!" Chase prayed. He was chomping at the bit. He *needed* something to field. Anything to get his mind off the empty seat.

The ball sped toward home, and the batter swung mightily, sending a line drive like a rocket between Chase and third base. Chase didn't even think; he rushed to his right, leapt out, and felt the ball sink into his mitt's pocket. He landed hard in the dirt and held up his catch in triumph. So much for a clean uniform. Zack cheered for him on his way to the dugout, and Brady slapped him on the back as he ran past. He'd really needed that.

"Woo, good job, Chase!" his mom hollered and clapped from the bleachers. Chase grinned, but his good mood didn't last; the empty seat was still there.

Where is he?

"Nice catch, dude!" Zack congratulated him when he walked into the dugout.

"Thanks," Chase replied curtly, even though he didn't mean to.

"Hey, you okay?"

"Yeah." Chase tried to say it convincingly, but Zack raised an eyebrow. Fine, no use hiding it; Zack always knew when something was bugging him anyway. Might as well tell him...

"No!" he admitted. "I don't know why he's not here yet!"

"He will be, don't worry," Zack assured him. "He probably just got stuck in traffic or something."

"Yeah, maybe," Chase said, though he wasn't entirely convinced. It wouldn't be the first time he'd been lied to.

"He will. Just keep your head in the game, okay? We need you!"

"Don't worry, I will," Chase insisted, knowing what Zack really meant. He looked past Zack to the fence line where Mr. Dzierwa sat. He wasn't sending Mikey anywhere!

The Rangers' second time up to bat wasn't any more productive than their first. They were getting hits, even getting on base sometimes, but Chase had to admit the Mavericks were pretty freaking good. The Rangers nearly got someone home, but a long hit to center field was caught, ending the inning before they had the chance to score. Zero to zilch. Time to take the field again!

CRACK!

Chase dove to his right, twisted his arm and reached as far as he could, but it wasn't enough to catch the high line-drive that soared over his head. Brady was backing him up, but it wouldn't matter; the Mavericks had a runner on third, and he was already on his way home. Bottom of the third inning disaster, and now the Mavericks were ahead because of him! Chase growled roughly and slammed his fist into the pocket of his mitt hard enough to hurt both his hands.

"Don't worry about it, Chase!" Brady shouted. Easy for him to say.

Chase knew it wasn't really his fault; it had been too far out of his reach for him to catch. But he couldn't help it. It was the bleachers, the still-empty seat. Maybe he shouldn't have gotten his hopes up.

PTINK!

"Oh crap!" Chase gasped, snapped back into reality by the sound of another hit and praying frantically it wasn't coming to him.

"Mine! *Mine!*" Mikey yelled from right field, waving off their center fielder, who was closing to intercept the pop fly. Mikey slowed, backed up two steps and put up his mitt, effortlessly catching the lazy ball. Thank God...

"Great catch, Michael!" Mr. Scott yelled from the sidelines.

"Get your head in the game!" Chase scolded himself, slapping his head with his mitt.

Why doesn't he want to see me?

"Stop!" Chase yelled at himself, drawing a look from their third baseman. Thankfully he didn't make a big deal about it, and Chase readied himself for the next batter.

Seriously? This kid?

Cameron. Chase already didn't like him and remembered the hit he'd made during their scrimmage that put the Mavericks three runs up. Cole blasted a strike right down the middle. Good start!

One out. Runner on first. Play at second.

"Ooh ooh ahh ahh!" Brady monkey-called from the outfield. That distracted Cameron enough to make him fall for Cole's change-up. Strike two, but man, the look Cameron shot Brady's way after sure looked anything but friendly...

One more. C'mon, just one more!

PTINK!

Chase sprang, covering the ground between himself and second base in the blink of an eye. He caught the lightning-fast grounder on a bounce and deftly tossed it to Ander, who touched second and whipped it to Zack before Cameron could cross first base.

"Yes!" Chase yelled, pumping his fist. Double play! The Rangers' side of the field erupted in cheers, and Chase looked hopefully toward the bleachers. Still empty.

"He didn't even see it..." Chase grumbled, pulling his hat low and staring at the ground as he meandered to the dugout.

He dimly heard the congratulations as he walked through and collapsed on the bench, but he didn't care. It didn't matter anyway...

"Chase. Chase!" a voice called to him from outside the dugout. He knew that voice! He shot up and shoved his way through his teammates, bursting from the entrance at a full sprint.

Mark grunted as Chase leapt into the air and slammed into him, wrapping his arms around his uncle's neck and burying his face into his shoulder.

"Hey, little nephew," Mark greeted warmly. "That was an amazing play!"

"You saw me?" Chase asked, barely able to contain his joy.

"You bet I did! Just in time too." Chase released his grip, and Mark lowered him gently back to the ground.

'What are you doing here?" Chase sniffled.

"You kidding? This is your big game! No way I'd miss seeing you play!"

"My dad's not coming, is he?" His uncle looked back at his mother for a moment, then back to him and shook his head slightly.

"I'm sorry, buddy," Mark said, and Chase nodded sadly.

"I never really thought he'd come, but I really hoped he would," Chase explained. "I guess he really doesn't want me..."

"Hey, don't say that." Mark placed his hands on Chase's shoulders and looked him square in the eyes. "You're a great kid, Chase. Your dad has no idea what he's missing!"

"Thanks, Uncle Mark." Chase smiled gratefully.

"I know you're disappointed, but you're playing great out

there!" Mark encouraged him. "Go kick some butt with your buddies, and we'll do something fun after the game, okay?"

"What?" Chase demanded, his spirits rising.

"You'll have to wait and see. Just keep playing like that so you earn it."

"I will, don't worry!" Chase beamed, running into his uncle again with something more head-butt than hug.

"I lead off this inning. Watch me, okay!" Chase insisted.

"I will, I promise."

Chase ran back to his team and stuffed his head into his helmet. He grabbed his bat and strode with purpose out onto the deck circle to get in a few practice swings before his time came. Now the empty seat was full with someone never too busy for him, someone who actually wanted to see him! Chase looked back to make sure his uncle was watching and stepped up to the plate. The Mavericks' pitcher wound up, Chase swung, and the sound of his mom and uncle cheering was all he could hear when he slid into second.

31 To Keep a Promise

"**YES**!" Zack yelled frantically when Chase made it to second. That was how you started an inning! They were only down by one; not too bad! Another good hit or two, and they'd be tied up or even ahead! Next up was Brady, then Ander and Mikey. They were all good hitters for sure, but Cameron was pitching. Chase had made it look easy, but it wasn't. He threw *hard* and had a good curveball like Mikey did. Brady had trouble hitting curvers.

"Single or better, Brady!" Zack called out when Brady walked to the plate, spinning his bat round and round like usual.

"Ooh ooh!" Brady greeted Cameron. Man, he was starting to take it too far again!

"Brady must *really* not like him," Zack commented to Mikey, who was standing next to him.

"Yeah, he never makes fun of people on purpose," Mikey agreed. He thought for a moment, then shrugged. "Usually."

"Hopefully it messes Cameron up. He looks like he's getting

really mad," Zack observed as Cameron prepared to throw.

The wind-up was slow, but *man* did he throw hard! It sped faster than any of Mikey's pitches, but it was way inside.

"Woo!" Brady yelped, barely having time to hop back out of the ball's path just before it hit him.

"Uh oh..." Zack said.

"He did that on purpose!" Mikey commented. "No way he'd miss that bad!"

Brady cautiously stepped back into the batter's box, tapped home plate with his bat, and took his stance again. Cameron's next pitch was a strike clean down the middle, followed by another that came way too close. Was Mikey right, or was it just a crummy pitch? Zack watched carefully as Cameron wound up and whipped it toward home. The ball flew straight, then curved hard to the right. Brady tried to turn and move out of its path, but there just wasn't enough time, and he was beaned with a meaty *thump* right in the side of his rear.

"Oww, my *butt*! My beautiful butt!" Brady yelled, clenching his eyes shut and stumbling away. Leave it to Brady to try to make it funny even when it was obvious he was hurt.

"Shoot," Coach Nolan remarked as he stepped from the dugout. "Zack, get a helmet. I need you to run for him."

"Okay!" Zack said, hurriedly pulling on his helmet and running to first base. He high-fived Brady, who was slowly limping his way back, and jogged to first base. It sucked Brady was hurt, but now they had a runner on second and third. If Mikey could get a decent hit...

"Let's go, Michael!" Zack's mom and dad cheered from the

bleachers. Mr. Dzierwa looked up from his phone as Mikey walked up to bat. Though his eyes were covered by dark sunglasses, he didn't appear too excited; it looked like he was judging him.

Mikey swung hard at Cameron's first pitch but failed to connect.

Strike one...

The next was a ball, barely, and Mikey caught a piece of the next one, sending a foul into the fencing behind home plate. Zack growled under his breath and wished Mr. Dzierwa wasn't there. Mikey always played worse when he was at their games, even when he wasn't yelling!

"Come on, Mikey..." Zack whispered as his friend readied to receive the next pitch. Cameron threw perfect and straight, and Zack's heart leapt in his chest. Mikey had that for sure! But then suddenly, with only a short distance to go, it sunk suddenly. Mikey swung and barely missed.

"Strike three!" the umpire shouted. Michael threw his head back, and Zack could feel his disappointment. His dad just shook his head and went straight back to his phone like he'd expected him to fail the whole time. It wasn't fair. Why did Michael have to have a dad like him?

"Ump!" Chase yelled. Zack snapped back to reality quick enough to see Chase pointing to Cameron, who was holding his wrist and fake-crying at Mikey as he trudged his way back to the dugout.

"That's enough!" the umpire commanded Cameron, then turned to the Mavericks' dugout. "Coach, anything like that again and he's out of the game!" he ordered. The Mavericks' coach didn't waste any time, immediately pulling Cameron off the field and laying into him. Zack was happy to see their coach wasn't a bully too.

One out. Logan's up next...

Zack found himself sprinting to second after Logan hit into deep center field. He was going to hold up at second, but Chase, as usual, decided he could make it home. The Mavericks' center fielder hurled the ball into the infield toward home, and Zack decided he could make it to third after all. The ball bounced once near home plate up into the catcher's mitt, but Chase had already slid in.

"Woo, thanks Logan!" Chase hooted, hopping and clapping his way back to the dugout.

"Such a goober," Zack said, smiling. He was probably showing off for his uncle, but whatever, at least they were tied now! Zack and Logan would soon find their own way home, putting them up three to one, but a strikeout and a lucky catch on Ander's line-drive put an end to their streak.

Three to one, we got this!

"Looking good, boys!" Coach Nolan beamed. "Same positions, except McCormick, you're on break." Zack felt bad for Brady, who sat leaning heavily to one side.

"Wait, Dzierwa!" their coach said.

"Yeah, Coach?" Mikey answered.

"I know I usually put you in the last two innings, but I want to hold this lead. If you get tired later on, tell me, but I want you out there now. Can you do it?"

"Yeah!" Mikey perked up, grabbing his mitt excitedly.

"Hey, I know your dad's out there and he might get noisy again, but just tune him out. You got this!" Coach Nolan encouraged him.

"Thanks, Coach," Michael said gratefully.

"No hitter, Mikey! No hitter!" Zack shouted, a call picked up by his teammates. Zack knew he could do it, and he needed Mikey to believe it too, whether his dad was there or not. Just three more innings. Three more innings and Mikey wouldn't need to be afraid anymore. Three more innings and Zack would be free of his promise and could finally sleep without having to worry if Mikey was safe or not.

To Zack's relief, things started off strong. Mikey struck out the first batter with just four pitches and put two more past the next in rapid succession. But that was all the good news. After that, things started to go south fast. Zack failed to field the first hit, turning what should have been an easy out into a single. Then the next hitter blasted the ball into right field, a double that put a runner on second *and* third. Cameron's friend Ryan was up next, and Mikey put a strike on him, then a ball, another strike, then...

"*CRACK!*"

"Oh no!" Zack gasped as the ball sailed in right field. It wasn't a home run, but it was close enough. By the time the ball made it back into the infield, the Mavericks crossed home plate and the batter stood triumphantly on third base. Mr. Dzierwa didn't move, didn't yell, but Zack could see Michael wilt under his father's gaze. *He* was doing this to him. He wasn't even hitting him, and he was still hurting him!

Zack wished the wild cheering from the Mavericks side would finally stop, but it didn't. It would only quiet down, then pick up again when someone got a hit or scored a run. Two more crossed the plate with only one more out to show for it. Five to three now, and Mikey had nothing left. He turned toward their dugout, and though Zack couldn't see his face, he could feel how spent he was. Coach Nolan nodded understandingly, waved Mikey in, and sent Cole out to relieve him. As he warmed up, Mr. Dzierwa rose from his chair and walked to the dugout.

"Oh no. Dad, please see them!" Zack prayed when Mikey exited the dugout and his father took him by the arm and pulled him along roughly until they were out of sight behind the large building in the center of the ballfields. Zack waited anxiously as the game renewed, and thankfully Cole struck the batter out in quick order. Thank God!

"Coach, I need to use the bathroom!" Zack insisted as he came in full-sprint. He didn't even wait for permission and tore out the back toward the restrooms. He slowed as he reached them, looking and listening for where they might have gone, and when he reached the shed where they kept the field equipment, he found them. Zack slid behind the corner and dared to peek out.

"What is wrong with you?" Mr. Dzierwa asked sharply.

"I'm sorry!"

"I can't believe you gave up that many runs and *asked* to be pulled!"

"I said I'm sorry..." Michael whimpered.

"Your brother never did anything like this," Mr. Dzierwa

scoffed. "Pathetic..."

"But I..." Michael begged as he began to choke up.

"He never did *that* when things got hard either," his father sneered. "Man up!"

"Please stop..." Mikey whined.

"Man up!" his father ordered.

"Stop!" Mikey screamed defiantly. But before it could rise too loud, his father raised his hand into the air suddenly and violently. Mikey swung his arms up in front of his face to defend himself, cowering in front of his father, but thankfully the hand never came down. Whatever that was worth...

"Dad, don't! Please..." Mikey begged, his voice trembling.

"Didn't I tell you never to raise your voice at me?" his father asked calmly, but with an unmistakable anger behind it. Mikey nodded slowly, fearfully. Zack had never seen him so scared before. He was shaking so bad...

"You and I are going to have a talk tonight, Michael," Mr. Dzierwa said slowly. "Now stop crying and get back to the field."

Zack waited a moment behind the corner for Mr. Dzierwa to leave, but what would he say? What would he do? He couldn't let him know he'd heard, but he had to do something.

"Mikey?" Zack chanced, rounding the corner to see Mikey leaning up against the wall. He hurriedly wiped his eyes and turned away.

"Hey, Coach asked me to find you. Are you okay?" Zack asked.

"Yeah." Mikey sniffled. "I'm fine."

"Was that your dad?" Zack asked, trying to sound curious.

Mikey nodded slowly, his eyes staring forward into nothing.

"Zack, I'm scared," Mikey admitted. "I'm so scared."

"Why?" Zack asked, his worry growing.

"We're losing and it's my fault!" Mikey replied fearfully. "He's already so mad. I don't know what he'll do if we lose!"

"I promised we'd win, and we will," Zack said confidently. "But you're our best pitcher, and we need your help!"

"But I'll just choke again!"

"You won't! I know you won't. Just ignore your dad, and you'll be fine," Zack promised. "Besides, I'm captain, so I'm ordering you to pitch."

"You can't even do that," Mikey argued.

"Fine, then I'm captain and telling you to suck it up, Buttercup!" Zack commanded, finally getting a laugh from his friend. It wasn't much of a laugh, but it was better than nothing.

"Zack! Your coach is looking for you!" Zack heard Drew's voice ring out from around the building.

"Crap, I'm probably up. Come on!" Zack dragged Mikey back to the dugout, where Coach Nolan was waiting impatiently.

"You're on deck, Walden, let's go!" He handed Zack his helmet and bat while shoving him out the entrance onto the dirt. Cole had just hit a single, and he stood on first with Logan at second.

"How many outs are there?" Zack asked nervously.

"Not telling. You'll do fine," his coach said, but his attempt at calming Zack's nerves was foiled by Brady, who leaned forward with his fingers in a "V" and mouthed "two." Figured, he'd sucked at bat for weeks, and here he was back in the same situation.

"Thanks for the pep talk, Brady," Zack said, rolling his eyes.

"You're welcome!" Brady chirped. Zack didn't know why, but he found Brady's attitude strangely contagious. No matter what happened, Brady never doubted him. Every time he'd struck out, Brady had been right there to tell him it was okay, to keep trying, that he'd get it next time. Maybe he was right; maybe he would get a hit. Maybe it was time he stopped doubting himself and started leading.

"You know what, screw this rut!" Zack announced confidently.

"About time you said that!" Brady grinned, giving Zack a quick salute. "Hit em' home, Captain!"

Zack stepped from the dugout and marched to home plate, trying his best to steady his heart and catch his breath. He took out his necklace before he stepped up to the plate, gave it a quick kiss for luck, and said a quiet prayer.

Please help me keep him safe!

Down three runs, two outs, whatever! He took the first strike to gauge the pitcher, then let a ball go by. Good eye. Here came the change-up. Zack shifted his weight to his back foot and gripped his bat tightly. The ball came and broke low, just like he thought it would. Not this time…

The next thing Zack saw was a small white orb speeding into the sky. He wasn't supposed to watch it, but somehow he knew it was gone. Four seconds later, it took a sudden dive back toward the Earth and into a pine tree past the left-field fence. Zack dropped his bat casually and ran the bases at a leisurely pace, then through the gauntlet of his teammates straight into

Mikey, Brady, and Chase.

"Holy crap, you hit a dinger!" Chase shouted in disbelief.

"No way! No freaking way!" Brady babbled excitedly.

"Oh my God, Zack!" Mikey hollered over the raucous celebration. "You did it!"

He'd done it! He'd showed Mikey they still had a chance! They'd needed a rally, and he'd started one. That was his responsibility, to his team and his friends. But would it really make a difference? Even if they won, would Mikey's dad really stop hurting him? And even if he didn't hit Mikey anymore, his words crushed Mikey's spirit. In a way, that was almost worse.

Do what you think is right, son. That's all I'll ever ask of you.

But what was the right thing? Zack froze and thought of something he hadn't before. Was he really doing the right thing keeping Mikey's secret? Even if they won, would he really be safe? What else would his dad do to him if he didn't tell? Then, the worst of all, something he hadn't even considered.

What if I'm wrong?

32 safe

MICHAEL couldn't believe it; Zack changed everything! The Rangers rallied quickly, their confidence restored in the fifth inning, putting one more run on the board before the Mavericks finally made their last out. At the top of the fifth, Tyler did a great job on the mound, but the Mavericks still scored two runs and were now ahead by one. Now, at the bottom of the sixth and final inning, Michael clutched the fence anxiously. Zack was on third, so that was almost a guarantee, but Brady was on second, and he was still having some trouble running because of his "butt bruise," so it was anyone's guess if he'd make it home. Ander was up next, and after a nerve-wracking full count, he hit a single that got Zack home while Brady managed his way to third.

"Come on…" Michael whispered, biting his lip nervously.

Strike three!

"No!" Michael groaned. That was two. Only one left. This was terrible!

"It's gonna be okay, dude, don't worry!" Chase assured him,

the weight of his arm falling across Michael's shoulders.

"I hope so," Michael said. Chase's gesture made him feel a little better, a little safer. Somehow, he always felt safer with his friends around.

"Oh my God!" Chase yelled suddenly, startling Michael.

"Go, Brady, go! Go!" Michael and Chase shouted frantically, jumping up and down together and shaking the fence. Brady was going as fast as he could, but the ball was flying toward the catcher.

"Down!" they yelled together. Brady listened, but Michael would have bet anything he hadn't wanted to when he slid in, barely beating the tag. Now they were up one!

"Brady-Bear! Brady-Bear! Brady-Bear!" Michael and Chase took up the cheer as Brady hurriedly stood up and hobbled his way into the dugout.

"Ow, ow, it hurts! It really hurts!" he complained, half laughing, half whining. Michael went to congratulate him, but Brady walked right past him to the exit.

"Evelyn, do you have an ice pack?" Brady yelled.

"Why would I have an ice pack?" she shot back.

"Do you or don't you?" Brady asked again. Evelyn froze for a moment as if giving great thought to what Brady had said.

"Fine," she said, pulling open the bag she'd brought and digging through it. She produced her first aid kid, zipped it open, and threw a small white pouch to Brady.

"Crush it in your hands first, then sit on it," she instructed.

"Thank you!" Brady said gratefully, squeezing it between his hands, setting it on the bench and sitting right on top of it.

"Dude, are you okay?" Michael asked, trying to stifle a laugh.

"We'd better win, because I'm probably not gonna be able to sit for a month now!" Brady laughed.

A groan from the Rangers' bleachers signaled the last out and the end of their last time at bat. They were up, but only by one.

"Nice job, Brady!" Zack shouted, putting Brady in a fake headlock, but he pretended to be strangled and let his tongue roll out onto Zack's arm.

"Freaking gross, Brady." Zack recoiled in disgust and punched Brady's arm. "Anyway, you ready, Mikey?"

"What? No way!" Michael exclaimed.

"C'mon, dude!" Zack demanded.

"Yeah, I took a bullet for you!" Brady said.

"It was a ball, Brady," Michael replied.

"Whatever, that turd burglar Cameron's gonna be up, and you owe it to my butt to strike him out!" Brady insisted.

"Mikey, this means something to us too. We *need* you!" Zack said. "You want your dad to see you're better than Jason, right? So go and prove it!"

Michael couldn't argue anything Zack had said. He wanted to, but he couldn't. Zack believed in him. Brady and Chase too. His friends. His brothers. They hadn't let him down; how could he?

"Bring it in, boys!" Coach Nolan boomed, calling them into a huddle before Michael could answer or think of another excuse.

"Alright, guys, this is it!" their coach continued, looking as stressed and excited as they all were. "Brady got us the run we need, and now we need to hold 'em! Everyone got it?"

"Yes, Coach!" Michael and his teammates answered as one.

"Coach!" Michael piped up, squeezing his way into the forefront of the circle.

"Dzierwa, can you finish this and bring us home?" he asked Michael.

"No hitter," Michael answered without a shred of doubt in his voice.

"That's what I like to hear!" their coach hollered. "Captain, get 'em fired up!"

"Let's do this, Rangers!" Zack yelled. He put his hand out, and the circle was joined.

"One, two, three…"

"Rangers!" the boys yelled before dashing out onto the field to take their positions. But Michael stopped when he heard someone call his name. He knew that voice and was glad to hear it.

"Hey, I wanted to wish you good luck," Mr. Scott said warmly. "And don't worry, I'll keep your dad in line. You just do what you need to do."

"Thanks, Mr. Scott," Michael said gratefully. He gave Zack's dad an exploding fist-bump, their tradition, and jogged out to the pitcher's mound to start his warm-up. When he'd ensured his arm was loose and on target, he signaled that he was ready. This was it, their final inning. Time to show his dad what he could really do!

The Mavericks were just as strong at bat as they had been a month before at their scrimmage, but today things were different. Today, Michael was throwing without a bum wrist and with fire in his veins. Still, the Mavericks were solid hitters, and Michael took the first batter to a full count before the tall boy on the plate hit one flying out into left field. Brady sprinted after it toward the fence line but couldn't catch the speeding orb as it sailed over his head. Thankfully, he was quick on the turnaround and got it back into the infield just in time to hold the runner up at second.

The double flustered Michael. He tried hard to ignore it, but he could feel the doubt creeping back in. He sucked in a deep, calming breath and remembered everyone who believed in him, who was counting on him, who cared about him, and his confidence returned.

Michael struck the next boy out with only five pitches, and the following batter got a base hit off a hard grounder, which Chase stopped and held onto so a runner couldn't get to third. Now he had runners on first and second to worry about. This wasn't good.

Michael loosed his curver and a fastball for a pair of strikes on the next batter, then threw a ball on purpose. He readied his fourth pitch and sent it screaming back over the plate, beating the Maverick's swing by a good second. Two down...

"Way to go, Mikey. That's how it's done!" Mr. Scott yelled, joining the chorus of cheers and claps from the stands.

But now Michael was sweating, and not just because of the hot breeze that had kicked up. Cameron stepped up to plate, that same stupid smirk on his face, and glared at Michael.

"You're done," Michael swore under his breath.

He was focused now, but the parents and his teammates yelling encouragements to him went a long way toward calming him down, and he couldn't help but smile at Carter and Drew, who stood behind the chain link fence right behind home plate, doing their very best to distract Cameron.

Michael locked onto Logan's mitt like a target, wound up and threw a strike, then a ball. Back and forth he went until there was a full count. He stared Cameron down like a hawk, leaned forward, rotated the ball in his hand, and let his fingers find the place on the laces for his best pitch. He breathed out slowly, wound up, and the top-spin of his curver brought it twisting down at just the right time. Michael thought it was over, but Cameron's bat connected, barely, and sent a grounder careening right toward the pitcher's mound. Michael prepared to field it as he'd done hundreds of times before, but the ball bounced at the last second from a small divot in the grass. He got his body in front of it but couldn't get his mitt up in time, and the ball smacked into his chest. He fumbled with it for a split second before he got his throwing hand on it. Feeling pressured for the time he'd wasted, he threw to first base without getting his eyes on Zack's mitt first. Zack stretched as far off base as he could to receive the wild throw, but it flew just out of his reach and sailed into right field.

"No!" Michael yelped at the mistake he'd made. Stupid, stupid, stupid! He had to fix it. He had to!

The runner on second had made it to third and was on his way home just as their right fielder scooped up the ball and threw it in. It came in hot, and Michael sprinted toward home as he went for it, racing to beat the runner home.

Come on, hurry!

The ball landed a few feet in front of Logan, and he caught it on the bounce. He turned and whipped it to Michael. He caught it, twisted around, and threw himself into the path of the boy sliding into home plate. Life moved in slow motion as he hurled his mitt downward, feeling it slap against the calf of the boy as he careened toward him. Then came the pain, the full force of cleats slamming into his shin. It all happened so fast he didn't have time to dodge, to prepare, to yell out. All he could do was clench his eyes shut and bear it as he crashed to the ground, landing on his side in the reddish earth hard enough to blast the air from his lungs. It felt just like getting punched, and he knew what that felt like all too well. The dust was so thick! He couldn't see, he couldn't breathe, and his shin felt like it had been hit with a spiked sledgehammer.

Time stood still, and Michael waited, clenching his teeth and staring up through the cloud at the umpire, who leaned over, put his hand out and brought it down in a clenched fist.

"He's out!" His call thundered over the ballfield, and the screams of his teammates erupted all around him. Michael forced himself to take a short, painful breath and finally allowed himself to cry out in pain. Somehow he managed to push himself up into a sitting position as Zack plowed into him, with Chase and Brady not far behind.

"I knew you could do it!" Zack cried. "I told you!"

"I'm just that good, bro!" Michael said as his friends crushed him. It hurt, but in a good way.

The cheers of family and friends echoed all around him. Even Carter and Drew jumped up and down, screaming in celebration. It was the best sound Michael had ever heard. He didn't want to cry, but whether it was the joy or the pain in his leg, he couldn't help it. Now he was safe, and he'd never have to worry about his dad hitting him ever again.

"Come on Mikey, time to get up!" Chase said as he and Brady offered him their hands. They hauled him to his feet and helped him limp his way into line for the post-game handshake. He was glad for the help; his leg felt like it had been run over by a truck, and each step made him fight back tears. Coach Nolan said it wasn't broken, but it sure felt like it was. Maybe he'd ask Evelyn to look at it after the game, just in case. He stumbled his way slowly down the line and wished each player from the Mavericks a good game. But then he got to the end, and the poor sports.

"Wow, are you always crying?" Cameron smirked as he took Michael's hand, and Michael winced as Cameron squeezed it overly hard and wouldn't let go when Michael tried to pull back.

"Hey! Leave him alone, you jerks!" Chase yelled as he put himself between Michael and the two Mavericks.

"Make me, midget," Cameron replied, casually flicking the bill of Chase's hat, knocking it off his head and sending it tumbling into the dirt.

Cameron had more than a few inches on Chase and outweighed him too, probably by a lot, but that didn't seem to faze Chase a bit. Michael watched his face twist into an angry, red-faced scowl, and before he knew it, Chase balled his hand into a fist and smashed it into Cameron's face in a vicious cross. Everyone watched, mouths agape, as blood erupted from Cameron's nose, and he crashed to the ground with a muffled cry.

Ryan moved in on Chase then, shoving him back and nearly knocking him down, but Chase stood steady and strong. Chase easily danced around the haymaker he threw next before slamming his fist into Ryan's side. Then he rammed into his stomach with his shoulder, knocking him to the ground. The two of them wrestled fiercely until Chase's uncle intervened, grabbing Chase around the waist, hoisting him up and hauling him off the field like a piece of luggage.

"Screw you, assholes! That's what you get for messing with my friend!" Chase yelled as he was carried away. He never let up, yelling insults and curses and fighting to break away from his uncle the entire time.

Michael couldn't believe it. A few months ago Chase had nearly picked a fight with him, and now he was standing up for him. As his uncle dragged him off the field, Chase took a break from his threats and flashed a toothy grin at Michael that he couldn't help but return. They really were friends, no doubt about it.

The Rangers received their medals not long after, and nothing had ever felt so good. Now Michael wasn't just as good as Jason, he was better than him! He'd proven that much today. Dad would be proud of him for sure. Now he wouldn't need to worry about getting hurt, pretending he was okay all the time, or wearing long sleeves in the summer. He was the first one to the dugout to start packing his bag; he couldn't wait to get home so he could brag to Jason that he'd beaten his record. As he stuffed his mitt inside, he saw his dad coming toward him carrying his chair, neatly folded and inside its case.

"Dad, did you see!" Michael began.

"Finish packing up and let's go," his father said, his face a stone: cold and unmoving.

"But wait, what about...?" Michael tried to add but again wasn't able to finish.

"Get your things and let's go, Michael," his father replied curtly. Michael nodded; he wasn't going to chance anything.

Maybe it was nothing. Maybe he was just hot and wanted to get home. They'd won, and Michael'd gotten the winning out; his dad couldn't still be mad! That's what Michael tried to convince himself. But if everything was going to be fine, why was his heart beating so fast? Why did he feel like bricks were piled on top of his chest? As he left without saying goodbye to his team, Michael pulled his phone from his bag and followed slowly behind his father. He typed a message to Zack with trembling hands, desperately hoping he'd get it before they reached the car. Michael had made him a promise too, and hoped he could stall long enough for Zack to get it.

33 Doing the Right Thing

"**SEE** ya later, Brady-Bear!" Zack bid farewell to his friend.

"Bye, Zack! See ya next weekend at the party?" Brady asked hopefully.

"Definitely!" Zack replied. "I wonder if Chase will even be able to come, though. He's probably grounded forever. Or dead."

"Probably dead," Brady agreed, nodding thoughtfully.

"Hi Zack!" Evelyn greeted, walking up to join them. "You ready, Brady?"

"Ready for what?" Zack asked curiously.

"Me and Abby are taking her home first," Brady said. "And yes, Evelyn, I promise I won't be annoying in the car."

"*Right*. I'll believe it when I see it," Evelyn teased. "Bye, Zack!"

"Bye, Ev!" Zack said, trying not to laugh. She had to know there was no way Brady would be able to keep that promise!

Zack hurried back into the dugout to collect his things and hopefully catch Mikey. His mom had already left with his brothers, and he could tell his dad was anxious to get home, so he tried to hurry, stuffing everything inside his bag as quickly as possible. Flipping the heavy load onto his back, he looked around, but there was no sign of Mikey.

"Where'd he go?" Zack said aloud, scanning the area around their field. Nothing!

"Zachary, are you ready?" his father asked, looking somewhat impatient.

"Hang on!" Zack insisted. "I wanna say bye to Mikey first."

Zack stepped over to the bleachers and scanned the area, even out toward the parking lot, and that's where he saw him. It looked like he'd just done something on his phone, and now he looked to be pleading with his father about something.

Something's wrong.

BZZZ.

Zack's phone vibrated inside his bag. He swung it onto a bench, hurriedly pulled it out, unlocked it, read the message, and was running before he knew what was happening.

HELP!

"I'll be right back, Dad! I need to ask Mikey something!" Zack yelled, taking off down the asphalt walkway. His dad called after him, but there wasn't time for that now.

"Mikey!" Zack hailed him when he got close. His friend turned, and Zack stared into desperate, terrified eyes.

No...

"Mr. Dzierwa, can Mikey sleep over tonight?" Zack asked hopefully. "My dad wants to take us all out to celebrate."

"Not tonight, I'm afraid. Michael and I need to have an

important talk," Mr. Dzierwa replied.

"Dad, can I please? Please?" Mikey pressed. "We can talk tomorrow. I'll come home early, I promise."

"Tell your dad thank you, but maybe next time," Mr. Dzierwa said, trying to sound polite but really just dismissing him.

"Oh, okay," Zack surrendered. But what else could he do? He was just a kid.

"Bye, Zack," Mikey muttered, almost like he was saying good-bye forever.

"Bye..." Zack replied with a short wave. He watched Mikey's father grab his arm roughly and drag him along behind him toward his car, not seeming to notice or to care that he seemed to be hurting him. Mikey looked behind him, his mouth moving, silently pleading for help.

Mikey's dad was going to hurt him tonight; Zack knew it. Mikey couldn't go home! Zack turned and tore back down the path toward his father and ran to him at full sprint.

"Dad!" Zack yelled. "Dad!"

"Zachary, where's your bag? We gotta go!" his father said impatiently.

"Dad, you gotta come with me!" Zack demanded. "You have to ask Mr. Dzierwa if Mikey can sleep over tonight!"

"Zack, not tonight, buddy. Your mom and I are exhausted."

"Dad, please!" Zack pressed. He had to listen! He *had* to!

"Zack..."

"Please, Dad! Please! He has to stay with us tonight!" Zack insisted, hanging on his dad's arm as he tried to pull him toward the parking lot.

"Zack, what's up with you? Why is this so important?" his father asked.

"It just is! Please, Dad, he has to!" Zack yelled. He stared up at his father, silently begging him to ask one more question.

Come on, just come with me! You know something's wrong! You always know!

"Zack, what's going on? What's wrong?" his dad finally asked, his face worried and serious.

Tell him!

Zack struggled to steady his frantic breathing, trying to muster enough courage to say what he needed to. It came a second at a time until it was almost enough, until he realized he wasn't the same little boy he'd been months before; he was a young man, just like his father said he was. His responsibility wasn't keeping his promise, it was keeping Mikey safe. Telling the truth and doing the right thing, no matter what.

"Dad," Zack choked. "I need to tell you something..."

34 The Boy in the Mirror

"**LEMME** go, Uncle Mark!" Chase demanded, twisting and squirming to try to worm his way out of his uncle's grasp. But his uncle didn't pay him any mind and continued to carry him over his shoulder. It wasn't until they were far away from the ballfield that he finally set him down in the last place he wanted to be, in front of the one person he was actually afraid of.

"What is wrong with you?" his mother demanded.

"Nothing! They were making fun of Mikey being hurt."

"So you got into a fight with them!"

"Uncle Mark told me to always stick up for my friends, so I did!" Chase explained. "Right, Uncle Mark?"

"Well, that's not really what I meant," Mark said sheepishly.

"Oh my God, I can't believe this." His mother sighed and shook her head. But was she also smiling? She was! *And* she was trying not to laugh!

"Why are you laughing?" Chase asked curiously. And his mom turned to face him and his uncle, hands on her hips.

"I can't believe it, he's just like you!" his mom laughed, looking dead at his uncle.

"You say that like it's a bad thing!" his uncle retorted. Chase took a step back when his mom kneeled down in front of him. He was pretty sure he was about to get reamed.

"You're stubborn and a hothead…" she began.

"Hey!" Chase tried to interject, but his mother shushed him.

"But you're also kind, loving, loyal, and brave. And I'm so glad you're like your uncle."

"So does that mean you're proud of me and I'm not punished?" Chase pleaded with a hopeful grin.

"Oh you're definitely still grounded!" She laughed "But not until your uncle brings you home."

"Wait, where are we going?" Chase asked excitedly.

"Somewhere your mom hates. So when I bring you home, don't even talk to her until you brush your teeth," Mark explained. Yep, that *definitely* meant Ruby's!

"Yes!" Chase started toward his uncle's truck, slowing every few feet to remind his mom and uncle to hurry up.

Chase flung the door open as soon as it was unlocked, tossed his bag in the rear of the cab and hopped up into the passenger's seat as his uncle slid into the driver's. As the engine roared to life, Chase heard the knock on his window and rolled it down.

"You be good tonight, okay?" his mom said.

"I will, Mom," Chase promised, smiling thankfully.

"All right, you boys have fun!" she ordered. "Mark, I want him home by nine at the latest."

"Will do, sis," Mark confirmed. "You ready to roll, little man?"

CHAPTER 34

"Yeah!" Chase confirmed, yelling good-bye to his mom as they left the parking lot.

Chase kept the window rolled down and let the wind blow on his face as they drove by the farms and neighborhoods of Westerhill. His fingers moved at a feverish pace, hopping from one house to the next and taking whole fields in a single leap. He took in the landscape, looked in the mirror, and saw the smiling reflection of a boy both glad and hopeful. He might never have seen that smile again if it hadn't been for his friends. They forgave him, listened to him, helped him, and never gave up on him. Maybe his dad would come see him someday, maybe he wouldn't, but his friends would always be there for him. Maybe that was enough. Chase breathed the country air deeply, never more grateful for his friends, and sighed.

"You okay, Chase?" his uncle asked.

"Yeah," Chase answered, smiling peacefully. "I am."

35 Homecoming

WHAT'S *going on? What's gonna happen to me?*

The thoughts ran through Michael's head like a freight train. Just this afternoon, not even two days after their game, Ms. Sheridan and two policemen just showed up at his house and talked to his family. Then, only a few hours later, he'd been told he couldn't live there anymore. He clutched his backpack tightly to his chest. It was all he'd had time to pack: his mitt and enough clothes to last him a week, if he was lucky. His whole life stuffed in one small bag.

"They're good people, Michael, I promise," his case worker, Ms. Sheridan, assured him. Ever since he met her, she'd tried to make him feel safe, like everything was going to be okay, but he didn't believe her.

"What are they gonna be like?" Michael asked. He needed to know. Who were these people he'd be living with while his dad was "learning to be a better person," as she'd explained it to him?

"I only had time to talk to them for a little while, but they seem like a great family!" she replied.

"Why can't I stay at home? I don't wanna leave!" Michael protested furiously.

"You know why, Michael. It's not safe for you there," she replied. "Even your brother said so."

"Who cares what Jason thinks? I wanna go home!"

But did he really? Zack had been wrong; they'd both been. His dad hadn't changed at all; he had the shiner on his left eye from their "talk" to prove that. Ms. Sheridan said he'd been brave for telling someone, but she didn't know how hard it had been. If it hadn't been for his friends, he might never have found the courage to ask for help at all. He'd always kept things secret. He hadn't even told Zack everything. Asking for help was the first time he felt he'd had any control over what was happening to him. But that weight off his chest had been quickly replaced by the consequences of his choice. Would he ever see his friends again? Would he ever get to go back home?

Will I even have a home?

"I'm scared," Michael admitted. It was a lie; scared wasn't even close to what he was feeling, but he didn't want her to see that.

"I know you are. But I promise things will work out for the best."

"Yeah, right," Michael scoffed, burying his face into his bag to try to hide his eyes. Whoever he was going to meet today, the last thing he wanted them to think was that he was a crybaby. Especially if…

"Do they have any kids?" Michael asked curiously.

"Why yes, they do!" Ms. Sheridan answered. "In fact, I think they have a son around your age. Maybe you two can be friends!"

"Doubt it…" Michael mumbled.

"Maybe you'll be surprised," she replied warmly. "Just remember, Michael, we want you to be able to go back home someday, too. But for now, we need to keep you safe while your dad gets the help he needs."

"How long?" Michael pressed.

"However long it takes," she responded.

Can't you say anything else?

Michael glared into the rear-view mirror, but as much as he hated that she wouldn't give him a real answer, the welt across his eye reminded him she was right. As scared as he was, as lost as he felt, his dad couldn't hurt him now. At least he was safe.

I should've listened to Zack. I should've told someone sooner!

Michael blinked back angry tears as those thoughts swept through his head. If he'd told Zack sooner, if he'd told Mr. Scott that night, maybe he could have just stayed with them. Then he wouldn't be driving off to live with strangers where he wouldn't be able to see his friends ever again.

"How much longer?" Michael asked nervously.

"Actually, we're here," she answered, slowing the car to a stop. Michael turned, looked out the window, and gasped. White paint, gray shutters, and a small wooden ramp left on the sidewalk. All of it so familiar.

"Really?" Michael asked hopefully, almost unable to believe what he was seeing.

"Go on." She smiled. "I think you know the way."

Michael got out slowly, his mouth still ajar. He hoisted his backpack over his shoulder, closed the door behind him, and slowly walked up the lawn. Mr. Scott, Ms. Hannah, Zack and his brothers all stood on the front stoop, the boys lined up from youngest to oldest, each holding up a piece of cardboard. Carter looked back at his mother and whispered something excitedly to her. She nodded, and the boys flipped their cards, each spelling one word of the best sentence he'd ever heard.

"Welcome home Mikey!" Zack and his brothers shouted enthusiastically and horribly out of sync.

"What do you think, Mikey-Man?" Mr. Scott asked. "Do you want to stay with us for a while?"

Yes!

He wanted to say it, but the lump in his throat wouldn't let him. So he nodded; it was the best he could do. A cheer sounded from the boys, and he soon found himself being squeezed to death by the Walden brothers. His brothers now.

"Do I really?" Michael asked joyfully, wiping his eyes. "Do I really get to be part of your family?"

Zack smiled broadly and crushed him in another hug.

"You derp," he sniffled. "You always were!"

36 All That Mattered

THE party the weekend after their last game of the season was pretty much Brady's favorite tradition. After his birthday and Christmas. Well, Halloween too. But it was up there! Every year when the season was over, the four of them would stay at his house, go swimming, and have a cookout with their families. But the bonfire after? That was his absolute favorite part!

No, that was a lie. Being with his friends was definitely the best part...

"Morning, Mom," Brady greeted his mother as he strode in the kitchen, his bed-head a sight to behold, and saw her smirk.

"Looks like you slept good," she noted, trying to stifle a laugh.

"I really did!" he agreed.

She was right, he *had* slept good. He'd just laid in bed staring at his medal from regionals for what felt like forever, and the next thing he knew he was awake again. It was actually the first night in a while sleep had come easy, and there was good reason for it. Last Sunday morning, the day after the championship, his mom and dad had sat with him and Abby, and they'd talked for a long time. That was the first time he'd been able to really say how he felt, and his parents had promised they were going to see someone Mr. Scott and Ms. Hannah recommended to help them. They hadn't fought all week, they were trying, and Brady cheered them on every day.

"Morning, Brady-Bear," his dad greeted, ruffling his hair. Brady made a face and went about his business, gathering ingredients for breakfast from the fridge. Chef Brady had work to do!

"Morning to you, too," he heard his dad tell his mom, turning just in time to see them kiss. Gross. Good to see, but still gross.

"So what are you making for us this morning, chef?" his mom asked curiously. He thought she'd never ask.

"Spinach and cheese omelets," Brady relayed as he started whisking the eggs in a big steel bowl. "The special ingredient is super-hot sauce. At least for Abby..."

"Don't even think about it!" His father laughed. Fine, he wouldn't do it to Abby. He thought about maybe pranking his dad instead, but decided against that too. Things were different now, better different, and he wanted to keep them that way.

If the last few months of helping his friends through their struggles had taught him anything, it was that he was a helper, and he liked that. He didn't need to be a straight-A student to be a good friend, or to make people laugh and feel better. If he hadn't been him--crazy, goofy, sometimes annoying him--The Quad Squad might not still be together, and that was the most important thing. Maybe he'd help people when he grew up, be a doctor like his dad or something. Yeah, that sounded good! Maybe he'd start trying harder in school. Just in case.

Three hours of extreme impatience later, the party finally began, and like every year, the day went by too fast. When the hours of swimming ended, he and his friends all sat around a table outside on their porch, devouring the burgers, hotdogs, and ribs his dad had grilled along with anything else they could get their hands on.

They shared their stories from the week as they ate, and it was amazing what had happened in just six days! Brady had eaten fourteen cookies he'd baked in one sitting, Chase went paintballing for the first time with his uncle (which explained all the round welts they'd seen when he was swimming), but pretty much the craziest thing to ever happen to them *ever* was that Zack and Mikey were brothers now! Well, "sorta brothers" they called it, but still! How cool was that? Wouldn't be hard getting the squad together now that the two of them lived in the same house!

It wasn't long before the sun started to sink lower and lower. It wasn't dark, but it would be soon. Mr. Scott and Zack had got the fire going, and they sat around listening to his famous scary stories, all of them falling for the jump-scare *again.* Mikey had screamed like he usually did, but Brady did too on purpose so Mikey wouldn't be too embarrassed. Soon it would be time for the four of them to have the fire to themselves until bedtime, s'mores and all, but goodbyes needed to be said first.

"Zack, be good tonight, okay?" Ms. Hannah coached, giving him the long "behave" speech even though he probably needed it the least. Not like they were going to go TP someone's house or anything!

"I will, Mom." Zack sighed before she leaned down and kissed him goodnight on his cheek.

"Mom, not in front of the guys!" Zack complained while Mikey, who was standing next to him, smirked at his discomfort.

"What are you laughing at, Mikey?" Ms. Hannah asked, ambushing him in a tight hug. "You get one too!"

"No!" Mikey yelled, struggling and squirming, but he couldn't escape before he received his mom-kiss as well. Michael rubbed his cheek furiously, acting like he hated it, but his smile said different. It was the same when Mr. Scott and Ms. Hannah said they loved them before they left. Brady had never seen Mikey look so happy; it was like no one had ever told him that before. It was a little weird hearing Mikey call Zack's parents Mom and Dad though. Just something else he'd have to get used to!

Soon after the last goodbye, the sun finally finished its descent below the horizon, giving up its place in the sky to the July moon. The flames of their bonfire, skillfully maintained, crackled and roared, illuminating faces both eager and annoyed.

"Quit hogging all the marshmallows, Brady!" Chase complained.

"Hang on!" Brady said. He'd taken the last bag of marshmallows they had and gone over behind a tree out of the light. He wanted it to be a surprise, but he was giggling so hard he was certain they knew he was up to something.

"Yeah, Zack dared me to eat a double-decker with peanut butter cups!" Michael added impatiently.

"Hang on! Okay, I'm ready!" Brady announced as he turned and ran back into the light.

"Ho-ho-ho! I'm Santa Claus!" Brady announced, spreading his arms out wide and falling into a giggling fit. He'd licked a dozen or so marshmallows and stuck them onto his face like a beard. A fluffy, squishy, white beard.

"Wow, Brady!" Zack sighed.

"Did you use all of them?" Chase asked. Brady's breathless nods were immediately met with jeers and a hail of candy and pop bottles.

"You guys are on the naughty list now!" Brady scolded them in the best Santa Claus voice he could.

"Oh my gosh, you are so annoying!" Chase groaned.

"Don't hate me 'cause I'm awesome." Brady grinned.

"That's not why I hate you…" Chase sighed.

SNAP.

"Hey, what was…?" Zack asked, but he didn't have time to finish as a pale, long-haired, sharp-fanged figure burst from behind their chairs.

HISSSSSSS!

Chase yelled as his eyes shot open and he rolled from his chair, his arm flying up straight into Brady's nose. Mikey shrieked and tried frantically to stand, but he got tangled in his chair and fell onto Zack, whose scream was cut off when Mikey landed like a stone on his stomach and knocked the wind out of him. Chaos reigned for a handful of terrifying seconds until laughter filled their ears.

"Oh my God, you guys are such spazzes!" the figure howled.

The Quad Squad, hearing the familiar voice, managed to quell their terror long enough to freeze and focus on Abby.

Abby?

"Why!" Brady demanded angrily.

"Aww, poor Brady-Bear. Did I make you pee?"

"A little!" Brady admitted, and his friends roared. They probably thought it was a joke. Good, because he wasn't kidding.

"Wow. Oh, and by the way, you guys smell awful." Abby cringed. "Like chlorine, smoke, and feet!"

Brady hopped to his feet, quick as a whip, vengeful thoughts shining in his eyes.

"But sissy, I love you! Come gimme a hug..." he said creepily.

"I swear to God, Brady, don't you dare touch me," Abby warned as Brady slowly walked toward her with his arms outstretched.

"Let's all hug Abby, guys. She needs to smell our love," Brady suggested with a devilish grin.

"Brady, I *swear*!" Abby growled, but her bravado soon turned to panic when Brady and his friends rose to their feet and chased her around the yard. Brady was sure vengeance would soon be his, until Abby got the hose and let loose. Chase yelped in surprise as he was hit by the first icy blast, sending him stumbling backward while the rest of them scattered. Abby continued her counterattack, picking them off one by one.

"Retreat!" Brady yelled, trying frantically to get his footing in the damp grass. They all fell back toward the warmth of the fire, shivering and laughing. Brady couldn't help but grin even though his teeth were chattering violently.

What a great night it had been, and there'd definitely be many more like it. Sure, middle school was less than a month away, but why worry? The Quad Squad was still together, and they could handle anything when they were together! They still had each other, always, and that was all that mattered.

Made in the USA
San Bernardino, CA
26 June 2019